YOUR EVER LOVING SON

Your Ever Loving Son

– MIKE TENNENT –

UPFRONT PUBLISHING
PETERBOROUGH, ENGLAND

Your Ever Loving Son
Copyright © Mike Tennent 2009

All rights reserved.

No part of this book may be reproduced in any form by photocopying or any electronic or mechanical means, including information storage or retrieval systems, without permission in writing from both the copyright owner and the publisher of the book.

No character in this book has any existence outside the imagination of the author and any similarity with any person, alive or dead, is purely coincidental. Likewise all incidents related in this book are purely invention

ISBN 978-184426-502-2

First Published 2009 by
UPFRONT PUBLISHING LTD
Peterborough, England.

Printed by Lightning Source

I dedicate this book to my maternal grandparents, the Stevensons, whose lovely Victorian house and twelve acre garden in Surrey, was the inspiration for my setting the first half of my book in the "upstairs downstairs" mode. My grandparents' house was smaller than the Macaulay's mansion of my book, and befittingly became a children's home.

By the same author:-

Finance – *"Practical Liquidity Management"*
(Gower Press, 1976 – now out of print)

Romance - *"The Hesitant Heart"*
(SPA Ltd. 1988)

Cover designed and illustrated by Rosalind Tennent

Chapter One – 1952

The wind was so strong that it seemed to Anne as if the rain was driving at her horizontally, while the fading early evening light made the landscape even bleaker than it normally looked in November.

'We'll have some more trees down, Bill, if this gale continues for another day,' she remarked to her foreman of her market garden business, and having to shout to make herself heard. They were returning from inspecting a large elm which had been uprooted in one corner of her broccoli field. Her wellington boots were thick with wet mud, and she found it an effort to walk along the squelching track.

'I agree, Mrs Banks. Can't remember a worse autumn gale for many a year,' he shouted back.

As they approached the offices, which Anne had had built on to the back of her cottage, one of the young clerks, a cockney, ran out excitedly to them. 'Oh, Mrs Banks. You're wanted on the telephone. A Mr Stevens.' The girl paused for breath before panting on: ''E says it's urgent!'

'Thank you, Elsie. I'll take it in the cottage. Switch it through will you, please?'

'Yes, Mam,' she replied.

Anne took a deep breath. before she spoke to her retired lawyer and long time friendly adviser. 'Uncle Steve. Sorry! I'm panting. I was outside. I've just run into the cottage. Trouble getting my muddy wellies off! I'm soaked. We've a terrific gale here. You can probably hear it on the line. How are you?'

'I'm all right, thank you.' He paused, but she had already detected a distressed note in his voice. 'Anne, dear? Is Arthur with you?'

'No Uncle Steve. Arthur's up in the Midlands. On an audit up there. Is something the matter? Can I help?'

'Is anyone with you, Anne?' he enquired anxiously.

'No. Not in the cottage. Just the usual staff outside and in the office.'

'I would like to come up myself....' When would he get to the point, she urged, feeling herself tensing up? 'But I've become a lot less mobile this last year or two. My arthritis, you know.' He paused again. 'I was hoping you might have company.'

'No, Uncle Steve. I'm all alone. What is it?' She was becoming impatient.

'I'm the bearer of more bad news, Anne. Very, very sad news.' He spoke slowly and his voice seemed to fade away.

'It's almost as if there is a curse on the Macaulay family.' He suddenly stopped talking and she wondered for a moment whether the line had gone dead.

'What is it this time? Who?' she urged, but still he did not come to the point. 'Uncle Steve? Uncle Steve? Are you there? Who is it? Not.... Not.... Not one of the boys? Not Ronnie?' She felt her whole stomach turn as she tensed herself ready for his response.

'You must try to be very brave, Anne. I know how, having brought him up, you look upon Ronald almost like a second son.' She heard him cough, his words sticking in his throat. 'He's had an accident. In his car. It was earlier today. The police got in touch with his office. They rang his grandfather. Mr Macaulay has just telephoned me.'

Anne felt her chest tighten and for it to become almost impossible for her to breathe. She wiped her brow with her spare hand which was still wet from the rain. Her other hand clutched the telephone receiver which she now found an effort to hold steady against her ear. 'How badly hurt is he?' Her distraught voice sounded to her as coming from miles away.

'What hospital have they taken him to?' She did not wait for any replies. Suddenly, and uncontrollably, she blurted out: 'I knew it! I knew it! I never did want him to have such a fast car. A Sunbeam Talbot 90 was quite unnecessarily powerful for a youngster! It was all my fault – why did I ever agree to his buying such a high performance car? But how….? How, Uncle Steve? How badly hurt is he? Uncle Steve? Uncle Steve?'

'Anne, dear. I…. I…. I hardly know how to tell you.' He began……. She interrupted, without waiting to hear him break the news she intuitively knew he was about to reveal. 'He's not…. Not dead? Not killed? Oh no! God, no!' she gasped and let out a piercing scream, collapsing backwards over the small chair by the telephone and landing on the floor. Any pain she had caused herself she did not feel. It was a few moments before she collected herself enough to remember her caller. She stared at the receiver, now lying beside her, before summoning up enough courage to lift it again to her ear.

'Uncle Steve?' She whispered. 'Uncle Steve, please tell me he's not been killed. Please, Please, Please….' Then again, without waiting for a reply, she held the receiver away from her ear, and felt herself begin to shake uncontrollably.

'Are you all right, Mam?' It was Elsie, who had responded to the scream, which had reached the general office. She had knocked on the side door, but Anne had not heard her.

'Oh, God, Elsie!' She looked up towards the girl, but her eyes did not focus. Suddenly, not consciously knowing what she was doing, she held the receiver out to the clerk.

'He's been killed…. My Ronnie… My Ronnie's been killed!' With these words she took a deep breath and broke down, burying her head in her hands.

'Is that Mr Stevens?' Elsie asked nervously, herself beginning to absorb some of the emotional state of her employer. Anne looked up and stared at the girl as if her own mind had ceased to function. It was as if in the distance, she heard the girl speak.

'Yes…. Yes, Sir. Mrs Banks is all right…. I think so. Yes, she's sittin' down…. On the floor!' The young village girl's point-by-point report had no meaning for Anne and, having looked at her open mouthed for a moment, she again buried her head. 'She's got 'er 'ead in 'er 'ands,' Elsie continued before pausing to listen to the caller. 'Yes, Mr Stevens, I'll go and get 'er a drink. Yes, I do knows where it is. Sorry, what did you say? Just a moment, I'll get a piece of paper and a pencil.'

A moment later, Elsie again picked up the receiver. 'Yes, I'm ready now. You says the accident was at…. Yes, I got that. And 'e 'as been taken to…. Yes, I got all of that. No, Sir…. Mrs Banks don't seem no different. She still 'as 'er 'ead in 'er 'ands. Yes, Mr Stevens, I'll look after 'er. Yes, I'll get 'er to ring you when she's feelin' a bit better. Good-bye.'

'Why don't yer come into the sittin' room, Mam?' Elsie suggested, putting her arms under Anne's shoulders and, with treatment more befitting lifting a sack of Anne's potatoes, gave her a sharp heave.

'I can manage, thank you, Elsie,' Anne mumbled, turning on to all fours then climbing slowly to her feet. She felt distinctly unsteady as she stumbled to the sitting room, shedding her wet mackintosh in the centre of the hall carpet on the way. To the accompaniment of a noisy exhalation, she collapsed heavily into one of the large armchairs. Was she conscious or dreaming, she wondered? She turned her head and let her eyes follow Elsie, who silently crossed the room towards the cocktail cabinet. Anne watched with an expressionless face as if she had never seen her office clerk before.

'Mr Stevens says as 'ow I was to get you a drink, Mam.' She spoke quietly and Anne was impressed with her composure. 'What's it to be, Mam? I think I knows 'ow to pour some things.'

'A large whisky, please, Elsie,' she murmured, waving one hand loosely in the general direction of the cabinet, as her eyes went suddenly to the window in response to an extra heavy gust of hail beating noisily against the window. 'It's the decanter on top,' Anne instructed.'

The glass the girl placed on the coffee table in front of Anne a few minutes later had been filled to the brim. 'How much soda did you put in this, Elsie?' Anne enquired a moment later in a dazed voice, having taken a large gulp and almost choked.

'Soda, Mam? What's soda?' The girl pointed to the glass. 'That stuff's whats come out of the funny shaped bottle that is…. The one you said was on the top.'

'Thank you, Elsie,' said Anne wearily, already feeling the steadying effects of the neat spirit. 'I'm very grateful,' she added feebly. 'You may go back to the office now. What time is it?'

'Nearly five, Mam. Will there be anything more tonight?' The girl spoke with concern.

'No thank you, Elsie. I can manage.'

The girl paused at the door. 'Mr Stevens said 'ow yu was to 'phone 'im back later. When you was feelin' all right, Mam.'

Anne managed a slight smile. 'Yes. I won't forget. Thank you, Elsie.' Then, noticing the girl's worried expression, added: 'Don't worry about me, I'll be all right.' As she left the room, Anne called after her. 'I shan't be here tomorrow, Elsie. I want to go and see....'

Her voice died away. 'See what happened.'

'What? See the car, Mam?' Elsie took a pace back into the room and began shaking her head slowly from side to side. 'It won't look very nice, Mam.'

Anne blinked several times and let her eyelids remain closed. 'I want to see what happened,' she repeated slowly as if talking to herself. 'I gave the car to Ronnie. And I want to see what happened.' She opened her eyes again, but did not focus them on Elsie. 'Why shouldn't I see what happened.... if I want to?' she questioned no one in particular.

'I'll tell Mr Bill then, Mam.... As 'ow you won't be 'ere tomorrow. Good-night, Mam.'

'Good-night, Elsie, and again thank you for your help.'

Anne sat still in the chair for most of the evening. She consumed the remainder of the whisky and, for some hours, her brain was numbed from the shock and the sorrow. She did telephone Mr Stevens, but in her state of inebriation, she made little out of what he said to her.

★ ★ ★ ★ ★

Quite early the next morning, after what seemed to her as an almost sleepless night, Anne drove herself to the local station. She bought a ticket for London and, at Waterloo, boarded a bus in the direction of the crossroads where she had been informed the accident had taken place.

The bus ride seemed interminable and gave her insatiable brain the freedom to remonstrate against all she had done to, and tried to do for, Ronald during his all too short life.

Was this latest calamity to befall her God's punishment for her covetousness for the Rathbone family wealth, and her particular envy of their daughter, Dulcie, with her inherited social standing, who had married into the family of Anne's employers. What more was life to throw at her as punishment? What more could life throw at her, Anne wondered, with her beloved lover Charles, and now her Ronnie, both taken from her?

Anne knew Elsie had been right and that she was making a mistake by coming to the garage by the scene of the accident. She was already near to breaking point, and the journey could bring her only further heartache. What possible benefit could she gain from coming to look at what remained of the green coloured Sunbeam Talbot 90 sports car she had given to her "Ronnie"? But she could not help herself. She felt compelled to come.

She had chosen a seat at the front of the upper deck of the red London Transport bus in order that she could see the road ahead and would not miss the stop at which she had to alight. The journey was a new one to her, and on any other occasion she would have followed with interest the route taken by the bus.

But today her eyes were sunken from lack of sleep in cheeks still swollen from her crying. A sudden jolt of the bus brought her mind back to reality. She glanced at her bus ticket, rubbed back and forth nervously between her fingers, it now lay in shreds in the palm of her hand. She realised that there could not be much further to go and began to peer anxiously ahead, reading and re-reading the names of the roads they passed.

The park she had been warned to look out for came into view, deserted and windswept, it seemed cold and uninviting and Anne subconsciously pulled her scarf up higher around her neck.

She noticed a large tree, uprooted by the wind and lying across one of the park foot-paths. With its severed roots it seemed to her significant and, for the umpteenth time since the previous evening, she reflected on all that had happened during the last twenty-three traumatic years, a seemingly interminable period which had begun with the birth of her only child. 'I did it for his sake.' she murmured to herself unconvincingly. 'For his sake.'

At that moment she caught sight of the garage across the road, and immediately spotted down one side the twisted remains of a green coloured car.

Quickly alighting from the bus, she ignored the lights controlling the crossing, and only narrowly avoided being run over by a small blue coloured van she had not seen turn the corner. At the scream of its tyres, the man selling newspapers from a kiosk on the pavement looked up. 'You look out, lady! Don't want to kill yourself, do you?' he called, pointing a finger threateningly at her.

She heard him but made no reply. She passed quickly in front of the van as the irate driver, just managing to curb his tongue, muttered: 'You might look out where you're going, my good woman!'

Behind her, she heard the newspaper man call out to the driver: 'We had an accident here only yesterday. Car skidded on the wet leaves. Chap turned it right over. Killed himself.'

Out of breath, and becoming conscious of a feeling of sickness creeping over her, Anne looked about for somewhere to rest. In a belated effort to reassure herself, she spoke aloud: 'It must be put right. It must be. I only did it for his sake. It must be put right. Oh God.' At that moment she blacked out.

The garage office was cramped and lacked any pretence at comfort. As Anne opened her eyes the garage proprietor smiled. 'Don't worry, lady. We've called for an ambulance. It'll soon be here.'

'Thank you. Thank you so much. I'm sorry to be a nuisance.'

In the distance she heard the bell of the approaching ambulance. 'Mrs Banks is my name,' she replied in a hoarse whisper to the proprietor's question as she felt another wave of dizziness begin to build up. She lost consciousness again and came round as two men were lifting her on a stretcher into the back of the ambulance.

'We'll soon have you in a nice comfortable bed in hospital,' one of the men said.

'Whatever happened to me?' she queried.

'You just had a little turn, lady. I don't think it's anything to worry about, but the doctor will soon check you over.'

'That's good,' she murmured. Ten minutes later she awoke with a start as the ambulance doors were opened and her stretcher was dragged from its clips. She was carefully transferred to a trolley and a hospital porter then pushed her through a door marked "CASUALTY" Was she really a casualty?

She was conscious of the peering faces as she was pushed across the uncomfortably crowded A & E waiting room. 'Where are you taking me?' she enquired croakily.

'To female Ward D, Madam. We're almost there.' The porter sounded friendly enough. A ward sister directed him to one of the empty beds on to which he then lifted Anne.

'There you are, Mrs Banks.'

'Thank you. Thank you so much,' she replied quietly.

The sister was carrying a clipboard. 'Now Mrs Banks, if you're feeling up to it, do you think I could have some personal details?'

As Anne completed the list a man in a white coat arrived. He glanced indifferently at the clipboard and then spoke without much feeling. 'Good morning, Mrs Banks. I am Doctor Fox. Had a little turn, I hear. We'll soon find out what the matter is.'

'I don't want to be any trouble,' Anne said apologetically.

'That's what we're here for,' the doctor replied, drawing back her upper sheet.

As soon as the doctor had finished he left the cubicle with the sister who, a moment later, returned. 'Now, Mrs Banks, do you feel like a little lunch? Doctor Fox said it will be all right for you to have something light.'

'Oh, thank you. Thank you. I think I would like a little something.'

The sister smiled at Anne. 'What you most need, Mrs Banks, is rest. Have your lunch and then we'll give you a tablet that will make you have a really deep sleep this afternoon.'

'Thank you so much. You're all so kind.'

Half an hour later Anne swallowed the tablet and lay back on her pillows with a resigned sigh. Soon she became drowsy as she momentarily fought to keep her eyes open. In her subconscious mind two pairs of impenetrable white doors confronted her and restrained her from entering the land of plenty. A massive chain and a heavy padlock prevented her from opening the doors, but even as she struggled desperately with the chain, quite suddenly it fell to the ground at her feet. The doors were opened back by bowing slaves and she walked through. And as she did so, so the memories, like leaves off a deciduous tree, came floating down all around her.

★ ★ ★ ★ ★

'Mrs Banks, Mrs Banks?' A kindly quiet voice was saying beside her. 'Mrs Banks, are you awake?'

'What? What?' Anne's voice was still slurred from the effects of the sleeping tablet which the sister had given to her at lunch time. The ceiling over the bed was now a long way above her. This, she reasoned, was not where she had gone to sleep, nor was it her little bedroom at home.

'Where am I?' she queried, trying to sit up.

'I wouldn't try sitting up just yet, Mrs Banks,' the nurse spoke softly.

'But where am I?' she repeated, struggling against the nurse's hand.

'You're in a bed in hospital,' she smiled reassuringly.

'In hospital?' As Anne spoke, a few of the events which had led to her finding herself in a hospital bed came back to her.

'Don't worry, Mrs Banks. We'll soon have you well again' the nurse said encouragingly.

Anne looked about her and tried to take in the curtained-off cubicle and the unfamiliar background noises. The events of the last few days, culminating in her seeing the smashed up car by the garage, were coming back.

The nurse spoke again, more cheerfully: 'If you're feeling up to it, Mrs Banks, you have a visitor. One of your relations has come to see you.'

'One of my relations? Who is it?'

'It's your son,' replied the nurse, being totally unprepared for the startled effect this simple statement would provoke in her patient's behaviour.

'My son? No. No, it's not my son. It must be a ghost!'

Anne almost screamed out the last words and, grabbing her sheet, pulled it up over her face and held it there tightly.

'Mrs Banks, Mrs Banks. Whatever is the matter?' The thoroughly alarmed nurse exclaimed, trying to pull back the sheet. But Anne held it firmly in her hands. 'Your visitor's in the waiting room and he wants to come and see how you are. He's naturally very concerned about you.'

'Oh, no! No! No! It must be a ghost! I won't see him! I won't!' This outburst was all the nurse's reasoning produced as Anne pulled the sheet even more tightly over her head.

'Now, come on Mrs Banks,' repeated the nurse trying to sound sympathetic. 'I don't know what is worrying you, but do please come out from under there. No one's going to hurt you.'

Very slowly Anne began to lower the sheet. From the scared look on her face the nurse was left in no doubt that something was worrying her patient a great deal.

'How did I come here?' Anne suddenly asked, looking about her, then questioned in quick succession: 'And where did he come from? Has he come to punish me? How did he know where I was?'

'If he's your next-of-kin the hospital would have contacted him as soon as you were brought in.'

'My son? My real son? Is he all right? Is he in one piece?'

'I think, Mrs Banks, you are perhaps still confused as a result of the extra strong sleeping tablet you were given. And the turn you experienced earlier today. I'm sure we will soon sort out what is troubling you. Don't worry about it.'

Anne remained passive as the nurse began to prepare her. Suddenly she broke the silence again: 'Please, don't leave me alone!' Her voice had an almost hysterical tone, as she clutched at the nurse's arm. 'I don't want to be left alone with him.'

'All right, Mrs Banks. All right. I won't leave you.' The now completely bewildered nurse had a thought. 'I'm going to ask the ward sister if we can move you into an amenity room. The one outside this large ward was free this morning. If no one has been put in there since, we could move you across.'

'Why? What are you going to do with me?' Anne queried nervously. 'I'll go and have a word with the sister,' said the nurse, walking out of the curtained cubicle.

A few minutes later the nurse and the sister Anne had seen before going to sleep, entered. 'I gather there's some little difficulty,' said the sister in a kindly voice, coming to her bedside and immediately beginning to straighten her top sheet.

'I'm very sorry to be a nuisance,' Anne replied timidly. 'You see.... I'm.... I'm frightened.'

'Don't worry. We can do just what the nurse has suggested. We'll move you into a separate room. You can then see your son in....'

'Oh, but I don't want to see him alone, not alone,' interrupted Anne. 'Please, please don't leave me to see him alone,'

'Don't worry, Mrs Banks. One of us will be there if you need us.'

Ten minutes later Anne was safely tucked up in a new bed in a small separate single room adjacent to the ward.

'Nurse, you can go now and fetch Mr Banks,' instructed the sister.

'Mr Banks?' enquired Anne in a surprised tone of voice. 'Mr Banks?' She repeated, as if the name were a new one to her.

'Yes,' said the sister, taking one of Anne's hands in her own. 'Mr Banks, your son. Nurse is going to get him from the waiting room and he's coming in here to see you.'

'And you are going to remain with us? You promised!'

'I promise, Mrs Banks. Either I or nurse will stay with you for as long as you feel you need one of us.'

'Thank you. Thank you so much. You see…. You see…. Oh, I'm all confused. I….' Her voice died away, her incomplete thoughts not revealed.

Anne had almost gone back to sleep when the knock at the door immediately reawakened her anxieties. As the sister moved to the door and opened it, Anne only half turned her head and reached out once more for the sheet, seemingly to be ready to hide herself again.

A tall man, in his early twenties, stood in the doorway. He wore glasses and was wearing a business suit. He had on a black tie and carried a mackintosh over one arm and a furled umbrella in his other hand. He smiled at the sister with a nod of his head, and took two paces into the room.

'Mother, dear….'

'Oh!' responded Anne with a gulp. 'Oh! I thought…. I thought…. I thought it was going to be Ronnie.'

'Ronnie?' enquired the man in surprise, moving to the side of the bed. He leaned over and kissed her on the forehead. In a quiet, pained voice he said: 'Mother, you obviously haven't heard. A terrible thing has happened to Ronnie.' She stared at the man as if not wanting him to say what she knew he was about to. 'Ronnie was killed in a car accident yesterday.'

'I know,' she murmured, fighting back her tears. 'My darling, darling Ronnie. Why? Why? Oh why did he have to do it?'

The sister spoke quietly. 'Mrs Banks, I expect you'd like to be alone now with your son.'

Anne looked at the sister and smiled. In an almost inaudible whisper she said: 'But he is not my son!'

The sister turned and drew the man away so that Anne would not hear: 'Mr Banks, I do hope the nurse warned that your mother was still suffering from shock and the effects of having had a strong sleeping draught.'

The sister then turned to Anne. 'I think you need some more sleep, Mrs Banks. We might even give you another strong tablet for the night. Then, hopefully, when you wake up tomorrow morning, your sad bereavement, and all these little problems in your mind at the moment, will sort themselves out.'

'But I have sorted them out,' Anne insisted. She looked affectionately at the man. 'This is Arthur. He's been like a son to me, but he's not my son.'

Arthur Banks looked at the sister as if for support. 'Mother, dear. Of course I'm your son. I can see that Ronald's tragic death has upset you deeply, as indeed it has me. Why don't you do what the sister suggests and have another sleep? I'll come back to see you later.'

'I think that will be for the best,' the sister broke in.

'Good-bye for now, Mother. Take care.... And have a really deep recuperating sleep. See you tomorrow. I'll bring you in some flowers. I'll try and get some of your favourite chrysanthemums.' He once more leaned over and kissed the top of her head and gave her hand a squeeze. 'I love you, Mother. God bless!'

As Arthur moved towards the door the sister followed him out of Anne's earshot. 'There seems to be something deep down troubling your mother's mind,' the sister said. 'I don't think there is anything to worry about. But if we don't get to the bottom of it after she's had another good sleep, I'll suggest to Dr Fox he asks the psychiatrist to see her.'

'Thank you, sister. I'm sure she's in very good hands here.'

'Please tell me, Mr Banks,' enquired the sister. 'Who is this "Ronnie" whom you said was killed in a car crash yesterday? Was he a relative?'

'No,' he replied with some emotional difficulty. 'Ronnie was my closest friend. He was the son of someone my mother knew well. We boys, being about the same age, and living not far apart, grew up together. He was almost like another son to her.'

'I see,' she replied. 'I am sorry, but as you can see I had to ask. Thank you for explaining that part of the mystery.'

The sister returned to the room. 'Now, Mrs Banks. We're going to leave you in this room. It's much more cosy, isn't it, than the big ward? And we want you to have another nice deep sleep. Then, when you wake up, perhaps not even until tomorrow morning, I think you're going to feel a lot, lot better.' The sister smiled reassuringly.

'It seems as if you are always sending me to sleep,'

'Sleep is one of the best cures for everyone. Now, do you feel as if you'll have a good sleep without the help of another tablet, or shall we give you one to make quite sure?'

'I'll have one if you think it will make me feel much better?'

'That's very sensible.' The sister turned to the nurse. 'While I go and fetch another draught, Nurse, will you please wash Mrs Banks and attend to her other needs?'

Anne gave the sister and nurse a smile. 'Thank you so much.'

Ten minutes later the sister shut the door quietly behind her, leaving her patient once more alone with her memories. Anne felt physically tired, but her mind continued to fight for attention.

She was worried that certain things which she had firmly resolved many years ago never to tell anyone, might have slipped out in that unguarded few moments. If only she could be sure of both what had actually happened and what she had said had happened!

The more she let her thoughts ramble, the more confused she found herself again becoming. She tormented herself over Ronnie's death. 'If I hadn't done it,' she questioned. 'Would he be alive now?'

Ronnie? Was this his way of punishing her? Of already getting his own back on her? If he were not to appear in tangible form, was he to haunt and confuse her mind for the remainder of her life? The words she kept saying to herself on the bus, came back to her now: 'Yes,' she had tried to convince herself. 'I did it only for his sake. For his sake alone.'

She slipped into another deep sleep.

★ ★ ★ ★ ★

'And how is Mrs Banks today?' It was the same sister from the day before who stood beside her bed. 'Do you feel more rested? You're certainly looking better.'

'I feel very much better, thank you,' Anne smiled.

'I even feel clear in the head, which I certainly didn't yesterday.'

'Good! That's excellent news,' the sister smiled back.

'I feel….,' continued Anne apologetically. 'I feel I must have made an awful fool of myself. I really am most sorry.'

'Don't worry, Mrs Banks. You'd had a very unpleasant and a very sad experience, hadn't you?' she replied with a broader smile, holding a thermometer out towards Anne. 'Pop this under your tongue, please.'

She watched the sister's expression carefully as she withdrew the thermometer a minute later and read it. 'When can I go home?' she asked tentatively.

'Oh, I don't know about going home. Not just yet. We have to get you completely better first. Can't have you going and having any more nasty turns like yesterday, can we?'

'But I do want to go home. And, besides….' She gulped and seemed on the point of breaking down. 'I've got a funeral to attend.'

'Mrs Banks,' replied the sister in a more serious tone. 'It will be up to Dr Fox when you can go out. But, if my assessment is correct, I don't think he'll want to release you for several days yet.' She smiled understandingly. 'And I don't think he'd want you incurring the strains of a funeral either, not right after what you have just been through .'

'What I went through?' Anne repeated with a frown.

'Certainly you can discuss your options with Dr Fox, but he'll tell you, I'm sure, that you had a mild stroke. What is called a "T.I.A." Not very serious. A sort of warning shot. A warning to take things easier in the future.'

Anne noticed a frown cross the sister's face before she asked: 'Have you been under any great strain, Mrs Banks? I don't mean just what happened to your son's best friend. I mean for some time. Perhaps, even for a long time? You appear to be suffering from a degree of hyper-tension.'

Anne responded evasively, reflecting on the years of torment dating back to when a certain Mrs Dulcie Rathbone had married into the family of Anne's employers.

'Don't you think, Sister, that the whole of life is something of a strain? I have my own business and, like all businesses, it has its fair share of problems…. And worries…. And….'

'We'll have to see,' replied the sister, walking towards the door. 'Now, how about some breakfast? What do you feel you would like, Mrs Banks?'

'Just whatever you have, thank you,' she replied, grateful for the opportunity of being waited upon.

'Scrambled egg?'

'That would be very nice, thank you,' she agreed.

'Good. I'll call nurse and she can attend to your needs. And then you stay there in bed until Dr Fox has been in to see you. You can ask him if he'll let you go out, but I'm pretty sure I know what his answer will be.' As the sister opened the door she turned. 'Your son's coming into see you later on, isn't he?'

'Arthur? I shall look forward to that,' she nodded, feeling her eyes begin to cloud over.

'He told me yesterday that he'd look in this morning, and that if you were all right he would catch the mid-day train back to Birmingham.'

'Kind Arthur,' Anne replied, giving the sister a smile. 'He's all I've got now.'

It was four more days before Anne was told by the hospital that she could return home. She missed the funeral, but Arthur managed to get down for the day from Birmingham.

★ ★ ★ ★ ★

Those four days gave Anne the opportunity, not only to rest physically, but to sort out the salient happenings, both pleasurable and not so pleasurable, which had featured in her lifetime. Happenings, some of which she was proud, whilst others of which she was ashamed.

In her mind, Anne chronologically went through her life for the umpteenth time, beginning with what had been, perhaps her saddest year – 1918.

Chapter Two – 1916/1918

For the three years leading up to the outbreak of the Great War in 1914, Anne's father had been head gardener at the Macaulay's large estate, known as "The Grange". Her mother had herself lately taken up employment at The Grange, part-time as a seamstress.

At the age of eight, in 1916, Anne had joined the choir at the local parish church, St Mary's. Her elder sister, Kitty, had been a member for two years and Anne had waited impatiently for the vicar to agree that she, too, could join.

★ ★ ★ ★ ★

This Sunday the sisters were late and ran and walked as fast as their legs would carry them, their mother hurrying some way behind. Their route lay past The Grange and, as they neared the main gates, Anne heard the crunch of car tyres on the shingle drive. The Macaulay's large Rolls slowed as it passed through the impressive gateway just ahead of the two girls.

Anne gazed admiringly at the Macaulay parents sitting grandly on the back seat. Their two daughters were on the folding seats just in front of them. The Macaulay's son was seated beside the chauffeur, Mr Roberts. At that moment, and to the astonishment of both girls, the boy turned his head towards Anne, put up his hand so his parents would not see him from behind, and blew her a kiss.

'Did you see him?' Kitty gasped as the car was driven off.

'He blew me a kiss!' replied Anne thoughtfully.

'I'm going to tell Mummy after church,' Kitty stated.

Ten minutes later the choir filed out of the vestry and, proud in her maroon coloured surplice, Anne reached her seat and glanced towards the congregation over the top of her hymn book. Her eyes fell on the Macaulay boy who stood in the front pew between his mother and one of his sisters.

Later, kneeling in her place at the lower end of the choir stall, Anne found that by slightly parting her hands she could see the boy. She wondered if he had noticed her. She parted her hands a little further.

BANG! One of her heavy music books toppled over the edge of the choir stall on to the stone floor. The vicar glared at her and Anne felt the eyes of everyone were upon her.

The sermon was on covetousness, but despite the vicar beginning by explaining simply that this had to do with people not being content with what they had in life and, instead, being envious of what other, seemingly better-off people had. Anne admitted to herself that she did not understand what he was talking about. And it was not long before her mind was again centred on the boy who, it looked to her, was equally disinterested in the vicar's droning address.

As the three made their way home, Kitty told of how the boy had blown Anne a kiss.

'Oh that Mr Charles is a naughty lad. Always up to something,' her mother commented gruffly. 'At his age, he should know better. Don't take any notice of him, either of you. He's a bit too full of himself if you ask me.'

"Charles," thought Anne, saying the name several times to herself. That is a nice sounding name: "Charles". Her thoughts were of nothing but the boy as they passed the now empty drive of The Grange and headed for their own humble terraced council house.

'He never plays on the common, Mummy,' remarked Anne.

'Those class of boys and girls don't play with the village children,' she replied. 'They're sent away to boarding school and, during the holidays, keep themselves to themselves.'

'I'd like to live in a large house like The Grange when I marry. Wouldn't you, Kitty'?

'Mummy,' asked Anne thoughtfully a few moments later. 'Why do they live in a big house and we live in a tiny one?'

'That's just how life is, dear.'

Not satisfied with so general an answer, Anne extended her questioning: 'Why do they have a great big car and we don't have a car at all?'

'I can see the vicar's sermon didn't make much of an impression on you today, my girl,' rebuked her mother mildly.

Anne ignored the remark. 'Could we have a car? Then we could go to church in it on Sundays. Kitty and I wouldn't have to hurry, and when it's raining we could get there in the dry. Mummy? Could we?'

'I don't think you understand, dear,' sighed her mother. 'Some people, as the vicar was saying, have a lot of money while…. Well, other people don't.'

'Was the vicar telling them off? For having so much money?'

'No Anne, dear. He was trying to tell people like us that we shouldn't be envious of families like the Macaulays who have more money than we do.'

'I think it's all very unfair,' remarked Anne abruptly. 'Don't you, Kitty?'

'I hadn't thought about it.'

'I'm going to have a lot of money when I grow up,' Anne stated defiantly.

'Are you, dear?' Questioned her mother with a light forced laugh. 'And where is all your money going to come from?'

'I don't know. But I shall have lots, because I want to have a bigger house than we've got. And I want a car.'

'And a chauffeur?' teased her mother.

'Yes. I might want a chauffeur, like Mr Roberts.'

'You'll have to marry a very rich man then, dear,' her mother replied with a broad smile.

As they reached their small terraced house in the village, Anne said, more to herself than to either of the others: 'I think Charles is rather nice.'

★ ★ ★ ★ ★

It was June, two years later. when for the day, the grounds of The Grange were opened to the public for a parish fête in aid of war orphans. Anne was showing excitement as she reached the gates of The Grange, accompanied by her mother and sister, and began to walk up the long drive. Soon they came across a trestle table where they found Mr Roberts selling programmes.

'Hullo, my dears,' he said cheerily. 'Hullo, Mr Roberts,' replied their mother, 'Yes, we'd better have a programme. How much are they?'

'Three pence, please. And that includes the draw. See,' he said, to Anne, whilst pointing to the corner of the programme. 'Here's your lucky number. You may win a prize.'

The sisters were anxious to reach the stalls and take part in the side-shows. And Anne was hoping to see Charles Macaulay.

After being unsuccessful at the housey-housey stall, and failing to win a goldfish, their mother offered to buy them each an ice cream as a special treat.

They were on their way to buy these when Anne spotted Charles at the coconut shy, and immediately hurried over to have a closer look. Charles had three coconuts left, and though the second of his shots grazed one of the balanced nuts, it failed to dislodge it.

As he reached to pick up his last nut, he caught sight of Anne watching him. He took the remaining coconut and, with an unnecessarily exaggerated action build-up, put all his strength into throwing it. The shot was well off target. Indeed, to Anne's unconcealed amusement, it went right over the top of the screening and, a second later, an ominous crash told those in the vicinity that a pane of glass had been broken.

But Anne had no eyes for this. The boy, looking thoroughly disgruntled, turned to face her. 'That was your fault, you…. You, stupid girl!'

'No it wasn't my fault!' she snapped back indignantly. 'And I'm not stupid either!'

'My father will be very cross with me,' he said dolefully, turning away.

'I'm sorry,' she said quietly. Then, regaining her composure, she asked more breezily. 'Can I help you clear up the bits?'

'No point. One of the servants will do it.' Then, as if to put the matter out of his mind, he changed the subject, 'You haven't been here before, have you? Would you like to see our garden playroom?'

'Yes, I would. Yes, please,' Anne responded eagerly.
'Follow me then.'

They reached a barn-like building standing on its own. Charles went in. Anne followed and found herself in a sort of gymnasium. There was a pair of climbing ropes, bars along one wall and a vaulting horse. But what caught her eyes were toys. Her eyes widened even further as she took in the dolls house, the dolls and rows of soldiers, two tricycles and a fine pedal car.

He noticed how admiringly she was taking everything in. 'Of course,' he boasted. 'The more expensive toys are kept up in the nursery. That's up on the top floor of the main house. I can't take you there.'

'But how wonderful this is,' she exclaimed as she pulled a curtain back and peered into a curtained-off corner of the room.

'That was my sisters' Wendy House. They used to have their pretendy dolls tea parties in there.' The boy spoke with derision and sighed audibly: 'I think girls are silly to play with dolls.'

'I have a doll. She's called Betsy and my daddy gave her to me when I was quite small. She's awfully old looking now, and she's lost one eye and one arm's nearly off. But I love her.'

'How old are you?'

'I've just had my tenth birthday,' Anne replied proudly.

'I've just had my thirteenth. Too old to play with any of the toys in this place. Most of them belong to my two sisters anyway. I expect they will be given away soon. To the poor.'

'I think it's all so wonderful,' she bubbled excitedly, oblivious to his manner and comments. 'You are so lucky. I'd love to have a playroom.'

'I'm not allowed to have people in from the village. Today's different because of the fête. We ought to go back. now.'

'Yes,' said Anne. 'My mother may be looking for me.'

'Come on then. Race me!' he called, hurrying from the building..

She found it impossible to keep up. 'Slower, please, Charles! STOP, please. I may get lost. please , Charles.'

'BOO!' He exclaimed, jumping out from behind a tree. 'What did I hear you call me?'

'Oh! You made me jump.' she was panting. 'Please don't leave me alone again.'

'You called me Charles.'

'That's your name, isn't it?'

'Yes, it is, but the staff have to call me "Mister Charles".'

'I'm not one of your staff.'

'Ah, but your mother is, isn't she? She does our clothes mending and things like that. Doesn't she?'

'Yes, she does, but I don't have to call you "Mister Charles".'

'What's your name?'

'Anne, Anne Jones.'

He grunted something inaudibly and turned away. 'Let's get back to the fête,' he added. 'I'm bored. 'Sorry I called you stupid. Goodbye.'

'Goodbye.' She walked slowly back to the centre of the fête activities and began to search for her mother.'

'Ah! There you are, Anne dear! Where have you been?'

Anne told her mother what she had been doing, and it was immediately impressed upon her that she was not to go off alone again at her age. 'That Mr Charles is not the nicest of boys. He's the type who might choose to lock you in a cupboard. Play with the boys and girls from the village. There are plenty of nice children of your age there.'

Anne did not reply. "Village boys" she had already decided, were not for her after a handsome thirteen year old, who lived in a large house with lots of staff, had befriended her.

It was six o'clock when Mrs Jones suggested they should think about going home. 'Oh, we can't go yet, Mummy,' cried Kitty. 'They haven't drawn the numbers for the programme prizes.'

'Nor they have. We'll wait until they've done that. just in case we've won something.'

Fifteen minutes later everyone was summoned to the largest tent and the draw began. There were ten prizes laid out, which Anne and Kitty had inspected earlier in the afternoon. A cuddly sailor doll was what had caught Anne's fancy. The first prize went to a Mr Thompson who chose a box of coloured soaps. The second prize was won by a lady from the village. She chose a rolling pin.

'The third number is....' Said the vicar, dipping his hand once more into the inverted hat in front of him: 'One thousand, four hundred and thirty-two. Will the holder of that numbered programme please come forward and choose his or her prize?'

Anne and Kitty glanced once more unhappily at the programme their mother held in her hand.

'I've got it! I've got it!' came a boisterous voice from the back, and a moment later all eyes were on Charles Macaulay as he elbowed his way to the front.

'He would win,' muttered Kitty indignantly. 'As if he hasn't already got all he needs.' Anne felt pleased that her idol had won.

As Charles surveyed the prizes, Anne guessed he would choose the large box of crayons. Instead, and much to her instant dismay, he chose the cuddly sailor doll. He picked it up and, with a nod to the vicar, walked towards where Anne was standing. 'Here, this is for you.' With a slight blush he held out the doll and, as Anne took it, he pushed past her and was at once swallowed up in the crowd.

'Oh thank you. Thank you,' Anne gulped as she recovered from her surprise. She looked up from admiring the doll, but her benefactor was nowhere to be seen. 'Mummy, look!' She cried out.

'I know, dear. I saw what happened. That was very kind of Mr Charles. I never expected him to do a kind thing like that. Do you want to keep the doll?'

'Keep it? I'm going to keep him for ever,' she pronounced.

The fête had surpassed her highest expectations, and she could not wait to meet her new won friend again.

★ ★ ★ ★ ★

For most people in England, Armistice year was one of great rejoicing at the ending of the carnage in the trenches of Northern France. But for many, if not most, families there was a rampant killer loose, one which was to take even more lives than the bullets of war – that killer was the 1918 pandemic influenza bug.

For Anne, as for thousands of European families, the latter part of 1918 was to see their loved ones becoming caught up in double tragedies. Anne's trauma began with her being sent away to stay with a widowed aunt. She was already aware that something was wrong because of the concern being shown towards her sister. The two shared a small bedroom and Anne had found it increasingly difficult to sleep on account of Kitty's seemingly endless coughing.

Her aunt was a kind person, and Anne enjoyed the change having only rarely stayed long at the seaside. 'You are lucky, Auntie, to live so near the sea. I wish we did.'

'Do you, dear?' she replied 'You live in the country, and that's nice too.'

'I suppose so,' agreed Anne unenthusiastically. 'I wish, too, we lived in a nice house like yours. Ours is ever so small'.

Her aunt smiled understandingly before replying, choosing her words carefully: 'I only live in a larger house than you do, Anne, because I married someone who earned more money.'

'Uncle Howard?'

'That's right. Do you remember him? He was a very clever engineer, and made a lot of money. This house is one of the nice things we were able to afford. Your daddy is a very clever gardener, but gardeners, however expert they are, don't usually earn quite as much as engineers do.'

'However, marrying the right man, someone you truly love, dear, is more important than how much he earns.' Her aunt paused and smiled again at her niece. 'My sister, your mother, and I were both very lucky in the people we married.'

'I'm longing for my Daddy to be home again,' sighed Anne. 'Perhaps he will earn some more money. Then we could have a bigger house, also a car. You've got a car, Auntie.'

Her aunt then changed the subject. 'Your mother tells me you're a clever girl, and that you're second in your class despite being the youngest. That's very good. Do you like school?'

'Yes I do, Auntie. Did you like your school? Where did you go to school?'

'Your mother and I went to a private school in Eastbourne.'

'I go to the school in the village,' Anne stated proudly

'So I hear,' replied her aunt. If she disapproved or had other views on her sister marrying below her family's expectations, she did not reveal the fact. 'What do you want to become when you grow up, Anne? Or is it too early for you to have any ideas?'

'I want to be a librarian.'

'Your mother told me you borrow lots of grown up books from your village library. Do you read fact or fiction? Do you know what the difference is?'

'I do know the difference. And it always makes the ladies in our library laugh at what I borrow, as the other children of my age all borrow from the "Junior section".'

'It sounds as if you have an insatiable thirst for knowledge, Anne?' Her aunt commented. 'It should stand you in very good stead through out life. A fine asset to have.'

'I love learning about new things.'

'I'm sure none of your Uncle Howard's engineering books would interest you, but I know he had several encyclopaedias and other similar books. They're in the study. When we've finished our meal, shall we go and see what we can find? I shall never read them, so you are most welcome to take some of them home with you. I say only "some" of them as they are very heavy tombs to carry far.'

'That's very kind of you, Auntie. Do you really mean I can keep the books?

'Yes, I do. And I'm sure your uncle would be happy to see them put to good use again.'

Anne was delighted when, after some weeks, her aunt told her that her mother would be coming down the next day to see them both and to take Anne home.

'Isn't Kitty coming with Mummy?' Anne quickly asked.

'I don't think so, dear,'

'Why not? She enjoys the seaside as much as I do.'

'Your mother will tell you the reason when she gets here,'

The next morning, at breakfast, Anne showed mounting excitement. 'What time will Mummy get here, Auntie?'

'Her train gets in at 11 o'clock and then it's another ten minutes on the bus.'

At precisely eleven-ten, Anne asked her aunt if she could go and wait by the bus stop. 'All right, but don't cross the road and don't go further than I can see you from here.'

'I won't, Auntie,'

Some minutes later, as Mrs Jones alighted from her bus on the opposite side of the road, Anne shouted: 'Mummy! Over here!' She waved her arms up and down gleefully.

Mrs Jones crossed the road before responding, in a very subdued sounding voice: 'Hullo, Anne, dear. How are you?'

'Where's Kitty, Mummy?' Her mother did not answer but put a hand firmly on her daughter's shoulders, drawing her tightly into her side.

'Let's go inside Auntie's house and I'll explain.' After a few words with her sister, a very subdued Mrs Jones sat down on the settee and drew Anne down beside her. In a voice which was breaking with emotion she spoke in little more than a whisper. 'I have some very, very sad news to tell you, Anne. Our darling Kitty has died.'

'No!' exclaimed Anne. 'Died? She's dead?'

'Yes,'

'Has she gone to heaven, and we won't see her again?'

As Anne buried her face in her hands her mother answered. 'Yes Kitty's gone to heaven, my dearest one, and we know that gentle Jesus will take the greatest care of her.' Mrs Jones herself then broke down, tightly hugging her surviving daughter 'We all need to be brave and be thankful Kitty's now out of all the horrid pain she has had to endure,' she sobbed. 'It's a truly horrible disease.'

Their arrival back home, later that day, was as unnerving for Anne as it was distressing for her mother. Their little terraced council house seemed lifeless.

'Where is Kitty's bed, Mummy?' Anne asked, going into the bedroom the two sisters used to share.

'We won't be needing it any more, so I've sold it,' replied Mrs Jones, seeming to be on the point of breaking down again.

★ ★ ★ ★ ★

After some months, Anne felt life had returned to as much normality as it was ever likely to and, with favourable news flowing in from France of the Germans being driven back, her father was confidently expected home for Christmas. But that was not to be, and a brief impersonal telegram delivered at the front door was the means by which Mrs Jones first learned that she, like her sister before her, had become a war widow.

'Mum?' shouted Anne, opening the front door after skipping home from school one day. 'Mummy, guess where I've come out in class this month? Mum? Where are you?'

A weeping Mrs Jones emerged slowly from their small kitchenette.

'Whatever is the matter, Mum?'

'It's Daddy,' sobbed her mother.

'What's happened to Daddy?' Anne begged, anxiety showing plainly in her voice.

'He's been killed. I've had a telegram, just like the one Auntie received during the early part of the war. When your Uncle Howard lost his life.'

'Oh, no! Not my Daddy!' Anne exclaimed, coming over to be hugged by her mother. 'Are you sure it's our Daddy?'

'I'm afraid so, Anne. There is no getting away from this second blow. First, the consumption pandemic took our Kitty from us. Now the war has taken your father's life on the battlefield.'

After a few minutes of hugging each other, Mrs Jones blurted out: 'I don't know what we shall do financially. We certainly won't be able to afford to keep renting even this little house. All the income I shall have will be a miserly war widow's pension, and my part-time earnings as a seamstress up at The Grange. I don't know what I'm going to do.'

'We could go and stay with Auntie?' sobbed Anne.

'I don't think Auntie would want us for very long, perhaps to have us for a short holiday, but that would be all.'

The summons to The Grange reached Mrs Jones as she and Anne were eating their high tea in silence the following day.

"Ere's a note for you, Mrs Jones,' said Tommy, the Macaulay's boot-boy at the door, one of his seemingly perpetual grins covering his face. 'Mrs Macaulay wants to see yer. Been naughty, 'ave yer?'

Mrs Jones opened the note nervously. It was written on heavy quality paper and Anne at once noticed that it bore a family crest at the top, It read:

Dear Mrs Jones,
My husband and I were shocked and distressed to learn of your husband's tragic death in France, and offer both you and your daughter our deepest sympathy. Mr Jones gave us faithful service over many years, most recently as head gardener, and he will be sadly missed by us all.
If convenient, we would like to discuss with you and your daughter some suggestions we have for relieving the difficult financial position you may now experience. Can you manage to see me tomorrow morning? Shall we say 10.30?
Yours truly,
R.A. MACAULAY (Mrs)

The next morning Anne, clutched her mother's hand as, dressed in their best Sunday clothes, they made their way up the back drive to the staff entrance to The Grange.

'What do you think the lady will say, Mummy? Why can't we go and live with Auntie?' Anne pleaded for the fourth time in as many hours.

Mrs Jones replied: 'As I've already said, I don't think Auntie would want us permanently. And there is no point in going to her temporarily. I would lose my job here,'

They reached the house and Mrs Jones opened the back door and guided Anne in. 'Now make sure your shoes are clean, dear. I know Cook, and she'll be after you if you put as much as a speck of mud on the floor of her kitchen. We'll go and find Mrs Lines,' said her mother.

'Who is Mrs Lines?'

'Mrs Lines is the house-keeper. One of the two most important members of the staff.'

'Who's the other important person?'

'Shhh! Not so loud. Cook.'

At that moment, a loud and authoritative voice suddenly broke the silence. 'Come here, Tommy! You take these potatoes here back down the garden again. I've told you, and I've told that lazy Simon, I will not have him sending potatoes up to the house which haven't been properly washed first! Now, take them back again. And don't be long, the scullery maids have ten pounds to peel for lunch today.'

Anne felt herself shaking at the knees at this verbal onslaught.

Cook had her rotund white-aproned back to them as they entered the kitchen, and Anne sensed her mother's equal unease. 'Oh, good morning. Good morning, Cook.' Cook turned to stare at them, a rolling pin brandished in mid-air.

'Mrs Macaulay has sent for us,' said Mrs Jones timidly. 'May we go through and find Mrs Lines?'

'Yes, you may go through, Mrs Jones.'

Anne felt Cook's eyes inspecting her from head to foot as she walked by. 'So this is your daughter, is it Mrs Jones?' She enquired without feeling.

'Yes,' mumbled Anne.

'Say "Yes, Cook",' corrected Mrs Jones nervously.

Cook suddenly looked stern again and, pointing to Anne, said: 'If she's going with you to talk to Mrs Macaulay in the morning room, I hope her shoes are really clean.'

'We made sure of wiping them very well by the back door,' replied Mrs Jones timorously.

'Good! Well, you'd better get along. Mrs Lines is in the store cupboard. Good luck!' Cook turned once more to the enormous scrubbed table which dominated the centre of the kitchen and began to knead the bread she was making, putting the extra stones of her over weight body and the strength of her muscles into each pummelling movement.

As soon as they passed from Cook's sight, Mrs Jones gave her daughter a reassuring smile. 'Mrs Lines is very different. You'll like her.' Further down another brown linoleum covered passage Mrs Jones stopped and tapped on a half-opened door.

'Come in!' The voice was gentle and welcoming.

A lady, dressed smartly in a plain black close-fitting dress, and some years older than her mother, was standing on a pair of steps. She turned and descended with both hands clutched firmly around several tins.

'Hullo, Mrs Jones.' Then, turning, added with a warm smile: 'And this must be your Anne. How are you, dear?'

'All right, thank you,' Anne smiled, appreciating the friendly reception.

'Let me finish putting out the lunch order, then I'll take you along to the morning room,' Anne continued to survey the tightly packed shelves with amazement. 'This is like a grocer's shop!' she squeaked, having temporarily forgotten the sad reason for their visit.

'Yes, it is a bit like a shop, isn't it, Anne?' replied Mrs Lines.

'We have a lot of mouths to feed. And today the Macaulays have visitors to lunch. This is what Cook requires today. She gives me a list each morning and I put out the items.'

'I wish Mummy's store cupboard was like this one.'

Mrs Lines locked the door. 'Now, let us go and find out if Mrs Macaulay is ready to see you, shall we?'

With Mrs Lines leading the way, the three walked to the end of the passage where Anne watched with fascination as Mrs Lines first pulled back a pair of heavy plain white painted doors to reveal, only a few inches behind, a second much grander, mahogany panelled, pair of doors.

'This is where the private side of the house begins,' whispered Mrs Lines. 'And I must ask you, Anne, if you'll please be extra quiet.' She spoke in a friendly manner and Anne was intrigued as Mrs Lines then had to use her strength to push apart the second pair of doors,

'It seemed to Anne that they passed from the world she knew into a kind of fairyland. The plain brown linoleum floor cover gave way immediately to thick carpets, which she at first found quite difficult to walk upon. With her mouth wide open, Anne stared upwards at the ornate plaster ceilings and the highly decorative and priceless chandeliers.

Mrs Lines noticed her expression. 'The Grange is a lovely house, isn't it?'

'I've never seen anything like it,' sighed Anne. 'I thought it would be something like my Auntie's house, but bigger.' As she spoke, she gazed around at the portraits, as old bearded and heavily wigged gentlemen, and expressionless but beautifully dressed women, stared coldly back at her. Who were all these people, she wondered?

'Come on, dear,' whispered her mother, as Anne lingered.

'Coming, Mummy!' she whispered back. Across the hall they walked, past the grand staircase. Not even in her picture books, Anne reasoned, had she ever seen a setting like this.

With a discreet hand movement, Mrs Lines indicated she wanted the two visitors to wait a few yards from one large and impressive looking closed door.

'Don't worry, dear,' Mrs Jones said reassuringly, as she observed her daughter's anxious gaze. 'Mrs Macaulay is very nice. Like Mrs Lines.'

'I like Mrs Lines,' she murmured. Then, as much to herself as to her mother, she added: 'Cook gave me the creeps.'

'Yes, Cook can be a bit frightening.'

Five minutes passed before Mrs Lines drew the door open. 'Do come in. Mrs Macaulay will see you now.'

Anne's hand reached out for her mother's as Mrs Lines formally announced them. 'Do you wish me to stay, madam?'

'Oh, yes. Do please stay, Mrs Lines,' replied the tall elegant lady who had risen from her chair in front of a large Victorian bureau. She seemed to Anne to glide rather than to walk across the room towards where, with a welcoming smile, she held out her hand. 'Mrs Jones, I am so pleased you are able to come in to see me.'

'Good morning, Madam,' responded Mrs Jones conscious that she herself was feeling somewhat weak-kneed.

'And this must be Anne,' said Mrs Macaulay quietly, as Anne peered round the side of her mother into the eyes of a simply but smartly dressed lady with a particularly gentle sounding voice.

'Hullo,'

'You're a big girl. Ten years old I'm told.'

'Yes,' she replied,

After enquiring where Anne went to school and some other introductory details, Mrs Jones began to feel more at ease. 'Mrs Lines tells me you are a wonderful seamstress, and I must say I've never had anything to complain about on that side.' She smiled agreeably at both of them in turn.

'Thank you, Madam,' Mrs Jones replied quietly.

'But we have no extra work of that kind to give to you at the moment.' Mrs Macaulay paused. 'You of course know dear old Mrs Plummer?'

'Very well, Madam,' nodded Mrs Jones.

'As you know then, Mrs Plummer is responsible for cleaning all the silver in the house. She had pneumonia last winter and I feel, and Mrs Lines here shares my view, that perhaps the time has come to let Mrs Plummer retire.'

'Yes, Madam,' nodded Mrs Jones, following the purpose of these comments.

Mrs Lines lent forward and took up the conversation. 'Mrs Macaulay and I were wondering if you would like to take over Mrs Plummer's work. It is a highly responsible job since much of the silver at The Grange is very valuable. With your seamstress duties, it would provide you with a full-time job here. What do you think?'

'That would be wonderful. It really would. Thank you, thank you so much, Madam,' responded Mrs Jones.

'I am so glad you like our idea, Mrs Jones,' continued Mrs Macaulay. 'I will leave Mrs Lines to go into the details with you.'

'Thank you, Madam, thank you so much,' repeated Mrs Jones.

Mrs Macaulay went straight to the next point. 'Now we have one other suggestion to make. We like to have the majority of our house staff living on the premises. It so happens that we have a staff flat, only a small one I'm afraid, free at the moment.'

Mrs Lines took over the explanations. 'Above the stables block, which is, of course, now used by Mr Roberts for garaging the cars, there is some living accommodation.'

'So I've heard,'

Mrs Lines continued: 'One group of rooms houses the unmarried parlour, chamber and scullery maids. The other group of rooms, which is quite separate, is, as Madam has just said, more like a small flat. It has its own kitchen.'

Mrs Macaulay, who had been watching Mrs Jones's facial expressions closely, asked: 'Do you think you and Anne would like to have that flat as your home?'

'It sounds a wonderful idea, Madam. I'm sure Anne and I would like it.' Then turning to her daughter, she asked: 'You'd like that wouldn't you, dear?'

'I don't know, Mummy! Does it mean the lady is giving the flat to us, for ever and ever?'

Mrs Macaulay smiled. 'Well, not exactly giving it. Not in the same way as you give someone a present. Our staff pay what is called a token rent. So they really lease the accommodation from us for as long as they remain members of the staff.'

'I see,' Anne replied, a frown appearing on her face.

'Mrs Lines will go into all the details with you, Mrs Jones'

'Thank you Madam. Thank you very much. I'm sure it will all work out very nicely. I'm….We're both very grateful to you for helping us so much,' Mrs Jones stammered.

'Don't mention it,' replied Mrs Macaulay with a smile at each of them. 'We are delighted to be able to help in this small way.' then added: 'And we are very pleased indeed that you can help us by taking over the important silver cleaning work. That is a load off our minds, isn't it Mrs Lines?'

'It certainly is, Madam,' agreed Mrs Lines, rising to her feet.

Mrs Jones also stood up and, turning to Anne, said: 'Come along now. We mustn't take up any more of Madam's valuable time.'

'Goodbye,' said Mrs Macaulay. 'And if you have any problems, don't hesitate to discuss them with Mrs Lines.'

'Thank you, Madam. Thank you very much.'

The three left the morning room and retraced their steps back through the house. Mrs Lines spoke first as she closed the second pair of double doors into the staff quarters behind them.

'I expect you'd like to see the flat.' Anne was not listening. Instead she stopped and was making a further study of the two doors, putting a hand out to feel their surface.

'And what is it that's puzzling our Anne?' enquired Mrs Lines in a jocular tone.

'Why,' she replied. 'Do you live this side of the house and not in the nice part?' Mrs Lines merely smiled her silent acknowledgement as Anne glanced again about her. 'I hate all this brown colour everywhere.'

'Now come along, dear,' responded Mrs Jones sharply. 'We don't make rude remarks like that about other people's houses.'

'We're only the staff on this side,' replied Mrs Lines with a friendly smile.

'What's the difference,' queried Anne quietly, not expecting and not receiving an answer.

The stable block was several hundred yards from the main house and was not over generous in size. 'I was hoping,' remarked Anne, it might be more like Auntie's house at the sea, with more and bigger rooms.'

'I think when we've got the carpets down and the furniture in, we'll be able to make it nice and cosy and homely.' She crossed the room to give her daughter an affectionate hug. 'We'll just have to make the best we can of it, won't we?'

'I suppose so, Mummy,' she replied thoughtfully, then queried suddenly: 'Mummy, what do we do for a lav?'

Mrs Lines spoke: 'I'm afraid the main house's drains don't extend down as far as here.'

'Don't worry,' smiled Mrs Jones. 'We only have an outside one at our council house.'

'That's all right then,' replied Mrs Lines. 'You'll have your own here. You turn left at the foot of the stairs and it's round the back of the first garage. It's totally private there and it will be emptied once a week by the gardeners.' Mrs Lines continued: 'Of course you can always use the staff facilities up at the main house, if you prefer. There's a bathroom there as I'm sure, Mrs Jones, you will have noticed, next to the staff hall.'

'Auntie's house has two proper toilets in it, one upstairs and one downstairs,' commented Anne, still not giving up hope of improving on the cards life had seemingly dealt her.

Two weeks later the Jones moved into their new accommodation.

Chapter Three – Christmas 1918

Christmas, Mrs Jones had been warned, was always a busy time for the house staff at The Grange, and 1918 was to be no exception. The Macaulay family and their close friends would be staying at The Grange over the holiday. Every bedroom in the house would be occupied, and many other acquaintances would be coming in for the grand Christmas Day dinner and dance.

Mrs Jones was kept fully occupied in the days leading up to Christmas with every piece of silver being brought out from the safes for the dinner. Anne spent much of Christmas Eve morning with one of the gardeners, gathering holly from the trees in the paddock.

'I think that should be enough, my dear. Now I'll have to get one of the men to help me take it down to the house.'

An hour later the last of the holly had been placed in the conservatory under the watchful eye of Mrs Lines. 'Anne, if you would like to help with the decorating this afternoon you may do so, but you must keep quiet and do what the staff tell you. That's a good girl. I expect you like Christmas time, don't you?'

'Yes, I do, Mrs Lines. And thank you.....for letting me help.'

After a hurriedly eaten lunch, Anne set to work with the staff. When the holly decorating had been completed two of the gardeners brought in a high pair of steps and began hanging paper streamers from the centre chandelier out to the gallery. The last item to be carefully positioned was a gigantic Christmas tree. Dressing it with glittering streamers and paper chains and a variety of highly coloured gewgaws and fairy lights occupied all the helpers. 'Now, to complete the tree how about Anne fixing the angel for us on the top?' suggested Mr Roberts as the work neared completion.

'Could I?'

'If you promise to be careful on the high steps. I'll hold them for you.' When all was finished, Mrs Macaulay was invited to inspect the result. Anne felt proud to have been allowed to help on this occasion.

Punctually at ten o'clock on Christmas Day morning, the staff were gathered together in the staff hall. Anne was there with her mother, as were the children of several other members of the staff. On a signal from Mrs Lines the staff lined up in a crocodile formation and followed her through the staff quarters into the main hall and took up positions in a large semicircle.

The Jones had barely reached their places when Anne's attention was drawn to Mrs Macaulay emerging from the morning room. She was followed by Mr Macaulay, then by their two daughters and lastly, to Anne's delight, but sudden pang of embarrassment, by Charles.

Mrs Macaulay began coming down the line, shaking each member of the staff by the hand and wishing them a happy Christmas. Mrs Lines followed her, pushing a large wicker laundry basket on wheels. Out of this she took and handed to Mrs Macaulay, wrapped and individually addressed presents for everyone there.

'Just think of that!' exclaimed Mrs Jones in a whisper. 'Everyone on the staff, and even their children, getting their own present. I do think the Macaulays are a wonderful family to work for.'

Anne made no reply. She had noticed that Mr Macaulay and all three children were following their mother's lead and were coming down the row shaking everyone in turn by the hand. Anne hardly noticed when Mrs Macaulay handed to her a brown parcel. Her eyes were riveted upon the approaching Macaulay children.

'Happy Christmas, Anne. Here's a little something for you, from our family,' said Mrs Macaulay. 'I do hope you like it.'

'Happy Christmas,' Anne replied. 'Thank you very much.'

Mr Macaulay was a tall man and leaned slightly as he took Anne's mother's hand. 'A happy Christmas to you, Mrs Jones'

'Thank you, Sir. And a happy one to you and your family.'

'And this must be Anne Jones,' he said, taking a pace sideways. 'A happy Christmas to you, Anne.' He spoke with an authoritative but not unfriendly voice. 'My! You are like your mother, aren't you?'

'Happy Christmas,' Anne replied formally.

The seasonal greetings with the two daughters were quickly exchanged as Anne eyed with mounting apprehension the approach down the line of their brother.

'Happy Christmas, Mrs Jones,' Charles said pleasantly.

'Happy Christmas, Mr Charles,' she replied. Then, as he was about to step sideways, she added: 'This is my daughter, Anne. I believe it was you who so kindly won that doll for her in the raffle two years ago. Such a nice doll. It's given her so much pleasure.'

Anne frowned. Why, she questioned to herself in visible annoyance, does my mother have to go and raise that very old matter just now?

'That's right,' he replied, his face spreading into a broad grin as he moved opposite and took Anne's hand. It seemed to her he held it for an extra long time and she felt herself turning crimson. 'Do you still have it?' he enquired,

'Yes, I do,' she replied awkwardly. This long looked forward to meeting was certainly not going the way Anne had hoped it would develop. Why had her mother messed it up?

'I'm pleased to hear that.' Then, holding out his hand again he added: 'So let me also wish your doll, a very happy Christmas!'

'Thank you,' she stammered. He turned to walk away as she suddenly remembered what she was meant to say: 'A happy Christmas to you, too,' she called after him

He turned back. 'Thank you, Anne. Thank you.' He had the same broad smile on his face. Her heart, she realised, was beating very fast.

Mrs Jones, who had been closely observing this encounter, remarked to her daughter: 'Mr Charles is growing up into a very nice young gentleman. Boarding school has done him a world of good. He was very nice to you, dear, wasn't he?'

'Yes,' she mumbled. What a stunner he was, she thought to herself, giving him a final glance as the staff, now led by Cook, who was clearly anxious to get back to her Christmas Day cooking, made their way back towards the staff quarters.

'Now, Anne dear,' warned Mrs Jones, 'You'd better hurry otherwise you'll be late for your Christmas Day Matins'.

It was Mrs Lines who, later on Christmas Day, thoughtfully suggested that Anne might like to peep in at the dancing. 'If your mother brings you over to The Grange at about nine o'clock, all the guests will be so busy talking and dancing, no one will notice you. You'll have to go up the back staircase. I'll get one of the chambermaids to show you. You can then go through to and stand in the corner of the gallery. You can see everyone from there. Would you like that?'

'I certainly would. Thank you. I must go and tell Mummy.'

'You'd better put on your best frock, dear,' Mrs Jones advised. 'You'll be less conspicuous if you're in a frock like the young lady guests.'

An urgent request for Mrs Jones to help with the washing up had been sent down to their flat earlier in the evening, so Anne now found herself sitting alone in the staff hall waiting for the dancing to begin. During the dinner the orchestra had been playing, and she could hear the music in the distance as she waited. Suddenly she was aware that the tempo had changed. It was also now louder she realised. Then listening carefully, she recognised the strains of Strauss's BLUE DANUBE WALTZ. The dancing must have begun.

She walked quietly from the staff hall. The kitchen was deserted, but there was a lot of clattering of dishes coming from the scullery. She would not bother to find someone to show her which way to go, she decided. She knew roughly the way Mrs Lines had suggested. The service stairs leading from the kitchen quarters were narrow, uncarpeted and very steep.

At the top she found a landing and a small tea dispensing area. She passed this and pulled open two large white painted doors which spanned the end of the short passage. Like the ones on the ground floor, these two doors had a second one immediately behind each of them which was heavier and of better quality, being panelled in Mahogany. On pushing the doors open, she found before her a wide carpeted and more luxurious corridor. Various doors led off on each side, but these she ignored as the sounds of the music indicated the direction she should head.

The corridor was only half lit, but this did not worry her. A pair of heavy curtains hung partly across the further end and some light along the bottom of them guided her. When she drew one curtain aside she found herself in a dimly lit corner of the gallery.

And what a sight revealed itself to her. The big hall was packed with couples dancing vigorously around. But what caught her eyes immediately were the dresses. The most beautiful brightly coloured dresses she had ever seen. For some minutes she stood quite still absorbing all before her.

Then, as her confidence grew, she began to move, very slightly to begin with, then more adventurously, with the music. She swung to and fro and began to visualise herself down on the floor dancing with the other people.

And when the orchestra started playing the VALETTA she began counting her twirls. It was not until she had lost count that she suddenly realised she was no longer alone. Someone had entered the area from the opposite corridor, but she could not see who it was, since the person remained in the shadows.

'Hullo, Anne,' came a voice she at once recognised. 'I didn't know you were a dancer.'

'Oh! You made me jump.'

'I'm sorry. I didn't mean to break into your fantasies. You seemed lost in a dream. Were you?' asked Charles.

'I suppose I was.... A bit,' she replied, hanging her head and not knowing what to say or do. Feeling suddenly guilty, she added formally: 'Mrs Lines said I could stand here for a little while, and watch the dancing.'

'Of course you can. And how would you like to dance yourself? Properly, I mean. Have you been taught?'

'Yes. Sort of at school.' He looked even more handsome than when he had shaken her by the hand that morning.

'The same with me,' he continued. 'At school. I'm no good. But you, Anne.' Now it was his turn to be hesitant. 'If I may say so, you are a very pretty girl. We don't have pretty girls to dance with at college. There are only other boys.' He shrugged his shoulders. 'And who wants to dance with another boy? They make us just practise the steps, over and over again. But, as I said, there's no point in dancing without girls. Is there?'

'There are boys and girls at my school,' responded Anne with a light laugh, thinking what an odd school Charles must go to.

'I wish there were at mine. Would you like to try here?'

'Oh! No! I couldn't go down there,' she replied, horror at the idea reflected in her voice. 'Not where everyone would see me!'

'We don't have to go down there. We could dance up here. There's plenty of room.' With that, he approached her, holding his arms up somewhat stiffly in the position to take hers.

Conscious of her heart once more beating fit to burst, rather clumsily she slipped her left hand up into his much larger one and placed her right hand uncertainly on his shoulder. She felt his arm slide around her waist and his hand draw her slightly towards him. How big and strong and very masculine he seemed, and the long coat of his tails, she soon discovered, had a satin face to its lapels. She found the garment soft as she occasionally brushed her cheek against it. Could this really be happening, she questioned, or was she just having the most enchanting of dreams?

'Do you know what mistletoe is, Anne?' he whispered. 'Did you notice the sprig hanging across those two curtains when you came on to the gallery?' He jerked his head to indicate the direction, but kept hold of both her hands.

'No,' she replied, glancing up at the curtain behind him and wondering if he were just teasing her. 'I don't see any.'

'Come over and have a closer look,' he replied, leading her by the hand. He stopped close to the curtain and pointed upwards. 'There, do you see it now?'

In the half light she could discern the piece of mistletoe which had been pinned to the curtain where the two met over the entrance to the corridor. She was still gazing upwards when she felt him move closer and pass his arms partly around her waist. She felt herself catch a short breath.

'Look at me, Anne,' he said very quietly. Slowly and very nervously, she lowered her gaze from the mistletoe and found herself looking straight into his eyes. 'The mistletoe is one of our family traditions. It's put there every Christmas,' he stated. 'My father says it's so any of the family who fancies giving someone, a kiss, has every excuse for doing so.'

'Oh,' was the only word Anne felt able to offer. She stood quite still and tried to decide whether she was frightened or merely unsure of what to do next. She did neither, but remained, quite still, as she felt him bring his body closer to hers, and felt his warm breath near her face. 'I.... I don't.... I don't know that we should,' she stammered as she felt herself powerless to resist the brief kiss he placed upon her cheek.

'I hope you didn't mind my doing that,' he added apologetically, drawing himself back. 'As I said, Anne, and I meant it, you are a very pretty girl. But you're still young and I have no wish to frighten you. As I'm now thirteen, you must be ten, the same three years separate us as when I showed you our garden playroom.'

He sounded so grown up to her. Again words failed, and she said no more than: 'Oh! I really think I ought to be going now.'

Then, as she went through the curtains and started to retrace her way towards the staff staircase, he came up beside her. She felt his arm go around her waist again, but he made no attempt to restrain her. He then spoke, again very quietly. 'It might be better if you didn't tell anyone I accosted you on the gallery. My father doesn't take kindly to his children getting too familiar with the staff and their families.'

'I won't tell anyone,' she whispered, once more feeling herself in a dream. 'I promise.'

'That's jolly decent of you.' Then, after a pause he added: 'There's no mistletoe here, but what about one more kiss?' She did not answer, but stood quite still. He bent forward and again she felt his lips against her cheek. 'Thank you, Anne,' he whispered as he released her. 'I do hope you've enjoyed your Christmas.'

'I have,' she replied promptly. 'I've had a wonderful time, and thank you for dancing with me.'

'Good-night.'

'Good-night.'

He pulled the first door open for her and held the second back against the wall. She was soon making her way, noisily down the uncarpeted back stairs wondering what to say if her mother wanted to know what she had been doing. She had, she reminded herself, given Charles her word. And that she would not break.

She entered the kitchen and went straight across to the scullery. Her mother and four of the maids were still washing glasses. 'I've had a look at the dancing, Mummy. Just as Mrs Lines said I could.'

'Oh, I'm glad you saw it, dear,'

'Weren't the dresses lovely, Anne?' commented one of the maids. 'Really beautiful.'

Anne went up closer to her mother. 'How much longer are you going to be, Mummy?'

'I'm just about through. You've had a long day. Are you wanting to get to bed?'

'Yes,' replied Anne, conscious for the first time that she was now feeling very tired with all the excitement.

'We've got the Boxing Day staff dinner tomorrow night, so you shouldn't be too late.'

Fifteen minutes later Anne was walking beside her mother down the back drive towards the stables block. 'Isn't the moon lovely tonight?' she remarked, as much to herself as to her mother. 'And the stars, aren't they clear and bright?'

'My! You're a proper romantic tonight, aren't you?'

Anne barely heard the remark nor anything else her mother said to her that night, and was soon asleep.

★ ★ ★ ★ ★

The Boxing Day staff dinner did not rise to Anne's expectations and she found it difficult to keep her mind on the events going on around her. Seated opposite her was Tommy whom she normally found to be good company and he often made her laugh. But on this occasion his jokes hardly seemed to be funny at all.

'Are you all right, Anne?'

'Yes, Mummy.'

'You seem so quiet. You hardly said a thing during the meal. I was watching you from down the table. Are you sure you're feeling all right? There's quite a lot of flu about.'

Before she could reply, Tommy grabbed her by the hand. 'Come on, Anne. Like to help clear the room? We've got to take all the chairs into the kitchen ready for dancing in here.'

Mr Roberts set up the gramophone in one corner and placed a pile of records beside it. Anne decided that this evening she would prefer the company of someone more mature than Tommy, and walked across the room 'May I help, Mr Roberts?'

'Why, certainly, Anne. What type of music do you like best for dancing?'

'May we have the VALETTA?'

'I don't see why not. We've got to start them off with something. You see if you can find the VALETTA record.'

She watched as Mr Roberts carefully placed the record on the gramophone and wound up the machine. 'May I start it?' Mentally, she was on the gallery above the grand staircase, in another world of riches and of swirling beautiful long dresses, of handsomely attired gentlemen. And in the arms of one extra handsome young man.

She hardly noticed as Simon, one of the young gardeners, came up to her. 'Would you like to dance, Anne?' At first she did not appear to hear him. 'Anne....Ooooh!' He spoke louder.

'Oh! Sorry, Simon! What did you say?'

'I asked you, if you would like to dance?'

'I.... I.... I was dancing, I....' She suddenly collected her thoughts. 'Oh! Sorry, I was sort of lost in the music. Yes, I'll dance if you want to.'

There was not much enthusiasm in her voice, and she soon found the young gardener's idea of dancing to be uncomfortably jerky. Though Charles had modestly claimed he was no good at dancing, to Anne she had seemed to glide effortlessly over the floor with him the previous evening. 'Sorry, Anne!' mumbled Simon, as she felt his shoe land on her toe for the umpteenth time.

Not even the sight of Cook trying to dance with Mr Roberts amused her. Whenever she could, she busied herself in the corner with the gramophone. This, she found, helped to keep her mind off comparisons with the previous evening.

She was bending over changing a needle when, quite suddenly, everyone in the room stopped talking. Anne turned to see Mr and Mrs Macaulay entering the staff hall. Had they, as in front of the tree on Christmas morning, brought their family?

'Good-evening to you all,' said Mrs Macaulay with her customary smile. 'We do hope you're enjoying yourselves.'

'Good-evening,' replied the staff and their families in unison.

'Please don't stop your party,' added Mr Macaulay. 'We just wanted to see you have all you need.' As he spoke, he went over to the side of the room. 'Got all the beer, squashes and other drinks you want? Eh?'

Mrs Lines moved beside him. 'Yes, thank you, Sir. And the staff have had a wonderful meal.'

'Good! That's good!' he muttered, stretching out for a glass.

'Would you like a port, Sir?' asked Mrs Lines.

'Yes, please.'

'And Madam?' Mrs Lines said turning towards Mrs Macaulay. 'What can I get you?'

It was clear to Anne that this was part of a customary ritual which was re-enacted each year. Once both employers had charged glasses in their hands, they moved to the centre of the room. 'May we wish you all, our loyal and hard-working staff, and their families, a very happy evening?' said Mrs Macaulay.

'All the very best to all of you,' added Mr Macaulay. 'It's not too early, is it, also to wish you all a happy New Year? A very, very happy New Year!'

'Happy New Year,' responded everyone. After ten minutes to Anne's relief, the ritual seemed to be ending. 'Well, we mustn't keep you from your dancing. Good-night everyone.'

'Good-night,' added Mr Macaulay.

Anne was about to mumble her response when Mrs Lines alone spoke. 'I know I speak for all the staff,' she began, in a rather high pitched voice. 'When I say how much we all appreciate the wonderful dinner... And presents.... And, and all the lovely decorations and other things Mr and Mrs Macaulay have so kindly given to us.' There was general muttered agreement and nodding of heads, which Anne found mildly amusing. 'I am sure, also, you would all wish me to thank them....' How long did this performance go on for, she wondered? 'And to wish them and their family a very happy New Year in a few days time.'

'Thank you very much,' echoed around the hall as the two left the room.

Anne was at once joined my Mr Roberts at the gramophone. 'Let's get a record on, as quickly as possible, and start the dancing going again,' he said, hurriedly winding up the machine.

A few minutes later, Anne went over to her mother. 'Would it matter if I went off to bed now, Mummy? There doesn't seem to be much going on.'

Mrs Jones had a word in Mrs Line's ear and, to Anne's relief, she came back to say it would be quite all right.

The two of them slipped away unnoticed from the hall. 'I'm glad that's over!' sighed Anne. In her mind there was now no doubt at all, that her place was on the Macaulay side of the double doors, not amongst those who, collectively, constituted "the servants". "Servants", she decided, was an unpleasant word. "Staff" was a little better.

'You are a funny child. All the other children enjoyed themselves,' commented Mrs Jones. 'You're very lucky we have such employers.'

They walked on in silence until Anne suddenly remarked: 'I wonder where the Macaulay children were tonight?'

'I expect they were getting ready to go away,'

'Going away?'

'Yes. I overheard Mrs Lines telling Cook that all three are going off tomorrow. Down to their cousins at Badminton. For the remainder of the school holidays. Aren't they lucky?'

As they neared the stables block, Anne looked up at the sky. It did not seem nearly as lovely as it had the night before.

Chapter Four – 1923

The years 1919 to 1922 passed quite quickly for Anne, though disappointingly they included no opportunity for her to talk alone to her idol. She saw him each holiday on Sundays in church, seemingly growing more mature and more handsome on each occasion, and she spoke briefly to him at the annual Christmas Day present giving ceremony. But as the months and years passed Anne became more reconciled to the fact that he lived on a higher plain than she was ever likely to.

Early in 1923 the engagement of the elder of the two Macaulay daughters, Mary, was announced. The wedding was to take place at the local church with a reception afterwards in a marquee on the East lawn.

The evening before the wedding a rehearsal of the church ceremony was held. The service was to begin with a bridal procession, so the rehearsal began with most of those present congregated at the back of the church.

'We'll start with the bride's mother,' called out the vicar. 'Now, where is Mrs Macaulay?' Anne watched with interest as Mrs Macaulay and her younger daughter, Sarah, came forward from the back of their family group.

'You should take up your place in the front pew,' the vicar directed. 'You're not part of the bridal procession. No! Not you, Sarah. Goodness me! Whatever next? Ha! Ha! You're a bridesmaid! Please stay where you are.'

'Now we're getting a bit more organised!' commented the vicar, looking about him. 'Oh no we're not! We haven't got a groom! Where's the groom? Ah! There you are. Your name is Robert? Is it? Good, I have to be careful I don't marry you to the wrong bride. Goodness me. Whatever next Ha! Ha! You shouldn't be back here where the bridal procession forms up. You and your best man should be down in the front right hand pew waiting for your bride-to-be. Saying a prayer that she hasn't at the last moment changed her mind! Ha! Ha!'

Anne was amused at the way the vicar ordered people around and was reminded that before taking cloth and becoming a vicar he had been an army sergeant-major,

'Now let us have the choir. Usual formation, please.'

Anne took her place in the aisle and was pleased to notice that Charles was standing only a few feet from her to one side. She gave him a hesitant smile and was delighted to be given a friendly grin back.

'Now,' continued the vicar. 'Now we need a stand-in for the Lord Bishop. Any volunteers? I'll tell him just what to do. The stand-in I mean, not the Bishop! So there's no need to be afraid.' Someone from the groom's family stepped forward and took his place in the procession.

'Now we only need the bride, her farther and the attendants, and the procession will be complete.' Mr Macaulay and Mary stepped forward, followed by Sarah holding the hands of two very small young girls.

'Tomorrow you'll have a service sheet, but this evening we'll sing one verse please, from the hymn book as we move forwards. I hope you've all got one. A hymn book I mean.'

The organ music began and the procession moved slowly up the aisle. No one put much effort in to their singing. 'I hope we shall all sing a lot better than that tomorrow,' said the vicar. 'It's a wedding we're rehearsing for, not a funeral! Ha! Ha!

The vicar looked somewhat dejected but managed a smile. 'Thank you all for being so patient. I think tomorrow we shall have a lovely wedding for, if I may say so, a very lovely bride.'

Anne came out of the church's side entrance and began her walk back to The Grange.

Soon, a heavy step behind her was accompanied by a voice she immediately recognised. 'My, Anne! You walk quickly.' Her hero drew alongside her as she continued walking.

'Hullo,' she said quietly, feeling a little unsure of herself.

'I don't seem to have seen you for a long time. Except of course on Sundays, but then only at a distance in church.'

'No,' she replied, not sure what interest to show.

'I'm due to go up to Cambridge later this year.' he went on after appearing quite happy to prolong the conversation. 'I'm going to read modern languages.'

'I heard you were going to Cambridge,' she responded, feeling him looking at her closely as they continued walking. She knew she had grown up a lot in appearance, as had he.

'Let's go through here,' he said, reaching out to open a lych gate almost hidden in the hedge. 'This way's a lot quicker than going round by the road.'

'I'm not allowed to go through this part of the garden,' Anne replied quickly, holding back.

'Oh, rubbish! Whoever said that?'

'The staff and their families aren't allowed to go into the private part of The Grange grounds, not unless they're on duty,' she recited bluntly.

'Well....?' Charles paused to reflect. 'You are on duty! You've been practising to sing at my sister's wedding tomorrow. And now you're accompanying me home!

How's that for two very good reasons for you to come this way?'

They had stopped at the gate and she knew it was up to her whether they walked on together or they went their separate ways. 'You may get me into trouble, but I'll risk it!' she smiled, blinking her eyes shyly.

'That's what I like to hear. Anyway, if anyone says anything to you, you refer them to me, OK?' He clearly meant business, and she was impressed.

'Really?' she questioned, broadening her smile.

'Yes. I mean it. Truly I do.' She looked up at him again, and considered he had lost none of his charm. as he stepped aside and politely indicated with his hand that she was to go first.

A few minutes later he said: 'This, regrettably, is where I must branch off and get back to the house. I suppose you'll be going that way?' he enquired, pointing to the path which led to the stables block.' He then changed the subject. 'Anne, I don't quite know how to put this.'

'Put what?' she asked.

'Just to say that… Well, I just wish you didn't live down the bottom of the garden in the stables block but, instead, lived in the main house. Where… Where I feel someone like you belongs.' He paused and looked attentively at her.

'I think you've grown into one hell of a wonderful looking girl, Anne. And…. And, well…. I just wish we could see more of each other.' He paused again. 'You're not like any of the other staff families. You're…. Somehow, you're more like my family type of person. Gosh!' he added quickly. 'I do hope that doesn't sound as pretentious as it might.' He followed his remark up with a forced laugh,

'I'd like that, too. That we could meet again. But is it possible? What would your father say? '

'When I'm up at Cambridge I'd love you to join me for a weekend. You'd make me the envy of all my friends. I know you would.'

'I couldn't possibly do that!' she replied with a shake of the head. 'What would my mother say? And your father? And, besides, I'm only fifteen.'

'Fifteen? Goodness, I keep forgetting. You look so grown up these days, I feel you are grown up. What will you look like when you're a few years older? Gosh!' She looked away as she felt his gaze focus affectionately on her. 'Fifteen the day after tomorrow!' she added quietly. 'I leave school at the end of this term. And….' She looked away at the large house in the distance. 'I start working up at The Grange in the autumn.'

'You start work? For our family? Become one of the staff?' His voice depicted a strong note of indignation.

'Yes. Why not? My mother does. And my father used to.' She dropped her voice to little more than a whisper. 'I'm to be a chambermaid, under Hilda.'

'I! Oh. I just don't know what to say. I really don't.' He shook his head violently and waved his hands in the air as if seeking inspiration. 'I feel so ashamed. You? Cleaning? You're not the working type.' Then, quickly he added: 'Oh, I'm sorry. That may sound a bit rude. I just mean…. Well, you…. And your mother. Neither of you are like the other staff, except perhaps Mrs Lines.'

'I understand.' Anne said almost inaudibly, pondering once more the injustices of the world.

'And you say it's your birthday the day after tomorrow?'

'Yes,' she replied, not raising her head.

He paused uncertainly, then added abruptly: 'Oh, I must go! This has been all too much for me.' He turned away and almost at once turned back. She looked up into his eyes and hoped her pleading thoughts were not as obvious as she felt them to be. 'It's been lovely to talk to you again, Anne. Take great care of yourself. Goodbye!'

'Goodbye…. Charles.'

Anne immediately turned away and, deep in thought, walked slowly back to the stables block. How many girl friends would he have once he got to Cambridge, she wondered? All of his type, no doubt, with parents endowed with all the wealth and trappings they could ever want?

The wedding went off as planned. Anne's mother was assisting at the reception, as were most of the staff. Anne therefore found herself alone in their small and silent flat in the stables block. She lay on her bed, gazing at the ceiling. Should she, she debated within herself, go into service and spend the remainder of her life working as a maid? What other options had she? Was she not cut out for something better? Her school results had been well above average, she recalled. What a waste of what the head teacher had referred to as "An Imaginative And Logical Brain". Of all the possible careers she had discussed with her other teachers, she most liked the sound of becoming a librarian..

She thought of her mother and father. Was her mother not above cleaning other people's silver and mending their torn bed linen? She thought of her aunt, with her comfortable roomy seaside house and her car. Had her father, whom she remembered with lasting affection, really been such a poor earner?

She looked around her room. It was very small but, she reminded herself, in the post war year circumstances, perhaps she and her mother were lucky to have even this. She knew of other village families who had been turned out of their homes because the bread-winner had been killed in the war. An ungrateful and heartless country appeared to care little for the dependants left behind, she reflected bitterly.

She saw it was nearly six o'clock and judged that the reception would soon be over. Her mother should not be long. She heard someone approaching and looked out of the window. It was Tommy.

'Hullo, Anne,' he called up cheerily as soon as he saw her.

'Hullo, Tommy.'

'I've got something for you. A parcel! It was left up at the house.'

'I'll come down,'

Tommy handed her a very small parcel. 'Doesn't look much, does it?' he remarked with his customary grin.

She debated whether to invite him up, but seeing the parcel had no stamps on it she sensed it might be better for her to find out its contents in private.

'Thank you, Tommy. It's probably just something for my birthday tomorrow. Thanks very much for bringing it to me.' She closed the door on a disappointed friend whose efforts to please, she knew, she too readily and too frequently rejected.

She tore the brown paper from the tiny package and saw inside a small flat and expensive looking case. She opened this and a card fell out on to the floor. She picked this up and read:

To someone special on her fifteenth birthday. Very many Happy returns of the day. See you again – soon I hope!

There was no name, but there was no doubt in her mind from whom the gift had come. What gift? She realised she had put down the case without seeing what was inside. The bracelet she gazed at was quite the loveliest piece of jewellery she had ever seen, let alone owned. She put it on and was admiring it closely when she heard the front door being opened and her mother's tread on the stairs. 'Anne, dear?'

'Yes, Mummy. In here,' she called back.

'Ah, you are here. I thought you might've gone down to the village.'

Should she show the bracelet to her mother? How could she possibly explain away so expensive a gift? Her mother would want to know from whom it came. Could she say it had come from the Macaulay family?

She decided she would keep quiet about it, at least for the time being, so she quickly gathered up the wrappings. The bracelet, the box and the card she just had time to slip under the corner of her mattress.

'How did the service go, dear?' Her mother enquired, panting somewhat and heading for the upright chair in the corner of Anne's bedroom.

'Oh, it was fine. Didn't Mary Macaulay look lovely in her dress? How did you get on, Mummy?'

'Hard work, but rewarding.'

'What were you doing?'

'I was in charge of the hats and coats. I was only busy at the beginning and at the end, so I managed to sneak off. There were some amusing speeches, especially that best man. I hear he's going up to Cambridge with Mr Charles.' Anne glanced guiltily at the edge of her mattress. 'Let's have our tea, dear,' her mother continued. 'My feet are killing me.'

'I'll get it, Mummy,' she responded immediately. 'You go and change out of that uniform. I don't like you in it.'

'You've never minded me in it before? Who've you been talking to? Tommy, I bet. Whatever next?'

'I don't think it suits you, Mummy.' Anne repeated.

'It's the uniform for the job, which you wear whether you think it suits or not. When you start your chambermaid work up at The Grange in the autumn, then you'll be in a uniform.'

Seeing the puzzled expression on her mother's face, Anne elaborated: 'Speaking for myself, I have no wish to spend the rest of my life with so small a chance of bettering myself than we have here, Mummy.'

'If it's not all right here for you where, may I ask, does that place me?' There was an unfriendly edge to her mother's question.

'Am I included in your redefining of our prospects? What ever has suddenly got into you?' Her voice trailed away.

Anne woke early the following morning. She drew the bracelet out from under her mattress and looked at it for a long time. Her mind was still confused when her mother came in with her own present.

'It's a really beautiful frock, Mummy. Thank you so much,' she said with enthusiasm, since the frock did please her. 'I'll wear it to church today.'

Later that morning the frock was concealed below her deep maroon-coloured surplice which, for once, Anne was pleased had long sleeves. For also concealed under the surplice, was her bracelet. She had had difficulty in taking it to the church unnoticed and now, as she walked in procession from the vestry, she could feel it on her wrist.

To her immense relief, Charles was standing beside his mother in the front pew. She glanced at the bracelet then looked straight at Charles who, she was delighted to notice, was watching her carefully. He slowly bowed his head to acknowledge that he understood the purpose of her movement.

After the service she waited inside the church for her mother and other members of The Grange staff as she was to be given a special birthday lunch in the staff hall.

She learned in the kitchen that Charles was going that afternoon to Cambridge to meet his future tutors. 'What's he going to do after he's finished at Cambridge?' Anne cautiously enquired of Betty who was sitting next to her.

'I expect he'll go into Lloyds, Anne. Like his father.' Mr Roberts offered across the table, overhearing the question.

'What's Lloyds, Mr Roberts?' she enquired, trying to sound casual and not too interested.

'Lloyds is the biggest insurance centre in the world. Mr Macaulay is an underwriter there,'

'An undertaker? I thought that was someone who buried you!' commented Betty.

'No, silly,' corrected Mr Roberts. 'An underwriter. Someone who underwrites insurance.'

Anne was glad of this partial explanation as she too had never heard of an underwriter. 'Mr Charles will probably join his father in their box,' continued Mr Roberts.

'Their box?' Exclaimed an even more puzzled Betty. 'A wooden box or a cardboard one?'

'Now, don't be silly. Underwriting is a very serious business. The various syndicates, groups of people, each has a small area of the large room, and they work in that space with a partition most of the way around. They're called boxes.' Mr Roberts smiled as he realised he had now gained the attention of all the staff.

'How do you know all this, Mr Roberts?' enquired Hilda.

'Though Mr Macaulay generally goes up to London by train , I've taken him up to the City by car many times. I've been right into what they call the "room" with him. It's very interesting.' He then added with a smile: 'And very profitable!'

'Do they make a lot of money?' enquired Tommy jocularly, joining the conversation.

'Yes, Lloyds is highly profitable. Look at The Grange, this house. Ourselves, his staff. We wouldn't be here if it were not for Mr Macaulay's interest in Lloyds. It pays all the bills and we should be thankful for it,' Mr Roberts concluded.

'I ought to be in Lloyds,' remarked Tommy with an accentuated laugh. 'I would then be rich. And all of you would be working for me! How about that Mr Roberts?'

'It's not many people who get the opportunity to become underwriters. You have to have two things. First, connections, You have to know the right people or have the right father. Secondly, you need a great deal of money to begin with.'

'That rules me out then!' joked Tommy. 'Why do you have to have so much money to begin with, Mr Roberts?'

'Because it's your money which is at call if the risks accepted by your syndicate result in too many claims.' Mr Roberts paused to let his lesson sink in. 'Underwriters make a lot of money only if the losses on the business they arrange do not exceed the premium income they earn. If it's the other way around, they have to use their own capital to pay off the losses.'

Anne followed the conversation with growing interest. 'Does that mean that underwriters, like the Macaulays, could lose all their money?' she enquired.

'Yes,' nodded Mr Roberts in sombre reply. 'It does mean just that. But, thankfully, it's a very rare occurrence.'

As Anne climbed into bed that night, her mind reflected on all that Mr Roberts had said. She had often wondered where Mr Macaulay went to work, and what he did.

Chapter Five – 1923

At the beginning of September Anne, clothed in her new daytime uniform, reported to Hilda, the senior chambermaid, immediately after breakfast on the first floor at the top of the back staircase. Her school days were over and so was the short holiday she and her mother had had down at Bognor with her aunt.

In common with all but the most privileged children, at the age of fifteen, she was about to begin earning her keep, in Anne's case, with the Macaulay family.

'We'll start you off at six shillings and six pence a week,' Mrs Lines had told her. 'You'll be supplied with four uniforms, two for day use and two for when you are on duty in the evenings. You'll be given breakfast and lunch every day in the staff hall, but living out, as you do with your mother, other meals will be your responsibility.' Anne had nothing with which to compare these offers, and accepted all that Mrs Lines told her. 'You'll have one day off per week, and two weeks paid holiday each summer.'

Anne had always found Hilda easy to get along with. 'From tomorrow, Anne, you'll need to be on duty by seven-fifteen to help take the hot water cans into all the occupied bedrooms,' she explained. 'Today is your first day, and you'll come round with me and help with the first-floor bedrooms while I teach you the way Mrs Lines likes things done at The Grange. You're lucky there were no guests staying here last night. And Mr Charles is still on holiday. And, of course, Miss Mary no longer lives here now she's married.'

As she spoke, Hilda led the way through the double doors on the first floor and along the dark passage. Hilda parted the curtains at the end and led the way out on to the gallery overlooking the hall. She stopped outside the second door along. 'Never, never enter anyone's bedroom without first knocking and then waiting a reasonable time for an answer.'

Hilda then knocked on the door, paused, cocked her ear towards the room and turned the handle quietly. Anne followed her in. 'This is Mrs Macaulay's bedroom. Mr Macaulay's bedroom is through that door over there. And that door, the one over there,' as she again pointed. 'That leads to their bathroom.'

Anne crossed to look at the dressing table and caught sight of herself in the mirror.

'Now, come along Anne,' said Hilda in a kindly manner. 'We have work to do. Let me show you how to strip a bed and make it the proper way. And there is only one way, remember. The proper way!'

'Yes, Hilda,' Anne replied quietly, secretly vowing that, whilst she was prepared to undertake such work for the present, in no way was she going to devote her whole life to skiving for others, not even for a family as nice as the Macaulays.

The next morning Anne's alarm clock awakened her at six-thirty. She dressed, made herself and her mother a cup of tea and ate a small piece of toast. Fifteen minutes later she was hurrying down the path towards the staff entrance to the main house.

Her second day of working was to begin by helping one of the other young chambermaids, Daisy, to take hot water to each of the occupied bedrooms along with a tray of early-morning tea. She found no problems with the tea, but the hot water had to be carried in copper cans from the scullery, and she wondered how often maids slipped down the steep back staircase and scalded themselves. She soon discovered that the handles of the cans became very hot and that it was necessary to use the corners of her apron to rap around them.

The maids knocked at the bedroom doors in turn, helping each other in with their respective loads.

'Good-morning, Madam,' said Daisy and Anne together.

'Good-morning, Daisy; good-morning, Anne,' replied Mrs Macaulay, raising herself up to a sitting position.

Daisy went across to the window and gently drew back the curtains while Anne placed the hot water can on the stand beside a large china bowl, and placed a heat cover over the top.

'What sort of a day is it?' enquired Mrs Macaulay.

'Fine, Madam'. No sign of rain and quite warm,' replied Daisy

'That's good,' acknowledged Mrs Macaulay, leaning over to begin pouring out her tea.

The procedure was repeated in Mr Macaulay's bedroom, though it was obvious he had still been asleep when the maids knocked on his door. To Anne it seemed very strange to be seeing Mr and Mrs Macaulay not attired in their usual immaculate daytime clothes. Even in her nightclothes and shawl, Mrs Macaulay looked neat and, Anne felt, every bit a lady. Mr Macaulay, on the other hand, had his hair untidy and seemed to have lost much of his authoritative presence.

'Why,' she asked, when they were once more outside Mr Macaulay's bedroom. 'Why do they need cans of hot water when they've got their own bathroom leading off their two bedrooms?'

'No one has ever asked me that before. Suppose it's so each can wash and dress all in the same room,' Daisy replied, then added with a giggle: 'And, maybe, they don't likes the other one comin' in to wash when 'e or she's in the bath!'

Anne was still somewhat puzzled. 'I can understand all the other bedrooms needing hot water cans. The people sleeping in them would have to go along the corridor and wash in one of the communal bathrooms. It must mean we have extra basins to slop out later.'

'Suppose so,' was Daisy's immediate comment. 'Never gave it a thought, to be honest. I just does what I'm told to. No point in protestin'! But try if yer wants to.' Anne remained silent.

Waiting until the Macaulay parents went down to breakfast, the two maids went back into their rooms to make the beds and tidy up.

The only chore which Anne decided she did not care for was emptying the chamber pots. It was menial, if not degrading. Why could the users not go along the passage to the toilet? At least they did not have to go outside as she herself and her mother had to.

'We are called "chambermaids",' remarked Daisy, sensing that Anne was about to protest on another aspect of her duties and watching her out of the corner of her eye. 'You thinks this work's beneath yer, don't yer?' Anne did not reply.

Later in the morning she was approached by Hilda. 'I'd like you to give Mr Charles's room a good dust, Anne. He's coming in to dinner this evening and may be staying the night.'

This was the opportunity Anne had been looking forward to. She looked around at the personal possessions he had left out on the dressing table, She began to dust all the surfaces, and articles lying on them, slowly and methodically. When she got around to the bed head she could not resist pulling back the counterpane and running a hand lightly over the pillow. She then lifted up a corner and stared at the pair of neatly folded blue silk pyjamas which lay there. She quickly straightened the counterpane when there was a knock on the door.

'Come in,' she responded.

'You're taking your time, dear,' said Hilda glancing around the room. 'I only said dust it, not spring-clean the place!' she added in a friendly tone.

'Sorry,' Anne replied quietly,.

'You've got your corridors and stairs to do before lunch. And don't forget the toilets and bathrooms on this floor.'

'I won't,' she replied as Hilda turned to leave her.

★ ★ ★ ★ ★

Anne was already awake when the alarm clock went the following morning. Had Charles stayed the night she excitedly asked herself? 'How many cans of hot water are needed this morning, Daisy?' she asked as soon as she entered the kitchen.

'Dun 'know. Why don'ts yer looks on Mrs Lines's list?'

Anne had not been shown the House List which hung on the back of the kitchen door, and she now eagerly crossed over to it.

Against both Mr and Mrs Macaulay's names there were the words "dinner" and "night"; against Sarah Macaulay there were the same two words. Against Charles Macaulay there was "dinner" and "? night".

'I can't tell from this, Daisy. It's either three or four cans needed.'

'Take up four then. Who's the query?'

'Charles Macaulay. Someone's put a question mark by his name.'

'That one never does know what the 'ell 'e's, doin!.' Daisy stated sulkily. 'Not even when 'e's 'ere. Not that one!'

'What do you mean?' Anne snapped back.

''E's always comin' and goin' at the last minute. It's safer to assume 'e's 'ere. Bad tempered when 'e first wakes up, 'e is. An' 'e gets annoyed if 'e wants to get off early an' 'e 'asn't 'ad 'is 'ot water.'

'Oh,' replied Anne. 'All right.'

'But 'e don't 'ave no early tea though. That's one good thing about 'im.'

'No tea?'

'No. Just take 'is water in, and… Well… Get out quick!' sniggered Daisy.

'Get out quick?' Anne repeated indignantly.

'Yes. That's is unless yer wants trouble.'

'Trouble?'

''E's quite a man is our Mr Charles, replied Daisy, beginning to enjoy ruffling up Anne whose mind was now in turmoil.

Was this the charming Cambridge undergraduate-to-be she occasionally spoke to?

' We'll do Miss Sarah's first,' stated Daisy.

'All right,' replied Anne, wondering if Daisy would need to come into Charles's room at all as she had no tea tray to deliver.

'Are yer 'appy to go in alone, Anne?' she enquired with a slight giggle, as the two of them emerged from Sarah's room, and were approaching his bedroom.

'Yes,' replied Anne resolutely.

'See yer in the kitchen later then,' said Daisy with a grin. As she turned towards the stairs she whispered: 'Watch out for the early mornin' temper! Don't say as 'ow I didn't warn yer!'

Anne tapped lightly on the door. There was no audible response. She tapped harder and heard a muffled but distinctly irate reply. 'Come in! Are you deaf? Do I have to say everything twice over?'

She opened the door and immediately noted the reason for the muffled reply. Charles Macaulay still had most of his head underneath the blankets. Indeed, she was surprised he had heard her at all.

'What sort of a day is it?' The question was brusquely voiced without the speaker moving. Having placed the hot water can on the wash basin unit, Anne moved towards the window and drew back the curtains. 'Don't pull that nearest one back! How often do I have to tell you that?'

'The weather is fine, but there's no sun as yet,' Anne stated, ignoring the curtain instruction.

'Goodness! It's you, Anne?' He was fully awake in a flash and sat up in his bed. He paused as if only half believing what he was seeing, Anne clothed as he had never seen her before. 'I'm sorry.' He paused, then added apologetically: 'I was only half awake. I find the light rather bright when I first wake up if both curtains are pulled back fully. Sorry if I spoke abruptly!'

'I'll pull one across again if you wish?' she responded, determined to be wholly formal in her dealings with her employer's son.

'No, please don't bother.' By now he was sitting bolt upright in his bed. He had his pyjamas top unbuttoned and was exposing what she observed was a manly looking chest. He lent forwards. 'Come closer, Anne.' When she did not move, he added: 'I only want to see how you look.' She stood her ground. 'I don't think I like you in that at all,' he continued with a smile. 'Where are the lovely frocks I see you in going to and from church? They suit you much better.'

'I'm on duty. I have to wear the aprons and other items Mrs Lines requires us to wear.'

'I hate you in it, Anne. God, I wish you didn't have to wear those ghastly things. And I hate even more the thought of your having to come to my room bringing hot water.'

'It's my job,' she replied without emotion.

'Yes. I know it is. But can't we change all that?'

'We can't. And I must be going. I've other duties to attend to,' With that, she hurried across to the door. But he was out of bed in a flash and took her hand just as she was about to reach out for the handle. 'I'd like to go, please,' she stated.

'If you say so, Anne. But I do wish we could talk.' He immediately released his grip on her and stood aside to let her pass.

'Thank you,' she said, the relief and gratitude expressing itself in her voice. Then, feeling she may have been a little too hasty, she added: 'I do hope you appreciate that when I'm on duty I must….'

'Do your duty only?'

'Yes,' she responded.

After a moments silence, he said: 'May we meet again for a proper chat? Soon?'

'If you wish.' she replied, breaking into a broad smile. 'But not in this cap. I feel so…. So damned stupid in it!'

He moved towards her and lifted his right hand gently up under her chin. He lent forwards and gave her a gentle kiss, then immediately released her.

'Thank you,' she replied.

Having left the room, Anne hurried towards the back stairs and was somewhat taken aback to meet Daisy coming up. 'You all right, Anne? You' been some time. I was comin' to see nothin' wrong with yer…. And 'im.' Daisy pointed towards the bedroom door and Anne wished she could tell her not to refer to her hero as if "im" were a pet dog.

★ ★ ★ ★ ★

Anne did not see Charles for a further private, off duty, meeting throughout the years 1924 and 1925, which passed uneventfully for her. She soon got into the routine of housework and, having come to accept it as her at least temporary basic way of life, it bored but no longer displeased her. At least her hours were reasonable and permitted her time to continue her hobby of reading factual books borrowed from the local library.

Following repeated rumours of how Charles treated female members of the staff, though Anne never found anyone prepared to give her any specific details, she always played safe on the second floor when he was at home. If the other chambermaid on duty at the same time offered to, she always let the other one take the hot water can into his room. If Anne herself had to take it in, she always left the door wide open. And when she was delegated to clean his room she always made sure another chambermaid was with her.

As Mr Roberts had correctly predicted, on leaving Cambridge, Charles had joined his father at Lloyds. Though he had no other address than The Grange, from the comparatively few nights he spent there, Anne judged he now lived a "high life" in London, and had come to look upon his London club as a second home.

Nevertheless, it came as a complete bombshell to Anne, a bitter disappointment but not altogether a surprise, when she learned over lunch one day in the staff hall that Charles had become engaged.

'A Miss Dulcie Rathbone,' Mrs Lines informed the staff.

'She's stayed here several times, hasn't she?' enquired Cook.

'Several times,' confirmed Mrs Lines.

'Is she part of the well-known Rathbone shipping family, I wonder?' enquired Mr Roberts who always seemed to Anne to be well informed on City matters.

'She may be,' acknowledged Mrs Lines. 'Perhaps we'll know tomorrow. The formal announcement of the engagement will be in The Times. I hear, also, that Miss Dulcie's photograph is to be in next months TATLER, along with the family background of both partners.'

'Is my photo appearing in the TATLER?' asked Tommy jocularly.

'Not this time, Tommy,' Hilda laughed.

Anne listened in silence and began trying to resign herself to the fact that this might well be the end of her childhood dreams.

At the weekend the whole Macaulay family went to stay with the Rathbones so as to meet the future bride's friends and relations.

The following weekend the Rathbone family were invited back to stay at The Grange, and a cocktail party, with, fork-supper, was hurriedly arranged for the Saturday evening. The chambermaids were kept busy with the guest bedrooms to prepare, while the kitchen staff worked tirelessly in readiness for the buffet.

The early evening found Anne, like the other maids, dressed in her evening uniform, black frock with white lace pinafore and laced head band. The girls stood silently together to one side of the grand staircase awaiting the arrival of the first guests. The silver salvers of canapés, which were to be handed round with the cocktails, were laid out ready in a room behind.

On the other side of the staircase stood a number of waiters hired for the evening. Their job was to carry round the trays of glasses, which had been filled ready with a variety of exciting looking cocktails.

Three trainee chefs, hired from a leading catering school in London, had been working tirelessly under Cook's critical direction for the previous two days. The buffet had been laid out in the dining room, where the massive antique table had been moved to one side of the room.

Anne had managed to take a quick look at the buffet earlier in the evening, and was inclined to agree with one of the young maids when she had said: 'I've never seen such a spread. It's like the Macaulays wanted to impress their guests. I hope none of this food's wasted, but I do wonder if they'll finish it all. How ever much do you think it all cost?

And all just because Mr Charles has got himself engaged. What about the poor?'

Anne suddenly heard voices from the gallery above and Mr and Mrs Macaulay appeared from their respective bedrooms and were joined by the rest of their family.

'Ah! There you are,' Mrs Macaulay said a few moments later, turning towards the guest bedrooms, and welcoming her guests with the experience of the perfect hostess.

Mr Macaulay, with Mrs Rathbone resting a hand on his arm, then led the small procession slowly down the centre of the wide staircase. Mr Rathbone, with Mrs Macaulay resting her hand lightly on her guest's arm followed.

Next in the procession came Charles and his fiancée. They came down hand in hand and in silence. As the formal procession crossed the corner of the hall, Anne had her first close-up view of Dulcie.

She noted with some satisfaction that Charles's fiancée had almost the same coloured hair as herself, although it was not cut short as was her own in accordance with staff regulations. Although there was no more than an inch difference in their heights, Miss Dulcie was a lot slimmer.

But there, Anne reckoned, the similarities ended. Miss Dulcie, like the Macaulays, was obviously experienced in society. She carried herself gracefully and had the same regal air about her as did Mrs Macaulay. Anne felt she would be a credit to any man. Not a beautiful woman, but a fine looking one.

Miss Dulcie, Anne thought, lacked the lively streak which she had expected to see in Charles's bride-to-be.

Anne and the other maids spent the next hour moving about the main reception rooms with their trays of cocktail refreshments. An announcement then invited the guests to move to the dining room and to collect a selection from the buffet table. Anne was told to stand at the end of the table as the guests came away, and to hand to each a fork and a small napkin.

In due course, Charles and his fiancée filed past in the queue, and seemed to Anne to be having an argument.

"I can see you like your roast beef, Charles,' his fiancée rebuked him, glancing at his plate's contents. 'You've taken enough for several people.'

'I like all red meat,' he replied with a light laugh.

'If that's the case, you'd better take every opportunity to eat it when we're out, because I can tell you, Charles, that when I'm in charge of the catering in our home, I shall forbid our cook from serving all red meats. So you'd better take careful note!'

What a selfish person my poor Charles has landed himself with? Anne thought to herself, shaking her head slowly from side to side. I'd give him what ever he wanted to eat if I were going to be his wife.

They both took their forks and napkins without looking up. To Anne's disappointment, Charles seemed not to have noticed her.

Once the fork supper was completed, and the empty plates had been quickly collected up from the various reception rooms, Anne began helping clear up the remnants and take them back to the kitchen. Just before being directed to help in the scullery with the washing up, she heard through the closed doors several loud knocks, then silence fall upon the proceedings.

'Goin' to toast their 'ealth,' whispered Daisy. 'Silly word "toastin"' 'ain't it?'

★ ★ ★ ★ ★

The following day it was Anne's turn for evening duty. She had to turn down the beds and place hot water bottles in the beds of those who had ordered them. Only the Macaulays were at The Grange this evening, as Miss Dulcie and her family had gone back to their own home. Anne therefore got through her duties quite quickly and returned to spend the early part of the evening in the staff hall, on call if required.

'I'm off to bed, Daisy.' She stated an hour later. 'Aren't you tired too after last night?'

'I won't be long, Anne. Just want to finish this Chapter I'm reading'. Don't wait for me.'

'Good-night then, Daisy.'

'Night Anne.'

Anne closed the back door behind her and started making her way towards the stables block, where she knew her mother was spending the evening listening to her favourite music on their old wind-up gramophone.

Anne's thoughts were still on the previous evening, and her conclusion, envy apart, was still that she did not like the looks of Charles's bride-to-be who appeared to Anne to be stuck up, the very opposite of the Macaulay family members.

She was half way down the path when she heard the crunch of stones on a nearby path which lead off to the right. It made her start, and immediately she stepped on to the grass verge, pressed herself against the hedge and remained absolutely still, hoping whoever it was had not seen or heard her.

'Is someone there?'

She suppressed herself from making an audible response.

'I know you're there, whoever you are!' The voice sounded annoyed at not provoking an immediate response. 'I said I know you're there, so why don't you come out?' The voice was Charles's.

Should she shout out? But who was about to hear her? And what reason had she to be frightened about? It was no good she decided, she would have to come out of the shadows. 'It's me. It's me, Mister Charles.'

'Anne!' he paused. 'Why are you hiding from me?'

'I…. I didn't know who it was until you spoke,'

'Even then you didn't answer me?' His tone mellowed and he sounded more disappointed than annoyed.

'I'm sorry. I thought you'd…. You'd go away if I kept quiet.'

'Go away? You don't really want me to go away, do you?'

'I was just taking a stroll around the garden. I felt in need of some fresh air before turning in for the night.'

'Oh,' was all she said.

'Why did you call me "Mister Charles" just now? You've never called me that before.'

'No,' she replied, wishing she had waited for Daisy.

'No what?' he enquired.

'No, I haven't called you that before. I'm now staff.'

'Was it on account of my engagement that you called me the formal "Mister"?'

'I suppose so. I didn't really think. It just came out that way,'

'Anne,' he said, turning his head towards her. 'I'd love to have a chat with you. I really would.' He paused. 'Would you mind if we walked together for a little way?'

'I don't mind,' she answered indifferently, wondering what he had in mind.

He did not speak for some time and, when he did, it was with uncharacteristic hesitancy: 'My engagement must have been a surprise for you?'

'Yes, I suppose it was,'

'I'd always hoped we…. That is, you and I, might have had some times together. Perhaps you coming up to London, or something. I felt I owed it to you.'

'It would have been nice,' she whispered. 'But you didn't, as you say, owe it to me.'

'I wanted to, Anne. I would have really enjoyed it myself, showing you the best parts of London. You saw Dulcie, of course?' he questioned, changing the subject.

'Yes, I did,' she replied, then politely added: 'She looked very nice. And I hope you'll both be very happy.'

'Yes,' he muttered almost casually. 'I hope so, too.'

Anne was amazed by the tone of his remark. 'If I may say so. You don't sound very…. Not very sure.'

'No, I suppose I don't.' Then he added thoughtfully: 'It was one reason for my wanting to have a walk around the garden alone. It was to give myself time to think.'

'Shall I leave you then? To your thinking alone?' she asked.

'Good gracious no. No, please. I didn't mean it that way.' He stopped talking abruptly and, when he began again, it was in a much friendlier and more relaxed tone. 'I've always liked you, Anne. And I'm genuinely very fond of you. Please believe me. Amongst the many other qualities I guess you have, you're a very good listener. You're sensible … And… And very sweet, and… Well, you're a jolly nice person…And in case I should forget to say it, I think you're extremely attractive.'

They had reached the playroom. He went up to the door, unlocked and opened it. 'They always seem to leave the key in the door. I suppose there's nothing of any value for anyone to steal. Only a lot of old long discarded dolls and teddy bears.' His laugh sounded forced.

Without further comment he went inside and she followed. 'Somewhere over here I seem to recall we had a small settee. Yes, here it is. Can you see sufficiently to come across?'

'Yes,' she replied, tiptoeing in case she tripped.

'I'm afraid we can't put on the light; there never were any curtains. Someone might see it from the house,' She sat down in one corner of the settee and he sat himself down in the other. She did not feel afraid though she felt perhaps she should do. He then began to talk and, remembering his saying how he considered her to be a good listener, she remained silent.

'My trouble, Anne, is that I just do not know what I want out of life. I have a lovely home, and well-off parents. I've been to Cambridge, and now I'm in a ready-made job in the City. In a business which many men would give their proverbial right arm to be allowed to join. Because I'm me, my father's son, I have joined Lloyds, not as a "name", but as a well paid executive helping to run our family syndicates. And when all that's done? What have I achieved? Nothing! Everything's been found for me. Nothing by my own efforts!'

He paused before continuing: 'I sometimes wonder if I shouldn't throw it all in, and go and do something entirely on my own. The Far East…. Singapore perhaps. That's a great place I'm told for British gentlemen to be in business.'

He paused again. 'Even my fiancée….'

'Surely she wasn't found for you?'

'Not exactly found,' he laughed flatly. 'but if it hadn't been for Father's business, he does all the Rathbone shipping line's insurance, I wouldn't have met Dulcie.'

'I see,' she replied, turning her head away. 'Do you love her? I mean, despite the way you met her.' He did not reply and she turned to face him. 'Do you love her, Charles?' she repeated.

'I think I do,' he said nonchalantly. 'I think at times I do… . At other times I find myself wondering if I'm not just seeing her as a valuable business asset.' He broke his solemn speaking and laughed. 'Sort of "marriage of convenience".'

'She likes to have her own way, doesn't she?' Anne remarked quietly, unsure whether she were permitted to pass any adverse comments.

'How do you mean?'

'I overheard you being told you were not going to be allowed to eat red meat in your own home!'

'You overheard that little argument, did you?' he laughed.

'You'll have to watch out, Charles.'

'You're right. I mustn't let her get her own way too often.'

They talked on for another half hour by which time she felt she was beginning to understand the problem which was exercising his mind. She was debating whether there was anything constructive she could say when she felt his hand come across and take one of hers.

'I really am very fond of you, Anne. More than just a passing infatuation. I feel more serious about you than just having the crush I first had. Gosh, I was young then. We both were!'

She was about to reply when both of them froze stiff on the settee. Someone was approaching the door. The door handle was turned and, on finding the door unlocked, the person promptly locked it. They both remained rigid until they heard the footsteps withdrawing.

'Who the hell was that?' Charles gasped, letting out the deep breath which he had been holding.

'It may have been John, the gardener. I believe he does do a round of the buildings each night to make sure everything is locked up. Can we get out?'

'I don't think there will be any insurmountable problem,' he tried to reassure her. 'There are several windows. That's if they're not all rusted up with lack of use. It's only a short drop to the ground. I'll help you down. Perhaps we ought to be going now anyway. It must be getting late.'

They moved over to the window beside the door. He felt in the dark for the catch and, to the accompaniment of a certain amount of screeching, the window was persuaded to open. 'I think I'd better go first,' he offered. 'I can then help you down. Can you climb up this side?'

'I think I can manage to do that…..Just!'

Then, to her surprise, he was out of the window in one bound and immediately turned to help her down. 'I must be careful not to tear my evening uniform on the window catch,' she said anxiously, then laughed. 'It would never do for me to have to explain to Mrs Lines how I'd done it!'

'Don't worry. I'll see you come to no harm.' She climbed on to the window-sill. 'Now,' he directed. 'Turn round and come down backwards. That is unless you want to try jumping.'

She managed to turn in the kneeling position on the sill, and had just completed the manoeuvre when she felt his arms come up either side of her legs and clutch her around the waist. 'I think I can manage,' she gasped.

'I'll steady you,' he offered. She felt him take her weight, 'I don't think your legs are going to be quite long enough to reach the ground.' His arms were right around her now, and she felt his breath just behind one of her ears as she drew in the pleasant manly fragrance of his hair cream. He placed her gently on the ground, but he did not release her. Instead, he nuzzled his face into her hair and, leaning further over her shoulder, gave her a firm kiss on the upper part of her cheek.

'I think it's you I really love, Anne,' he whispered.

She made no attempt to move. Was he teasing? She wanted to believe not.

'I like you, too,' she whispered back.

He eventually did release his grip, then gently spun her around in his arms so that she faced him. One of his hands moved down and she was conscious of her own body stirring deep within her as she felt his hand follow the contours of her buttocks. Keeping her pressed closely to him with one of his hands, he raised the other and placed it gently on her left breast.

This was a sensation she had never before experienced. She made no attempt to move except to place her arms around his neck in order both to steady herself and because it seemed to her the natural thing to do. This had the effect of raising her chest and she enjoyed, more than she had ever imagined possible, the sensation of his hand stroking her still covered breasts. She felt his hand feeling through the material of her brassiere for her nipple and gently squeezed it with the tips of his fingers.

What, she wondered, should she do now? What was expected of her? She wished to respond, but was unsure if this were right. She ran her fingers lightly through his hair and was pleased when this incited him to grip her even more tightly to his own body, and to place his broad lips firmly on her own. She felt his lips part slightly and the tip of his tongue move along the length of her own lips, gently exploring their soft feminine curves. She slightly parted her own lips, and was immediately conscious of an even deeper sensation within her as the tips of their tongues began to caress each other.

'Anne, darling. Nothing would give me greater pleasure than to make love to you. Real love. Love with all my heart.'

She began to feel weak at the knees. She had read romantic novels, but never thought somehow that real life could be as wonderful. 'But I feel we perhaps ought to leave that for another time.' He paused and looked her full in the face, then took her face gently between his hands.

'Yes,' she whispered very quietly, not knowing quite what she was agreeing to, but relieved that the passion he was undoubtedly experiencing was not going to go too far on this the occasion of their first serious embrace.

He drew back slightly, but without letting go of her with his hands. 'I can't tell you, Anne, how much this meeting with you has meant to me. Thank you so very, very much for listening so patiently to me. For….'

'I've enjoyed it too,' she responded, drawing back from him and putting her dress straight. She looked up at him, the quarter moon providing sufficient light for her to see his affectionate expression. And how, she wondered, was their relationship to develop from this point? Were her ambitious dreams to be fulfilled after all?

'I think I had better let you go on from here alone,' he suggested as they reached the main path again. 'I'll keep in the background, and make sure you get to your front door all right.'

'Thank you. Thank you, Charles.' She turned to face him and to let him take the initiative in their last exchange of kisses.

'Good-night, Anne,' he said quietly as she drew away from him. 'You're a super girl. You really are!'

"He", thought Anne, was quite definitely the most super young man in the world. Just before reaching her door she realised that he had said nothing about meeting again. The implications of this suddenly worried her. Had she been foolish in thinking that she and not Dulcie Rathbone was now to be the centre of his affections, and his whole life? Surely not? The way he had held her, she recalled. What he had whispered in her ear. Surely, she consoled herself, surely she was now to be the real undisputed object of his love?

'You're late, dear,' said Mrs Jones as Anne, hoping her dress was not too creased, climbed the stairs. 'I thought after last night's party, you were going to get to bed early tonight.'

'Yes, Mummy, that was the idea. But....well, we got talking and it just seems to have got late. Anyway, I'm going to turn in now. Good-night, Mummy.'

'Good-night, dear. God bless. Sleep well.'

Before dropping into a deep sleep she puzzled over one aspect of her garden stroll with Charles who, earlier, had told her the key to the playroom was always left in the door.

Why then, she wondered, having got himself out of the playroom through the window, had he not just gone to the door, used the key and let her walk out. She smiled to herself reliving the pleasure his lifting her down into his embrace had given to her. Neither had she spoilt his pleasure by telling him he need not have done it.

★ ★ ★ ★ ★

Charles spent little time at The Grange during the remainder of the year, and Anne was left to wonder how much he was spending with Miss Dulcie. Her purposefully nonchalant enquiries in the staff hall produced no definite information and, as the weeks rolled by, she began to feel her one night of romance had perhaps been just that, a one-night affair. Her period of doubt was ended when the staff were informed by Mrs Lines that Mr Charles's marriage to Miss Dulcie would take place the following June.

'At least we'll not have to cater for that wedding,' remarked Cook with an undisguised sigh. 'The bride's family staff are welcome to it. Perhaps I'm getting old, but these big functions tire me out.'

'It'll certainly be a big occasion,' remarked Mr Roberts. 'The Rathbone's are a very well known family. Their house, which I saw when I drove Mr & Mrs Macaulay there, is almost on the scale of one of the big stately homes.'

'What? Bigger than The Grange, Mr Roberts?' asked Tommy in surprise.

'Oh, much, bigger,' replied Mr Roberts. 'You think The Grange is large, and so it is compared with most houses, but the aristocratic homes are really vast, more like palaces.'

'And Miss Dulcie's parents have one of them?'

'They do,' nodded Mr Roberts.

'Coo! Mr Charles is doin' all right for hiself then!' chuckled Tommy.

'I doubt if Mr Charles will gain much financially. Not in the way you're thinking, Tommy.'

Anne wanted to hear no more and, making her excuses, she left the hall and walked down the garden to the privacy of her own bedroom. She glanced indifferently at the cuddly sailor doll propped up in the corner of her room. Charles, her hero and idol, who in her eyes could do little wrong, now seemed to have failed her and, momentarily at least, had fallen from grace.

Had his and Anne's undoubted attraction for one another really been insufficient to surmount the difficulties which stemmed from their different backgrounds? Or had he, in the interests of his family business, just opted to play safe with the aristocratic Miss Dulcie?

Early in 1927 it appeared to Anne, on cleaning Charles's room one day, that his fiancée had given him a photograph of herself. Anne picked up the silver frame from the dressing table and studied it closely. Across one corner was written: "From Dulcie with love". The words made her writhe as she wondered if Miss Dulcie knew what real love was, the kind of love which she herself still felt for Charles.

"Miss Dulcie", Anne repeated to herself, squirming the words. Miss Dulcie, the woman who epitomised all she loathed in her contempt for upper class snobbery. Miss Dulcie who, in addition, had now confiscated her Charles, seemingly for good. Anne's resentment became unbridled. The fight back would be waged, she vowed. Then she paused in her thinking. Might she not also accidentally embroil Charles himself? That would not be intended.

Nevertheless, he was, she decided, partly to blame. If she were able to acquire some hold over him, would she be wholly averse to using a small measure of such leverage to her own advantage? To win him back? Would that be so inequitable?

She lay down on the bed on her back and her mind began, not for the first time, to dwell on the injustices of the Rathbone's inherited wealth.

★ ★ ★ ★ ★

As the June wedding day approached, Charles began moving many of his clothes and other personal possessions from his bedroom to the flat in Kensington, which his parents had given to the couple as a wedding present.

As Cook had correctly judged when his engagement was announced, the house staff at The Grange were to be in no way involved with either the wedding or the wedding reception. It would all take place many miles away at the Rathbone's Hertfordshire home.

'Now, Anne and Daisy,' spoke Hilda the morning after the wedding. 'I've an important job for you two. Mr Charles's bedroom requires emptying so that the room can be used for guests. I have had a number of cardboard boxes put in the room and into these I would like you to put all his remaining personal items, items which he has not yet moved across to his new home in Kensington. The boxes, when filled, I will arrange to be taken and placed together in the box-room….. for, if I know Mr Charles, he'll be up there after something or other every time he comes here to stay. And you know him! He doesn't like not being able to find what he's looking for!'

'Won't 'e be sleepin' in the same room no more?' enquired Daisy.

'Of course he won't, silly!' replied Hilda abruptly. 'He'll be a married man when he next stays here. Go in one of the guest suites on the first floor with his wife, he will.'

'Oh,' responded Daisy with a frown.

Hilda had been right in guessing that they would find the balance of his things strewn untidily around, and Anne worked hard with Daisy all the morning on the vacated second floor bedroom.

She found herself with mixed feelings as she touched his more personal possessions. In a drawer she found an old snap-shot taken of him when he was up at Cambridge. She debated what to do with it and, looking to see whether Daisy would notice her if she slipped it into the pocket of her apron. Later in the day it was transferred and hidden in the back of one of her books in her own bedroom.

★ ★ ★ ★ ★

Christmas 1927 was the quietest Anne had known at The Grange, and this was because the entire Macaulay family spent a whole fortnight, including the New Year, up on the Rathbone's country estate.

Likewise, the greater part of 1928 was without any exceptional happenings at The Grange. When Charles and his bride visited the family Anne used her best endeavours not to be involved with the couple, though she studied their behaviour towards each other whenever she could do this discreetly.

It seemed to her as if they had been married for a very long time and already took each other for granted. He seemed a lot more serious than she remembered his being. Had he had all his natural fun knocked out of him? Was their relationship a happy one, Anne pondered? How much happier, she was sure, she could have made him.

In the Autumn, the staff were informed that Christmas 1928 was to be on the grand scale again, with all sides of the family staying at The Grange.

★ ★ ★ ★ ★

A few weeks later, as Anne was returning from the village shop, she was momentarily startled by a sports car suddenly approaching from behind and drawing up beside her. 'Can I give you a lift, Anne?' asked her hero, leaning across the passenger seat and winding down the window.

She did not immediately answer. She noted that he was alone, but the tone of his voice made her hesitate. 'I'm on my way back to The Grange,' he continued. 'It's a cold day and it looks as if it's soon going to rain. Wouldn't you prefer a lift to walking?'

She wondered if she was imagining it, but was he being slightly patronising? 'Thank you, but I....'

'Oh, come on!' The door nearest to her was pushed open, and she felt it would be more embarrassing to refuse than to accept the lift.

'It's kind of you. It is getting colder,' she said, shutting the door and keeping her head facing rigidly forwards.

The car, a two-seater model, had not much room in it and Anne felt his shoulder rub against hers as he selected first gear. He let the clutch in with a jolt and her head was thrown back. 'Got a good performance these Talbots!' he remarked.

'Yes,' she replied, never having been in so small a car before.

'And how are you these days, Anne?' His question sounded forced to her, and lacking in genuine interest as to the answer it generated.

'All right, thank you,' she replied conventionally. As the car approached the end of the road leading to The Grange she asked if she should get out.

'If you want to, but I can take you to the bottom of the back drive.' She felt his eyes glance across at her. 'Are you going up to the stables block?'

'Yes. But don't bother. I can walk the last bit.'

He slowed down the car, then suddenly changed his mind. 'Hold tight! We're going for a bit longer drive!' With this, he put his foot on the accelerator and the car rapidly gathered speed as they passed the end of the main drive to the house.

He broke the silence a few minutes later as he steered the car on to a rough piece of ground. 'I've been waiting to find a suitable opportunity to speak to you, Anne,' he began, seeming uncertain how to continue. 'But… Well…. To tell you the honest truth, I've not known what I'd say if we did get a chance to talk privately.'

'Well, here we are in private as you call it.'

She noticed the troubled look he had, and at once felt sorry for his obvious embarrassment. 'I do understand,' she added quietly, immediately forgiving him for any part he had played in her unhappiness.

He reached out for one of her hands and began running his fingers through hers. He began to speak even more quietly. 'You do something to me, Anne. I tried. I can't tell you how hard I've tried…. To forget you.'

'Forget me?' she questioned, strains of indignation showing in her voice.

'Yes. I didn't want to forget you, because I am very fond of you,' he stuttered to explain. 'I wanted to forget you because…. Well, as you know, my marriage is all set for June. One cannot marry someone and still have half of your heart elsewhere,' he said philosophically.

'I suppose not. I'm sorry if I'm the cause of making life awkward for you. Perhaps you should have got your parents to dismiss me. Then I wouldn't be at The Grange any more, and you wouldn't be reminded.'

'Our family could never do that! Dismiss you? What have you ever done that's wrong? It's me. I'm the one who….' He paused and, lifting up his hand, used his fingers gently to turn her face towards his own.

'As soon as we're together, I feel as if I should never be without you.' He paused again, studying her deep brown coloured eyes. 'It may sound strange, but I never feel like this when Dulcie and I are together.' Anne thought it best to let him talk on. 'We get on well, but we somehow don't quite…. How can I put it? Let go. Relax….Be our natural selves.'

'I do want you to be happy, Charles,' she said without knowing if she really meant it.

'And I want you also to be happy, Anne.' He reached out once more for her right hand, drew it across between his own and began gently to stroke it. 'You don't deserve to be messed about by me. I am sorry, truly sorry, if I've, as they say, led you up the garden path.'

Anne was thoughtful. 'I suppose I did think for a time that we might, well….' It was now his turn to let her continue the talking. 'But,' she went on more quietly. 'Later, I came to realise that it was just a silly childish….Oh, I don't know. Just a dream.'

'Not silly, nor childish, Anne. I'm so sorry,' he replied apologetically. 'It was cruel of me ever to let you have such a dream. But if it's any consolation, I had just the same dream about you.' He dropped his voice to little more than a whisper. 'You were always my "dream girl", and I wanted you more than I can describe.'

She felt there was now little point in continuing with the apologies, and that if he talked any further she might breakdown and cry. 'I'd like to go home now, please.'

'Yes, of course,' he responded, dropping his hand from holding hers, and turning to settle down properly again in the driver's seat.

The rain began to fall heavily as they drove back in silence. He stopped the car just a few yards before they reached the back drive. No one was about and, as she was about to let herself out of the passenger side of the car, he lent over and gently turned her face towards his. He smiled affectionately and, leaning still further over, gave her a firm kiss on the lips.

She had not expected this. She was close to tears and found herself biting her bottom lip. She drew herself away, but could not bring herself to look him straight in the eyes. Before she even realised it, she found herself whispering, almost defiantly: 'I still love you.' Immediately, she reached for the door handle, thrust the door open and put her feet on the ground.

He just heard her final words above the first clap of thunder, as she stood up and moved away from the car. 'And I always will love you.' The words rang in his ears as, after a few moments of watching her run off up the back drive, he leaned across, closed the passenger door and then drove the car off at speed, crashing the gears as he went.

Chapter Six – 1928

'What a fuss over next to nothing!' Anne overheard Cook exclaim to Mrs Lines, as she walked in through the back door.

'It did seem as if Mrs Dulcie was making the most of it,' Mrs Lines agreed. 'Anyway, she's now back in bed in the room she and Mr Charles occupied. Mr Charles carried her there, and the doctor's been sent for.'

'The doctor? Just for an ankle sprain?' exclaimed Cook,

'Yes. Our Mrs Dulcie, it seems, is used to being well cared for! This means, of course, Cook,' added Mrs Lines. 'That Mr Charles and his wife will now be staying on here for a day or two.'

'It was as Mrs Dulcie was saying good-bye to Mrs Macaulay,' described one of the pantry maids. 'I was standing in the doorway with the last of her small luggage. When…. Woosh! Down she goes. Nothing too bad I thought but oh no! Mrs Dulcie…. You'd have thought she'd broken both her legs!'

'What happened then?' enquired Anne, not a little amused.

'Mr Charles. He didn't look too pleased. You should have seen him. Lifted her up as if she were one of his old cricket bats.'

'I overheard Mrs Lines say she's now back in her room,'

'That's right. She wouldn't hear of the idea that she be put in Mr Charles's car and taken back to their London flat. Oh no! Mrs Dulcie was not going to be moved until she'd been seen by a doctor!' continued the pantry maid.

At that moment Hilda came into the room. 'Ah, there you are, Anne. I can't find Daisy anywhere. Be a good girl and put your uniform on, Then please come up with me to Mrs Dulcie's room. She's staying an extra night or two.'

'So I've just heard,' said Anne, putting on an affected tone of voice. 'She's sprained her ankle, but not, regrettably, broken her neck.'

'Oh, you have heard?'

'Yes,' she replied sarcastically. 'Such news travels fast!'

Hilda tapped on the bedroom door and, with Anne following closely behind, entered.

'Ah, there you are, Hilda. Replied Mrs Macaulay. Could you and Anne please come and make Mrs Dulcie's bed.' She smiled as she added: 'I'm afraid you'll have to make it with Mrs Dulcie on it!'

'Don't you dare hurt me!' Mrs Dulcie spoke harshly, looking from one to the other threateningly.

'We'll try not to, Madam,' replied Hilda.

'It would be much simpler for everyone,' Charles said, walking to the bed side, 'If I merely lifted my wife off the bed for a minute. This would enable Hilda and Anne quickly to make the bed in the normal way.'

'No you don't! You'd hurt me!' snapped Mrs Dulcie. 'And don't you forget my condition. My condition. Do you hear?'

He ignored the request, bent over and lifted his protesting wife.

Hilda and Anne quickly made the bed. As Anne tucked in her corner, she looked up and caught her idol watching her intently. She felt herself blush and quickly looked away.

Mrs Dulcie had just been replaced on the turned-back bed, to the accompaniment of further groans and various blunt instructions to her husband to have more regard for her condition, when a knock on the door heralded the arrival of Mrs Lines accompanied by the doctor.

Hilda and Anne made their escape, but not before Anne was instructed to let Mrs Dulcie rest undisturbed for the afternoon and to bring her tea punctually at four-fifteen.

'Perhaps,' asked Hilda outside the room. 'You'd be kind enough, Anne, to bring Mrs Dulcie's tea up to her. The parlour maids are going to have all their time cut out on the Church Committee tea which Mrs Macaulay's got in the drawing room this afternoon.'

'Do I have to?'

'Be a dear', queried Hilda.

'All right, Hilda. It's just…. She's so awful, isn't she?'

'I shouldn't say it, nor is it your place to comment on such things, but I do agree she's a bit of a one!'

'It's not for nothing, Hilda,' Anne stated. 'That the junior staff now refer to her as "the DD", which stands for "The Detestable Dulcie". She talks to the maids,' Anne went on, 'as if we were all her slaves. Does she order you about like that? '

'Because I'm quite a bit older than you girls are, she doesn't put on quite the same superior airs that I've seen her use with the younger members of the staff.'

★ ★ ★ ★ ★

Punctually at four-fifteen, with a tray balanced on her outstretched hand, Anne knocked on the bedroom door. 'Come in.'

She entered and, after taking only two paces across the room, very nearly tripped. The curtains had been drawn across the widows and a pile of the packed luggage had been brought up from Charles's car and placed on the floor. It was a piece of this which she had almost fallen over.

'Can't you look where you're going?' retorted Mrs Dulcie.

'I'm sorry, Madam,' Anne replied indifferently. 'Someone's left a piece of your luggage right in the middle of the floor.'

'If it was in the middle of the floor, you ought to have seen it!' Came the haughty response.

'The curtains are drawn, Madam. It's dark in here,' stated Anne, having to make a positive effort to control her tongue.

'Well? I can see it!'

'I would expect you to be able to see it, Madam,' she replied, refusing to be out-talked by "The DD" whom she detested as much as the more junior staff did.. 'Your eyes are used to the dark. I've just come in from the daylight in the passage.'

'Don't you argue with me,' she snapped. 'Where's your respect?'

Anne was tempted, but did not reply. 'Will you have your tea tray across your knee, or shall I place it on your bedside table?'

'Keep holding it for the moment, I'm going to try and sit up.'

Anne watched as, once more to the accompaniment of groans, Mrs Dulcie sat herself up.

Anne moved forwards with the tray. 'Would you like me to fetch another pillow? It may help you to sit up more comfortably.'

'Thank you. That's the first sensible suggestion I've heard you make!'

Anne just restrained herself from answering this provocative statement. 'Thank you. I suppose Mrs Macaulay is still engaged downstairs with her committee.'

'Yes, I believe she is, Madam.'

'She's down there,' stated Mrs Dulcie venomously. 'My husband's gone out. There doesn't seem to be anyone who cares what happens to me!' Then, with a toss back of her hair, she added out of self-pity: 'I'm the only one who's in pain and cannot move, and I'm stuck here alone!'

'Is that all, Madam,' Anne enquired.

'Yes. I suppose I'll just have to manage.'

Anne left the room and closed the door quietly behind her. She made her way down the passage and out on to the open gallery. She crossed to the corner which led into the passage leading to the back staircase and, in so doing, passed the main staircase leading to the second floor. She glanced up the stairs and was surprised to see a light on.

Evening was approaching and it would soon be dark but, she reasoned, the light should not be on because none of the rooms on that floor should now be occupied, No one was about so she felt it her duty to go up and turn off the light. As she reached the second floor, her hand went to the switch and the passage was thrown into darkness. She turned to go back down the stairs when, with a slight gasp of surprise, she now noticed a light shining under Charles's old bedroom.

Why had the light been left on? She dismissed the idea of him being there himself because his wife had quite definitely stated, only a few minutes before, that he had gone out. Perhaps, guessed Anne, that light, like the passage one, had been left on accidentally. She tip-toed quietly to the door and listened. There was no sound. She paused again. Should she go in and turn off the light? Or was it on for some purpose?

Suddenly she was aware of feeling distinctly uneasy. Mrs Macaulay had her committee tea party downstairs, where all the other members of the staff were busily assisting. Mrs Dulcie was confined to her bed on the floor below. The rest of the house seemed deserted and eerie, and a feeling of foreboding gripped her. So intensely preoccupied was she with the situation that she did not react to the first signs of an approaching sneeze.

'Ah! Ah! Tishoo!' She found herself taking a quick deep breath in order to stop the second sneeze from maturing. It was too late! The noise of a chair being moved, followed by striding feet across the room and a roughly seized door knob, confirmed her fears. She was not alone on the second floor.

The door gently opened. 'Who's that?' There was neither time nor space in which to try and hide. Indeed, the light from the open door now lit up the very part of the landing where she stood. 'It's you, Anne!' Charles's voice sounded surprised and somewhat hostile. Then, on reflection, his mood changed. 'Thank God it is you, and no one else. '

'I saw the light.'

'Don't worry about that. Come in. Quickly And quietly!' He put his finger to his lips. 'Does anyone know you're up here?'

'I don't think so,' she replied, unsure what to make of the situation as he hurriedly, but quietly closed the door behind her.

'Look, Anne. I'm not supposed to be here. I'm supposed to be out! Do you understand?'

'Yes. I think so, I've just taken your wife her tea. She said you were out.'

'She did? I want it to stay that way. Do you understand?'

The two were now standing in the middle of the room. Anne cast her eyes quickly around.

'Shall I go?' she asked, unsure of what was expected of her. 'I promise not to tell anyone. No one knows I came up here.'

Charles seemed about to say something and then changed his mind. 'Do you mean, that no one knows you're up here?'

'No one,' she confirmed, glancing uncomfortably at him.

'And you won't be missed downstairs?'

She shook her head. 'Not for some time.'

He moved towards her and she sensed a pleasant feeling run down her spine and her heart begin to beat faster. 'Anne?' he began. 'If no one knows either of us is here, why don't we make the most of it?' She looked into his face which was warm with affection. A smile broke across her face as she vowed to make him speak first.

'Well?' he said with a broad grin.

'Well, what?' she replied teasingly.

He removed the book he was reading and placed it carefully on the floor. He then turned and sat down in his favourite armchair, left in the room from the days he used to have that room. Anne meanwhile remained still, though she guessed his next move and knew she wanted to be his if he wanted her.

He held out both arms straight towards her. Now she did step towards him. She stopped just short of his feet as if to ensure it was his initiative which led them on. 'Come and sit on my knee, my beautiful one, my darling,' he said, again holding out his arms invitingly.

She knew instinctively that this was to be no ordinary meeting for them. She turned and shuffled her feet backwards. He put up his arms and guided her down on to his knees and then guided her gently with his hand back into his waiting arm. Their faces were only a few inches apart as he once more looked straight into her eyes.

'Comfy?' he murmured.

'Very, thank you, Charles.'

With his left arm around her shoulders he drew her towards him and they kissed ardently and passionately for several minutes.

She sensed a thrill run through her whole body as he began gently to fondle her breasts.

'That's lovely,' she heard herself whisper in his ear.

'Darling,' he whispered back. 'I really do love you. I said I couldn't do without you.'

As they kissed, she felt his hand move off her shoulder to the centre of her back and begin to undo the buttons on her uniform frock. He then moved his hand up to push the frock forwards off her shoulders. She looked down at her bared brassiere, then longingly up into his eyes. She felt his hand once more behind her back and, a few seconds later, felt the firm support of her brassiere fall away. Gently, as if afraid he might hurt her, he pushed the straps forward off her shoulders and removed the freed garment.

She felt his eyes relishing her well developed body, as he cupped one breast gently in his hand, lifted it upwards and ran his fingers slowly over the sensitive tip, which quickly responded to his fondling. It was ecstasy for her as he placed his mouth over the stiffened nipple. She felt the lower part of her body stir in a way she had never before experienced, and she put her arm around his neck as she felt a need to grip him quite tightly.

'Darling, darling! I can't begin to tell you how much I love you.' His whispers were too much for Anne to answer vocally. Instead, she took his head and turned his mouth towards her breast again, an invitation to which he immediately responded. 'Let's go on the bed, shall we?' he whispered in her ear a few moments later.

'Yes,' was all she could murmur, unsure quite what was expected of her, but ready to give her all to her long loved idol.

'I'll be very gentle as it's your first time.' He spoke encouragingly as he slipped off his own clothes and joined her under the counterpane.

It was more than an hour later when she awoke. She was lying with one of his muscular arms around her. He, also, was awake and seemed to be gazing at the ceiling. He had been gentle and she had had to endure none of the piercing pains she had heard giggled about in her last year at school. On the other hand, the experience had not been quite as ecstatic as she had heard described. Perhaps, she reasoned, that would come on future occasions. She smiled contentedly to herself and snuggled up closer. 'I want to stay like this for ever and ever,' she murmured.

On learning that she was awake, he turned his head towards her and, with a loving smile, whispered: 'Why can't this go on for ever? Shall we run away?'

'Now, Charles. Now you're teasing me. You know we can't,' she whispered back, giving him a broad sensuous smile.

'I suppose not, but I wish none the less that we could,' he replied, reaching forward and giving her a slow purposeful embrace on the lips.

As he drew back he partly pulled aside the bedcover he had drawn up over them both. She had no clothes on and he stared admiringly at the young, firm and fragrant figure beside him.

'I do love you, Charles,'

'And I love you, my darling,' he responded, drawing back the bedcover a little further on his side so that she might see his whole manliness again. She sensed it would take little to arouse his passion once more, and that there was nothing and no one at this point of time to stop them, if they wished, again to make intimate love to one another.

He turned over to face her and nestled his whole body up alongside hers, again gently fondling her breasts. 'When's your next day off, Anne?' he asked, not lifting his eyes from the object of his fondling.

'Friday. Why?' she asked, relishing the attention and obvious pleasure her whole body was giving him.

'I don't know if I'll still be here,' he continued softly. 'Much depends upon my wife's ankle. I'm supposed to be back at work that day, but I could take it off and not tell anyone. Then you and I could go out somewhere together for the whole day. How would you like that?'

'I'd love to,' she whispered eagerly.

'Would you have any difficulty in getting off? What would you tell your mother and the other staff? About where you were going. Would they ask?'

'I think I could sort out some excuse. Where would we meet?'

'You can't easily get to a railway station. But it's not too difficult, is it, getting to a bus stop from here?'

'No. I could do that.'

After they had discussed and agreed a meeting place, it seemed unlikely to her that he would now want to make love again so she turned away from him, and climbed down from the high old fashioned broad bed. Conscious of her complete nudity, and his eyes upon her, she hurried across to the chair where most of her clothes lay.

He watched her every movement. 'Darling,' he suddenly said, raising himself up on one elbow. She turned and heard him catch his breath at the full frontal view of her standing with no more than a small handful of clothes held down in front of her. 'Don't put those on for a moment.' Smiling and anxious to please, she stood quite still, ready to accede to his next command, whatever that might be.

'Please come over here,' he called softly, beckoning her towards the side of the bed where he lay holding one of his hands outstretched. 'No, leave the clothes behind. I want to see you. All of you, in the…. Just in the beautiful way God made you. God! You're attractive… You do something to me, you really do!' He sighed almost inaudibly. Teasingly, she edged a few inches at a time towards him. 'A little closer, darling.' His voice sounded more urgent as he reached out for her.

'Do you want to do it to me again, Charles?' she whispered.

'I will if you want to?' As she awaited his answer, she pulled aside the counterpane and witnessed his equal eagerness.

'If you do, darling.'

'Yes. You were so gentle the first time.' He made room for her on his side of the bed and she was soon in his full embrace.

★ ★ ★ ★ ★

It was as Anne reached the bottom step of the flight of stairs leading to the second floor that she suddenly remembered Mrs Dulcie's tea tray. It should have been collected long before now, she knew, and it was with some trepidation that she made her way to the bedroom and tapped lightly on the door.

'Come in!'

'I've come to collect your tray, Madam,' She said, trying to sound calm.

'Why haven't you collected it before?' was the snapped response.

'I've had other things to do, Madam,' she responded tartily. And she was tempted to tell Mrs Dulcie just what she had been doing, but knew that that was more than her life, and that of her lover's, was worth. She moved to the foot of the bed and lifted the tray off the end to where it had been pushed.

'When I'm mistress of The Grange, there'll be a lot fewer staff and things will be done….' Began Mrs Dulcie in one of her most aggressive tones.

'When you are mistress of The Grange?' repeated Anne,

'Of course! You silly girl. Hasn't it dawned on you that when Mr Macaulay, Mr Macaulay senior that is, dies, my husband will inherit this place…. And I shall run it!' She then added, even more defiantly: 'And I shall run it very differently from the way it is run now!'

'Yes, Madam,' responded a dumbfounded Anne, observing the rather skinny form of the lady's chest, and longing to tell her what her husband had said about her own well developed breasts, and that less than an hour earlier. What a laugh, gloated Anne to herself.

'Well, what have you to smirk about? What are you waiting for? You know where the door is, don't you?'

'Yes, Madam,' she replied meekly, as she headed for the safety of the gallery outside.

How ever does Charles put up with that woman? She muttered to herself shaking her head thoughtfully.

As she closed the door behind her, she permitted herself a self-satisfied grin. Physical pleasure apart, and had Anne not succeeded that afternoon in getting one back on her *bete noire*? In terms of having slept with her husband was she not now Mrs Dulcie's equal, she reasoned?

Totally unexpectedly, a moral victory had been waged and won. Anne had not, at the same time, occupied a bed on the private side of the invincible double doors? Her vowed fight against the iniquities of working class life were demonstrably improved, she told herself. The outlook was altogether rosier.

As she reached the dividing doors at the end of the first floor, she pushed them aside contemptuously, no longer did they harbour the same significance for her. How much longer, she wondered, would she be using uncarpeted and steep service staircases?

Chapter Seven – January 1929

Two days later found Anne alighting from a bus, some miles from The Grange, into the waiting arms of the person she now regarded as her lover.

'I was afraid it might snow and we'd not be able to go,' she remarked as she glanced up at the handsome man beside her who, she relished the thought, was to be hers alone for the day. 'It's certainly got a lot colder.' Anne commented. 'I wish small cars had heaters.'

They were soon driving out into the country. 'Where are we going?' she enquire, not caring much where they went as long as she was with him. And how long would he be merely a lover? In her mind the previous evening, when she had put her head on the pillow, she had confidently concluded that Charles would not remain married to "The DD" for very long and that, after a divorce and no more than a polite interval, she would be asked to become "Mrs Macaulay", "Mrs Macaulay the Second", "Mrs Charles Macaulay"! The day Anne was sure, was full of promise.

'I've booked a table for lunch at a nice little hotel I know some way from here,' he informed her.

'I suppose there's no chance of our getting stuck up here if it does come on to snow heavily, is there?' She looked up at the sky. 'What do you think, Charles?'

'I must admit that I, too, have been getting a little worried.' Charles said, 'Would it be more sensible to go back nearer home?'

'Why don't we have a quick walk first?' she suggested, not wishing to curtail his carefully planned day completely. 'I need to get my circulation going. What about you?'

'Good idea.' Fifteen minutes later he looked at his watch. 'Twenty past one. Time's getting on. Hungry?'

'A bit.'

'I seem to remember seeing a small restaurant in the next village we drove through earlier. Nothing very grand, I'm afraid. I suggest we stop there as time's getting on,'

The restaurant was indeed small, more of a café. 'Not quite the romantic little place I had lined up for us,'

'Don't worry, Charles. Each other's company is the most important thing.'

Charles studied the menu before passing it across to his guest.

'Not a wonderful choice of main course,' he stated disinterestedly. 'But it'll have to do. Mutton or done-up turkey. Nothing else.'

'I'll have the soup to begin with, please. I'm still none too warm. Then the mutton.'

'Two soups and two muttons,' he ordered, handing back the menu. 'And let me see the wine list, please.?'

'We're not licensed, Sir' the waitress informed him.

'Oh God!' was Charles's abrupt response. 'That's the last straw. Just when I felt in need of a large Scotch I'm sure you could do with one yourself. I'm so sorry.'

'It doesn't matter, Charles. It's not your fault. Anyway, I'm not used to strong spirits. Water will do for me.' She smiled at him. 'But you seem to be in need of a stimulant,'

'I'm usually abstemious at this time of day. Anyway, it's too late now to go elsewhere.' He immediately dropped his eyes to stare at the table mat before him. Neither of them spoke for several minutes.

Even if, thought Anne, this was not the kind of weather or lunch he had planned for them, he need not look quite so depressed. What was he so deep in thought about? Surely not just having to do without Scotch? And where had her day of blissful romance disappeared to?

'Cheer up, Charles! You look as if you have all the cares of the world upon you.' His verbal reply was little more than a grunt. 'May be I have. May be I have.'

'It's said, Charles, that a problem shared is a problem halved. Can I help?'

'Not with this one, Anne, but thanks all the same.'

Most of the meal was eaten in silence, and it was not until she had finished her sweet course that Anne raised the subject she felt was probably the one casting its doleful shadow over their much looked forward to lunch together. 'Charles? What happens next? I mean about you and me?'

'I wish I knew, Anne, I wish I knew' was his only response.

'Are you…. Are you and Mrs Dulcie…. Are you going on living together?'

'We must,' he replied, stretching his hand out across the table, more, she felt, for his own comforting than for hers.

'Am I going to see you again, I mean, other than just when you…. you and Mrs Dulcie….Come to stay at The Grange?'

'Believe me, Anne, I do want to.' He again stopped talking and she was concerned at how troubled he now looked and, for him, how tired he also now appeared to be. 'You're not making this very easy for me, are you?' he enquired quietly.

'How do you mean?' she responded, unsure for what she was being blamed.

This time, as he paused before replying, he did look up into her face and was troubled by her anxious expression. 'This…. The wonderful time we had together the day before yesterday. You are an intelligent girl, Anne. Surely you must know. It can't be more than just an affair. Can it?' He then repeatedly questioned : 'Can it?'

'You mean, you're going to go on living with Mrs Dulcie? Just as if you and I, had never…. Never even…?' The expression on her face became intense as she studied his for some small indication of hope.

'I'll get the bill. Then I think we should go back,' he stated.

Anne walked back to the car alone and seated herself in it without saying a word. Had she been cruelly deceived? Had she been naïve? As the car moved off she spoke. . 'Charles? We've got to talk. We can't just leave it all in mid-air!'

He began to speak hesitatingly again.: 'Will you promise me, Anne, not to tell anyone? Not anyone at all? What I'm now going to tell you? Do you promise?'

'I'm not one of the staff who gossips,' she stated.

'Anne. One of the reasons my wife…. Why Dulcie made such a fuss, when she slipped on the steps. About her fall. It was because she's…. She's probably expecting a baby.'

Nothing he said at that moment could have hit Anne harder. Her throat became dry, and she felt unable to speak. He continued in the same serious stammering tone. 'I say "probably" because we don't know yet for sure whether she has conceived.' He dropped his voice to a whisper. 'It was less than a fortnight ago. We've been trying to start a family for several months. Unsuccessfully. Dulcie has….There are medical complications.'

They drove in silence for five minutes. Try as she did, Anne could not rid her mind of the mental picture of herself sharing his bed, and their sharing each others bodies only two days before, during what had been for her, her first ever such experience.

'I'm going to draw in here,' he stated, slowing down and sounding unsure of himself. He turned into a lane and stopped the car. 'We're getting near The Grange and I can't drop you off and…. And just say "good-bye".'

At this point her control broke down and she wept openly. 'Oh! Oh! I…. I…. I just can't. I just can't believe how anyone. Anyone could behave….'

Charles turned and raised his left arm and went to place it around her shoulders. 'Take your arm away!' she snapped, punching it away. 'Don't you dare ever touch me again! I hate you! I hate you!'

'Surely not, Anne?' His voice sounded frightened and he put out one of his hands to place on her knee.

'I said take away your hands. Your filthy hands away from me! I told you. Don't you dare ever touch me again! Ever…. Ever…. Ever again. Do you understand?' With this defiant outburst, and raising her voice to a crescendo, she lent forwards and began sobbing uncontrollably.

He sat uneasily wondering what he should do. It was Anne who eventually spoke: 'You made love to that….That woman!' Suddenly she raised her voice again, turning towards him and appearing about to strike him. 'You made love to that woman just two weeks…. Less than two weeks before you…. You….' She quietened down and turned away from him. 'Before…' she added almost inaudibly: 'Before you took away my virginity. You…. You…. Swine!'

'What can I say, Anne?' His voice trembled. 'I'm just so very, very sorry. Please….'

'Sorry! Is that all you have to say…. Very, very sorry!' she snapped again, clenching her fists.

'I was about to say that I wanted you to believe me,' he stammered. 'And that there's truly no person on earth whom I'd want to hurt less than you, Anne darling.'

'Darling! Darling!' Her tone was bitter with sarcasm. 'You can sit there and dare to call me "darling"! You…. You two-faced rotter. You….'

'I know what's happened,' Charles said quietly, deciding that the better course was to sit out the storm. 'I should have known how humiliated you would feel if I told you…. Told you about my wife's condition.' He swallowed hard. 'But I felt you deserved to know the truth. That's all.'

'That's all. Thank you very much!' She almost spat out the words. 'Humiliated, yes! That's it. In a word – humiliated!'

Again neither spoke for several minutes. 'I'm going to walk home,' she stated suddenly, putting her hand out for the door handle.

'You can't walk from here. It's now snowing hard.'

'I don't care!'

'How do you think I'd feel if some harm became of you?'

'Right now,' she snapped with venom. 'I don't care how the hell you feel about anything! You think only of yourself!' What about me? I think it'd be better….' She broke down again and completed the sentence in a whisper. 'For everyone if I died!'

'Oh God!' His voice became firmer. 'Look… I can't say more than I've said about how sorry I am. We can't stay here any longer. I have a responsibility to see you home safely. Now, please, pull yourself together. Here, use my handkerchief. It's larger than yours.'

She took the neatly folded handkerchief and immediately her eyes fell on the interwoven monogram in one corner. The two initials were 'D' and 'C'. She stared at them as if in disbelief and then threw the handkerchief back on to his knee. She was still in her aggressively defiant mood.

'I don't care a damn for you, Mister high-and-mighty Charles Macaulay! You think you can treat me like this. Well, I'm going to show you that….That…. You mean nothing. Absolutely nothing to me! Do you hear? Nothing! Now, please drive me home! At once'.

'You make me feel awful, a real cad,' he remarked quietly.

'And how do you think I feel? You deserve to feel awful,' she snapped. 'Yes, and you have behaved abominably!'

A nonplus Charles decided that silence was probably still the better course and started the engine without saying anything further. He drove her to the bottom of the back drive, as he had once before, and reflected that on that earlier occasion, their meeting had also ended on a less than cordial note.

Anne opened the door as the car drew to a halt. She said, quite simply before walking away with her head held high: 'Thanks for the lunch.' The even layer of pure white snow, which now covered the entire landscape, seemed a poignant reminder to her and, on reaching the stables block, she went straight to her bedroom.

'You're back early,' called out her mother. 'Had a nice time?' Anne did not immediately reply. She picked up her towel, her sponge bag and a clean set of clothing and made straight for the top of the stairs. 'I'm going up to The Grange, Mummy, for a bath. I feel filthy!'

★ ★ ★ ★ ★

By the end of the third week in January Anne had cause to become extremely worried. Her curse had been late before, but never more than a few days. She felt unable to discuss the matter with her mother, whose likely reaction she feared almost as much as all the other consequences, and there was no one else she felt able to confide in.

Knowing little about contraception beyond playground gossip at school, she had assumed Charles had done something to himself to stop anything not wanted from happening. A further week passed and Anne became reconciled to the fact that, almost certainly, she was carrying Charles's child. This, she realised, was bad enough in itself. But two other matters compounded her problem. Her last words with the father had been acrimonious to an extreme and she was apprehensive of his willingness even to talk to her again. The second matter, which occupied much of her thinking and anger, was the possibility, if not probability, that Dulcie, her rival for Charles's affection, was also carrying a child of his.

If nothing else, Anne assured herself, her child was going to be no less well treated by him than Dulcie's was. Determination in this respect rapidly became an obsession, and occasional thoughts of revenge crossed her mind. Born out of wedlock, her baby was not going to be regarded as some second-class citizen. Whether he would like it or not, Charles had equal responsibilities to both babies and both mothers.

Her immediate problem was how to get in touch with him. He and his wife had returned to their London flat and were not expected to stay at The Grange again until Easter. She did not know the address of either their flat or his office, nor did she know either telephone number She would have to write, she decided, and hope that if she posted the letter to him at The Grange, marked "Please Forward" clearly on the outside of the envelope, it would reach him.

She waited until her mother was out and then began composing a letter. She rarely wrote to anyone except her aunt at the seaside, and at first she made several quite unacceptable attempts. These ranged from seeking forgiveness for what she had called him to threatening to go and tell his mother and father. In the end, her letter was brief and to the point. It read:

Dear Charles, I have to talk to you urgently. You have got me into baby trouble. My day off is Friday. I will be at the same bus-stop we met at before, next Friday at aboit eleven o'ckock."

She decided she could not possibly end the letter with "love from…." the only ending she had previously used. In the end she just put her name. She needed to put that, she told herself angrily, in case the bounder received numerous such letters!

She took the envelope to the village post office, having remembered to print Charles's name and The Grange address in capital letters to prevent someone who knew her hand-writing at the house, from recognising the sender. As she pushed the envelope through the slot in the post box, she offered a silent prayer for help. Would he rescue her? Would he forgive her? Would he act like the gentleman she had always taken him for until their previous acrimonious meeting?

By the time the bus approached the stop where she would alight, Anne had become apprehensive. She did not know if he would be there, or had even received her letter. She had gazed absentmindedly out of the window for most of the journey, trying to weigh up in her mind what she could achieve from the meeting if he did turn up, and what, at heart, she wanted from their meeting.

And though the snow had melted, and the countryside looked wintry and inhospitable, she was not without some satisfaction at the cause for her journey and the opportunities which might shortly be opening up for her. She must, she warned herself, play her cards circumspectly.

Just one aspect continued to worry her thinking, making all the other issues not quite so clear-cut as she at first had thought they were. Was she still at heart as deeply in love with her idol as she had been for many years past? The interval since writing the letter seemed already to have mellowed the hostility she had felt towards him at their previous meeting, and she was ready to blame "The DD" for all the trouble they were in. Charles was no cad. His wife, she reckoned, had got at him and somehow changed him. It was all her fault.

It was with an immense sigh of relief that she saw him, just as the bus came to a halt, emerging from the same side of the road where he had parked his car before. He stood some yards back from the bus stop and waited for her to walk to him. From the expression on his face, she knew he was looking forward to their coming confrontation as little as she was.

'Hullo, Anne,' he said with half a smile.

'Hullo, Charles,' she replied uncomfortably, forcing an equally slight smile.

'How are you?'

'All right.'

'Let's go to the car.' He turned and walked beside her. 'If it's acceptable to you.' This, she thought, is probably how he opens conversations with his business clients. 'I thought we should find somewhere near here where we can park the car. Somewhere away from people so we can talk things over.'

When they got to the car she noticed that he was even more attentive than usual about opening the door for her, and placing a rug over her lap before getting in himself. Also, his driving was without violent accelerations. Was this out of consideration for her condition? They pulled up on the corner of a country road, where there was a spare piece of ground. He began, speaking very stiffly and keeping his head facing over the front of the car.

She turned to face him and started saying what she had planned to get off her chest at the first opportunity. 'Charles, before we discuss the main matter we're going to talk about, I want to say I am truly sorry for what I said and what I called you when we last met. I....'

The sigh of relief he let out was as audible to her as it was to himself. He turned towards her and took her gloved hand in his and gave it a gentle reassuring squeeze. For the first time that day he looked her fully in the face and gave her a genuine smile. The ice, she knew, had been broken. This would make their principal discussion that much easier.

'Let us say no more about the last time we met, Anne,' he said quietly. 'It was a day which just did not go right from start to finish? The snow, that rotten, grotty little restaurant!' 'Oh,' she cut in, feeling her tension falling away. 'It wasn't that bad, was it?'

'I suppose not. It was just the mood I was in, I suppose. I'd so much on my mind. Then the snow ruining my carefully worked out lunch arrangements was the final straw. I can't say I enjoyed one mouthful of that meal!' He looked serious again.

She kept her eyes on his face, studying his expression, and spoke in as relaxed a tone as she could muster. 'So we're friends again, are we?'

'Of course we are!' He lifted her gloved hand towards his lips as she bent forwards.

'I don't like formal kisses like that!' she said guardedly, with a slight laugh. 'Anyway, my gloves are probably none too clean!' She bent towards him and he accepted the invitation to be less formal.

His embrace on her cheek was not prolonged. He drew back and sat up straight in his seat. 'In the time since I received your letter, I've given your news very careful consideration. I stress this, Anne, because I want you to know that what I'm going to say is not being said on impulse.'

'I understand,' she said, anxious to know what was coming.

'First,' he continued. 'You must have the child. Please promise me that you'll give no thought to running off to one of these awful back-street abortionists. It's illegal and it's highly dangerous medically.'

'I hadn't even given that idea a thought,' she confirmed.

'I'm very relieved to hear you say that. The one problem we, that is you and I, don't have which most people who get into this sort of trouble have…. Is a shortage of money.'

'I've hardly any savings at all,' she responded, missing the point to which he was alluding.

'I mean on my side. Anne, I promise you one thing, if nothing else, you're not going to have any financial worries.'

'I see,' she replied, without knowing what limitations there might be to his apparent boundless generosity, but beginning to be aware that, like her, he appreciated the power that the situation gave to her. The conclusion to her own first hours of introspection at home had been to achieve as generous a settlement as possible, but that objective already had been substantially softened. Now her plans were more widely targeted. 'You know, Charles, there are other and much more important things than money to talk about?'

'I know, Anne. I'm well aware of that. I'm thinking of you. I just wanted first to put your mind at rest on the financial side before we begin talking about other considerations.'

'You make it sound all rather business-like, Charles. You must remember that what we're talking about is a baby, who'll come into this world because you and I did something rather special together.'

'I've not forgotten, Anne. I'd also remind you that the baby is as much mine as he or she is yours. Don't forget that.'

'I'm so relieved to hear you say that, Charles, I really am. I'd had thoughts that, with you expecting another baby at the same time, you might think our one did not count for very much.'

'On the contrary. I know my responsibilities and I'll not shirk from what I have to do.'

'But what about the baby? He or she is not going to have a proper father. People are going to talk. And what are they going to say about me?'

'It's those kind of questions which have been worrying me since I got your letter. Let me outline what I have in mind. But believe me, please Anne, I want you to be as happy as I can make you. If I weren't already married, there is no question but that I would want to marry you.' He dropped his voice. 'I think I'm a gentleman, a man of honour and that, at least, is a token of my feelings.' They exchanged glances.

'We're caught up in one hell of a dilemma.' Charles continued, a serious expression clouding his face. 'Or at least I am. For very different reasons, both you and Dulcie have justifiable claims on me, of which only one can be satisfied.'

'And that one's Dulcie's.'

'Yes, For the moment at least it is my marriage to Dulcie which holds sway.'

'You say for "the moment" How long is "the moment"?'

'That is the question, Anne. None of us knows. I certainly don't. Apart from loving you, I've always considered you a most sensible person. You've got your head screwed on the right way, as they say.' He paused again before changing the subject. 'I believe a scandal, which would reflect against my family as much as against you, Anne, can best be averted if you were to leave The Grange as soon as possible.'

She did not respond and waited for him to continue. 'I'll buy you a nice house, one in the country, which you and your mother can choose. To make this appear wholly plausible you could let it be known that either you or your mother has been left an unexpected legacy, or something like that. She and you would move to the new house and no one at The Grange need ever know that you're having a child.'

'You have it all worked out, don't you?' Before he could respond, she continued: 'And how am I supposed to earn a living to support my…. Our child?'

'I was just coming to that. I propose to enter into a legal commitment to pay you sufficient income each year. And I shall settle a capital sum in trust for our child. At least you can see, Anne, you should have no financial worries.'

She remained thoughtful, and ran quickly over in her mind her change of thought during the last few days. 'I understand that, but I feel somehow as if I'm being.... well "bought off".'

'Please don't feel that way. I know I may sound, as you said earlier, a bit too business-like today, but I do feel we have to deal with the money side.'

'And what about "The father-less baby" side? And love. Love, Charles!' She studied his expression carefully, ready to detect the faintest response. 'You and me. Is our baby not to have parents who live together, who love one another, and go on loving one another? If you don't give me love, who will?' Her voice grew in emotion. 'No other man will want me now!'

Sensing she was on the point of breaking down, he put his arm around her shoulder and pulled her closer to him. 'Would you ever want me again?' he enquired hesitantly.

'Yes,' she responded with unexpected spontaneity, immediately wondering what had led her to admit her decision quite so readily.

'You know,' he said softly. 'I can never promise anything on that side, but if you had your own little homestead I would want to visit you and our child.

'But am I not going to have a husband? I want someone to share my whole life with. I want you, Charles. To my very own!' Her eyes echoed the pleading tone of her voice.

'I wouldn't be able to share every moment of my time with you, Anne, but we could try and spend as much time as possible together.'

'But you'd have that other woman?'

'I'm married to her, and that is a fact we do have to accept.'

'As if I didn't know,' Anne responded sulkily. 'Why do I have to suffer? Why can't she? You don't love her, that's plain to see. Why can't you divorce her and marry me? It seems to be me who is doomed to come off second best.' She then enquired tentatively. 'I suppose she is still expecting?'

He nodded. It was Anne who then became business-like, venting some of her more carefully nurtured ideas. 'I shall want you to provide our child with everything you provide for your other child, Charles. There mustn't be any difference in the treatment they receive. You agree?'

'Well, I understand what you are saying,' he replied thoughtfully. 'But I have to say I hadn't thought of it quite in those terms. I can assure you, though, as I've already tried to, that our child will not want for anything which I can provide.'

'That's not quite the same thing, Charles. I want both babies to be treated. identically!'

'That would be impossible. Take The Grange, for example. There's only one of those for me to pass on to my eldest son.'

'Our child will be a Macaulay son if he is a boy,' she snapped back, taking him by surprise. 'And it's just medically possible that he may even be the eldest. Pregnancy lengths vary by up to a week or two, you know?'

'I know your baby, if he's a boy, will be a Macaulay, but it isn't the same is it?' He dropped his voice. 'Children born out of wedlock don't always inherit automatically.'

She ignored the innuendo. 'I want it to be the same for both of them, Charles,' she stated adamantly. 'I want you to promise that our child will get everything your other child gets. Do you promise?'

'No! I try never to promise things I may not be able to keep to,' he replied. 'And I don't think I'm in a position to keep to such a promise as you clearly want me to even if I wanted it myself, which I don't. You're intelligent, Anne. You must be reasonable.'

'Reasonable?' Then, feeling she might be losing out on her point of principle, she continued bluntly without thinking: 'If you don't agree I'll….' She bit her lip. She had so nearly been going to say: 'I'll tell your parents.' That would have been awful. The moment of shame passed as quickly as it had occurred. She knew subconsciously she had been treading on dangerous ground. Charles was too strong a man to be pushed in that way.

'Let's now change the subject completely: How are you going to break the news to your mother?'

'I haven't worked that out yet.'

'How do you think she'll take it? When her first reaction of horror has passed? Do you think she will look forward to having a grandchild?' He risked a glance at her, their eyes meeting only for a moment before she turned away.

'I just don't know,' she grimaced. 'I haven't given it much thought. Mummy will certainly scold me. Tell me I've disgraced the family and so on.'

'Oh, Anne.' He risked putting his arm back around her shoulders and she did not protest. 'I said when we were together at Christmas that I loved you. And I do. Whatever happens, or does not happen please remember that I do love you, and that I'll do everything I humanly can to make you happy, and to relieve you of all worries about our baby.'

She had felt the need for this reassurance and, on receiving it in what appeared to be a sincerely meant fashion, she turned her head towards him and waited for his embrace. 'That makes me feel ever so much better, Charles,' She said with a sigh of satisfaction as he withdrew. 'You don't know what I would have done. Killed myself perhaps?'

'No. I don't believe that Anne,' he said, speaking seriously. 'Not for one moment. You're far too plucky a type of person to take the so-called easy way out. You know how to stand up for yourself. Look at the way,' he added with a laugh, waving a hand in her direction. 'Look at the way you've stood up to me, even if you haven't had your own way on every point you've tried to negotiate.'

'Sorry, Charles,' she said, making a grimace and a forced half laugh. Silence fell again until she asked: 'Are you ever going to tell any of your family?'

'I think it most unlikely. I shall probably tell our family solicitor. He's the sort of father confessor type who knows and advises upon all the family secrets.'

'Are there any more secrets of this type?' she enquired, feigning genuine concern. 'Are there?'

'I can assure you, Anne. There are no more such problems.'

She was reminded of the staff hall gossip. How many other's had he seduced, she wondered, and made them pregnant? 'What about other affairs with other staff at The Grange?' She enquired tentatively.

'I've never even looked at another member of the staff.' he retorted indignantly.

'Honestly?' Her voice expressed surprise.

'Yes. Quite sure. Why? Do you think I chase after every piece of skirt?' A shadow of annoyance crossed his face.

She paused before replying. 'I had heard the odd remark in the kitchen quarters.'

To her surprise, he laughed quite heartily. 'What do they say? Poor bunch of girls! Jealousy, I bet! I can just see it. Trying to pretend to each other that they've conquered the owner's son! I really think that's damn funny! Who are the aspirants? Daisy? Hilda? Not Cook, surely!'

'Where am I going to have this baby? You say I'm to be put away in a house in the country so no one knows I'm there. Where do I have the baby?' Before he could answer, she asked: 'Where is your Dulcie going to have hers?'

'Oh, we've already booked her in at a rather old fashioned, but very comfortable nursing home. Conveniently, it's about half way between The Grange and our London flat. Almost all recent generations of the Macaulays have been born there, including myself.'

'Then,' Anne reacted quickly. 'That's surely where our baby ought also to be born!'

'On no it isn't! I'm not agreeing to that!' he assured her firmly with a pretence at laughing. 'Oh no! Not that.'

'Why not? Surely the place isn't too good for my baby and for me?' she responded quietly.

He ignored this challenge and instead replied: 'You and Dulcie, as you've said yourself, could both be there at the same time, at least for part of your two confinements.'

'What's wrong with that?' Anne continued, beginning to feel that on this topic, if she used it wisely, she could develop the relationship she wished to establish at the outset, and build on as other opportunities presented themselves. 'I'll keep out of the way, I presume,' she continued insensitively, 'In a nursing home which is good enough to be graced by the likes of your Dulcie, every mother has a private en suite room?'

'Yes they do, but Anne, that really is going a bit far.' He shook his head.

'No it's not!' she persisted. 'Not if the children are going to be treated the same whenever its humanly possible. That's what you said. You've agreed!'

'I don't need reminding of what I've agreed! And what I have not agreed!' Once more he spoke more firmly, irritation clearly evident. 'You can go into a nursing home. That I'm quite happy about. Just as nice a one, just as expensive a one, but not that particular one. How's that? No favouritism.'

'Did you not say all the Macaulays were born at that one?'

'Yes! Well?'

'Our baby will be a Macaulay. So surely he or she is entitled to be born there,'

Charles knew he had lost the argument. With a laugh and a shake of his head he said: 'You're a tough one, Anne.'

She smiled back, not wishing to antagonise him. It was against Dulcie alone she really wanted to get revenge. 'Not at all, Charles. Just that I think we should start as we intend to go on. Our baby's going to be born at the same place as your other baby is. Do you agree?'

He nodded. 'All right, I agree.'

'So now you will kindly make the necessary arrangements?'

'Of course. Which leads me to another subject. Your name.'

'My name?'

'Yes. You can't go to the nursing home and other places, as Miss Anne Jones. Nor, before you jump in with the suggestion, can you call yourself Mrs Macaulay.' He paused. 'I suggest you call yourself.... Mrs....' He looked closely into her face and a smile crossed his own. 'Mrs Brown. To match your big beautiful brown eyes?'

'That's too ordinary. Like Jones which I hate,' she responded quickly. 'I want something more classy,'

'Like 'Banks?'

'Why Banks?' Anne queried.

'Mrs Banks. To match….' He laughed. 'I was thinking of all the money I can foresee you're going to amass at my expense.'

'I'll go along with "Banks"

They talked for another half hour and then drove off, and were a lot more fortunate than the previous time with their choice of a restaurant for lunch. Afterwards, they went for a drive into the country so that Anne could get an idea of what houses there were. She came to an early decision that she wanted a centuries-old cottage with leaded windows.

He stopped the car near the bus stop, after ensuring she felt fit and well enough to see herself home. He gave her his private telephone number at his office, and promised to arrange for his secretary to get in touch with estate agents and obtain details of all the cottages for sale in the county.

'Anne, darling, you're being so brave and sensible. I am just so sorry it had to end up in this way. I'm to blame.'

'It was my fault too,' she smiled 'But it was lovely.'

'It was only your fault for being so attractive!' he said with a broad smile. Despite the lack of privacy, he put his arm around her shoulder and drew her close to him.

'I just wish my family circumstances made it such that we didn't have to suggest your moving away. But my father is a pretty important figure in the City. I owe it to him not to let the family down if we can possibly avoid doing so.'

'I do understand that, Charles. But I don't quite see why she, your wife, gets away with it all?'

'She's done nothing wrong!'

'She has! She's grabbed you and not made you very happy. If she hadn't grabbed you, you said yourself. You would ask me to marry you.'

It was a wholly sincere, if not passionate, embrace which they exchanged before she got out of the car and began running for the bus, which had suddenly appeared. Charles ran beside her. 'Should you be doing this? Isn't it bad for you in your condition?'

They exchanged one final quick kiss with Anne standing on the bus's rear platform. She took her seat and turned to give him a final wave. It seemed to her as if his eyes had been moist. He stood at the stop until the bus took her out of his sight.

Taking a seat, she began reflecting on the meeting which in most ways, she knew, had gone off better than she had dared to hope. Had she, she debated, perhaps been too hard on Charles? How did girls usually react to men who got them into trouble? Especially very rich men? Perhaps, she thought, she should have been a business woman, and not a chambermaid. Why were there so few women in business? Her father would be proud of her.

Charles, she acknowledged, had not been ungenerous. Indeed, he had behaved like a real gentleman. Had she been a bit too grasping about equality, and the insistence on the same nursing home? Was that insistence going to cause her trouble and worry in nine months time? She was, she admitted, a bit of an opportunist at times. Had she now gone too far? No, not too far! Why should her child not have every benefit that the other one was going to have lavished on it?

She loved Charles and did not want to harm him, but if only to snub Dulcie, she would keep Charles to his word on the subject of equality!

Yes, she told herself philosophically, she was going to make the best out of the interim situation. She would accept what Charles had proposed. But her two objectives were now clearly defined. First, to out-manoeuvre Dulcie for her husband's affections and, secondly, to get the very best chance in life for her own child. Her child, and no one else's, would one day, she vowed, be the proud and revered master or mistress of The Grange.

Chapter Eight – February 1929

Anne's immediate task, to which she was not looking forward, was to acquaint her mother with her predicament, and to tell her, in the best way she could, how that their employer's son was going to help them financially. She decided that she would not, on this occasion, tell her mother that Dulcie was also expecting. That would be revealed later. Charles had given Anne this piece of information in strict confidence but, that apart, it certainly added an irony to an otherwise already complicated enough situation.

'Well, I really don't know what to say. How could you, Anne, dear?' Was her mother's first emotional comment.

Anne had begun by asking her mother not to say anything until she had told her the whole story. Done this way, Anne had hoped that the idea of moving to a cottage in the country and her mother no longer having to work, would help to soften the blow. 'You'll be able to go and visit Auntie whenever you want to, Mummy.' Her daughter tried to enthuse.

'And whatever would your father have said?'

'I do realise that it's a great shock for you, Mummy,' replied Anne, taking up a seat beside her mother on their small settee, and putting an arm around her shoulder. 'But now that it has happened, there's nothing we can do but make the most of it.'

'Make the most of it? That sounds very mercenary, dear! I do hope you didn't give that impression to Mr Charles.'

'Oh, I didn't mean it quite like that. I mean that we, well…. we should look on the good side as well as on the bad. For one thing, Mummy, we will both be able to give up our demeaning work as cleaners.'

'I'm lost for words. I don't know what to say. It will take me several days to get my thoughts clear.' Mrs Jones sat with a stunned expression on her face. 'You seem to be taking it all so calmly. Almost as if you're pleased it has happened. I do hope you didn't lead poor Mr Charles on. Did you?'

Anne ignored the suggestion and went on to describe their need to begin to get the story about the unexpected legacy across to the staff.

'But that's a lie, dear. And I don't like telling untruths about anything. You know I don't.' Mrs Jones looked as if it were all too much for her and she was about to break into tears.

'We're only being asked to say this small fib for the sake of Mr and Mrs Macaulay's reputation. You wouldn't want to hurt them, would you, Mummy?'

'No,' she replied without conviction. 'But I'd hardly call it just a small fib.'

'I have to see Charles's solicitor on my day off, next Friday. Mrs Lines will let you swap your day so that you can come with me, won't she?'

'I think I'll be able to arrange that,' agreed her mother, still shaking her head to and fro in disbelief.

'Remember, Mummy,' Anne coached. 'You've had a totally unexpected letter from a solicitor telling you that you've been left a legacy by someone Daddy knew when he was a young man.'

'I'll try and remember to say that.' Mrs Jones looked around their sitting room. 'We've now lived here very happily in this little home for more than ten years.' She went on, as much to herself as to her daughter. 'I'm happy working at The Grange, and I shall really miss all the staff.'

The following day a letter arrived from Charles telling Anne that he had seen the solicitor who would be making all the necessary financial arrangements. Charles himself would not be at the meeting. He enclosed five pounds in the envelope to cover their fares to London and other incidental expenses, and ended the letter: 'I promise I will look after you financially and will do my best in other directions. And with this help comes all my love for someone who is very dear and special to me.'

'Dear and special?' repeated Mrs Jones, as she handed the letter back to her daughter. 'He's jolly lucky, if you ask me, to have had.... Had his indiscretion.... With someone like you, dear.'

'He really does love me, Mummy,' she stated breezily.

'That's maybe, but he's married to someone else,' said Mrs Jones.

'That's the only snag in the whole business,' replied Anne. But for how long, she wondered, would that state of affairs remain?

★ ★ ★ ★ ★

The following Friday Anne and her mother got up in their best clothes prior to catching the train to London.

At the solicitors' office, they were shown into a poorly lit waiting room, the walls of which were lined with shelves of heavy leather-bound tomes. They sat down in two dilapidated leather armchairs, which Mrs Jones found to be even deeper than they looked. 'I do hope I don't have to get out of this thing in a hurry!' she remarked nervously.

'Mrs Jones and Mrs Banks?' A tall man with a monotonic loud voice helped neither lady to regain her confidence. 'Mr Stevens will see you..' said the man from the door. 'Please follow me.'

Anne helped her mother up on to her feet and, in silence, they followed the man down a long corridor with doors on both sides. The man knocked at the last but one door and, holding it open for them to enter, called out their names in the same unvaried tone. 'Mrs Jones and Mrs Banks, Sir.'

The man who emerged from behind a very large knee-hole desk was short and plump. Once the frown had fallen from his face, he gave them both a kindly smile. 'Do come in, ladies. And sit yourselves down and make yourselves comfortable.' He guided them towards a small table at the side of the room around which three upright chairs had been placed. 'Now, how about a glass of sherry?' As he spoke, Mr Stevens opened one of the wall-cupboards and brought out a decanter, holding it out towards the two ladies as if to prove he meant what he had just said.

'Oh, not for me, thank you.' Mrs Jones responded immediately with a forced laugh.

'Oh do, Mummy. It'll do you good. I'm going to have one.' Anne's confidence had returned, and she was beginning to respond well to the apparent importance with which they were now being treated.

'All right then…. Just a very small one. Thank you,.'

Anne watched Mr Stevens closely as he poured the sherry and passed a glass to each of them. The scene of the two ladies seated at the small table, each sipping sherry and attended by this Dickensian character, seemed to her mildly amusing. She could see why Charles had said that all the family chose this gentleman, who seemed to exude confidence and security, to confide in.

As soon as he had poured his own glass, he joined them at the table. 'Now…. Eh? Ladies, Charles…. Eh? Ah yes! Mr Macaulay has been in to see me and has told me about the whole…. The whole…. Un…. Unfortunate matter. In complete confidence, of course.' He paused and began to fidget with his watch chain. Anne realised it was likely to become a long meeting since Mr Stevens appeared to weigh up each word before he uttered it.

'It is not for me to pass any comments whatsoever,' he continued, as she wondered what one could do to wind him up to go a bit faster. 'I am here only to deal with a few legal details of the settlement matters. Matters about which I understand there is already agreement between the parties. You, Miss….Mrs Banks, and Mr Macaulay, Mr Charles Macaulay.'

Mr Stevens sat back and drew out a gold watch from a small pocket in his bulging waistcoat. He looked at it, frowned, raised his eyebrows and then took a large sip of sherry. He replaced the glass slowly on the table in front of him, and looked up at the ceiling. His visitors waited in silence.

'I've known the Macaulay family for…. For almost all my life. I was an articled clerk in this firm in the lifetime of Charles's great grandfather, you know. A charming man. Very sound. So was Charles's grandfather. And, of course, Charles's father.' He paused again, and now appeared almost oblivious of the two ladies. 'Mr Macaulay is most highly thought of in the City. They want him to become an alderman and then Lord Mayor. I've known them all. Wonderful family, wonderful.'

His eyes rested momentarily on Anne before he closed them as if, she thought, wanting to shut out all thoughts of the problem from his mind. 'Very sad. Very sad. I love them all. Just as if they were my own family.'

Anne felt the need to break a further period of silence. 'Charles wants me to go ahead and get the house.'

'Ah, yes! Yes!' Mr Stevens returned from his reminiscences. 'Yes, the new house for you. For you and your mother here…. Yes. Yes. That is certainly one of the things we shall need to deal with.' He rose to his feet, looked at his watch again, went across to his desk and returned with some papers.

'Charles…. Very generous…. Very generous indeed. He has….Er…. Yes, here we are. Let me go through the list.' Mr Stevens re-adjusted his pince-nez glasses. 'He is going to give you one thousand pounds with which to buy your house. A cottage he told me you have in mind. And to furnish it.'

Anne nodded her understanding.

'And he has asked me to draw up a Deed of Covenant. Under this he will pay to you four hundred pounds each year. When your…. Yours…. Yours and his…. Child is born, he has asked me to draw up a Trust Deed under which he will initially settle…' He studied his papers again. 'Five thousand pounds on the child. You may use the income for maintenance until he or she is twenty-one, and then the income is to be his or hers. Charles intends, from time to time, to add to this Trust as the child grows older. Finally, he has asked me to prepare an Educational Trust which will enable his or her private school fees to be paid for.'

Anne and her mother had difficulty in following all that was said, though it was clear to them that their financial needs were to be well taken care of.

'I am given to understand,' continued Mr Stevens. 'That in return for what it is hoped you will feel is a generous settlement, that you are giving a solemn undertaking not to divulge to anyone, now or in the future, the…. The…. The little difficulty, shall we say, and who was the man responsible?'

'That's what I told Charles,' replied Anne confidently.

'Ah , well. That's good. That's very good.' Mr Stevens consulted his watch again, and then peered at the two ladies over his glasses and asked: 'Now have either of you any questions you would like to ask me?'

'How soon,' asked Anne, 'Can I go ahead and buy the new house?'

Mr Stevens studied his now empty glass with an expression of apparent dismay. 'Would either of you like another sherry?' he asked, totally ignoring her question.

'Not for me, thank you,' Mrs Jones promptly replied, glancing at her still almost full glass.

'I'd like another, if I may, please,' responded Anne, holding out her empty glass while avoiding her mother's disapproving stare. 'It's very nice.'

Mr Stevens refilled his own and Anne's glasses and, when all three were once more seated around the table, Anne repeated her question. 'Ah, yes,' he replied. 'Yes. You naturally want to know when you can go ahead and buy your house.' He paused then said : 'I don't see why you cannot go ahead now. 'Choose your house and ask the agents to get in touch with me. I will deal with the legal formalities. These take about three weeks. Completion very largely depends on the vendors. If you choose either an empty house or one where the vendors are in a hurry to vacate, you could move in a little over a month. Would that fit in with your other arrangements?'

'That would fit in very well,' Anne replied,

'We,' said Mrs Jones. 'That is both Anne and I, have to give in our notices to the Macaulays.'

'Yes, of course, of course.' Mr Stevens nodded as he replied. 'I don't see why…. Why both of you cannot get on and give in your notice.'

'We're going to say,' interposed Anne. 'That a friend of my late father has left us a large unexpected legacy.'

'Very suitable, very suitable!' he acknowledged with a nod. 'Wholly plausible reason for giving up service.' He consulted his watch yet again and rose to his feet. Anne and her mother took this as their cue also to get up. 'It will be necessary,' Mr Stevens added turning to Anne. 'For you to sign a number of documents as soon as they have been prepared. Is it easier for you if I send them to your present home, or would you prefer to come in here, in about a week's time, and sign them here?'

'I think we'd prefer to come here,' replied Anne. Then, as an after thought, she asked: 'Will Charles be here next time?'

'Oh, I don't know about that.' He looked at her quizzically, then glanced at Mrs Jones. 'He will, of course, have to sign the documents.'

'Do I have to sign anything?' enquired Mrs Jones.

'No,' he replied. 'We shall need only your daughter's signature.'

'I'll come alone then,' said Anne, whose mind was running ahead to the chance of meeting her lover at the same time. 'I'll give Charles a telephone call to his office.'

Mr Stevens looked taken aback. 'Would that be wise?'

'Why?'

'I.... I.... Well, it is perhaps not for me to say. I thought it would.... Er.... Be better if you two.... Did not see each other.'

'What? Not meet again? Never again, do you mean?' The tone of her voice surprised Mr Stevens and momentarily he looked pained.

'In circumstances such as these, my dear. That is not an uncommon course to pursue.'

'Charles and I are planning to see a great deal of each other. Obviously, he has not mentioned this to you.'

Mr Stevens appeared even more taken aback and moved towards the door. 'Perhaps I have said too much already,' he added quietly. He opened the office door and, with a waddling gait, which almost caused Anne to laugh aloud, led the way back up the long corridor without speaking. He handed them their coats and opened the front door for them. 'Have you any luggage, parcels or anything?'

'None, thank you,' replied Mrs Jones.

'Thanks very much for your help,' said Anne with a smile, .

Mr Stevens took it slowly and, looking straight into her face, said: 'I am so very sorry all this has happened to so nice a young lady. It really is all most unfortunate.... Most unfortunate.' He then turned to Mrs Jones. 'The Macaulays are a very honourable family, and you may rest assured that what Charles has said about looking after your daughter will be done.'

'Thank you,' replied Mrs Jones with a smile which showed her relief that the meeting was over and had been successfully concluded.

His final words, before closing the door, were to Anne: 'I shall expect to see you here next Friday and, please remember, if there is anything I can do to help…. Anything at all…. Now or in the future. You have only to write to me or telephone me. God bless you.' With that he turned and closed the door.

'What a sweet old gentleman,' Mrs Jones said as they walked away.

★ ★ ★ ★ ★

'I really don't know what we shall do without you both,' said Mrs Macaulay, looking genuinely dismayed. 'It came as such a shock when Mrs Lines told me you wanted to leave us.'

'We don't want to leave you, Madam,' emphasized Mrs Jones, not daring to look her employer fully in the face. 'Anne and I have been so happy here. And we shan't forget how good you were to us when I lost my husband.'

'You have both been wonderful and loyal members of our staff. And since you took over the silver responsibilities, Mrs Jones, we've had not a single problem on that side. And Anne?' She smiled almost affectionately.

'I don't want to leave either, Madam. I'm very grateful for all you've done for me, too.' She smiled as convincingly as she could.

'Leaving us, Anne, has spoilt the little plan Mrs Lines had worked out. Perhaps she has mentioned it?' She felt Mrs Macaulay's eyes upon her. 'When Hilda retires in a year or so, we'd planned that you should become head chambermaid. You are such a responsible person.' She broke off. 'You get that from both your mother and your father, I think.'

'Yes, Madam,' replied Anne, not knowing quite how to respond and glancing nervously at her mother.

'Anyway, we mustn't let our problems cloud your wonderful news, You must be looking forward to setting up your new home.'

'Yes, we are, Madam,' agreed Mrs Jones, hardly daring to reflect on the true circumstances for fear of letting something slip out accidentally.

'If that is all, Madam, we won't keep you,' Mrs Jones said, hoping to conclude the meeting as soon as possible.

'That's all right. It's not every day I have staff coming in to say they have struck gold!' This time Mrs Macaulay laughed aloud.

Anne and her mother rose to their feet and turned towards the door of the morning room. 'You must come and see me before you actually leave us at the end of the month,' said Mrs Macaulay. 'I know my husband also will want to wish you both all the very best of luck and good health.'

'Thank you, Madam,' they both echoed again.

As they returned across the hall, and passed through the familiar heavy mahogany dividing doors, Anne reflected on her first walk through from the drab brown coloured staff quarters to what had seemed to be a fairyland.

There would be few further visits through the doors for her, she reminded herself. For, very soon now, she would have her own home and would, for all time thereafter, be living on the "private side" of a house, mistress of her own domain.

★ ★ ★ ★ ★

A week later Anne was met at the end of the platform at Waterloo by Charles. 'How are you? Still keeping fit? You look the picture of health. No morning sickness?'

'No,' she replied with a broad grin, wondering if it were done to embrace someone in this place when, from Charles's style of dress, it was obviously "business hours".

'I've got the car round the corner. Let's go straight to Uncle Steve and get that part of today over.'

'Uncle Steve?' Anne queried.

'Oh, he's not a real uncle. He's just affectionately known as "Uncle Steve" by all generations of the family.' He took her hand and they were soon standing beside a shining black Daimler saloon. 'Office car,' he said, noticing the surprised expression on her face. 'Usually chauffeur driven.' Then, with a grin he added: 'Has a lot more space in it when required than my sports two-seater!'

Driving off through the maze of London streets, she sensed him glance at her. 'You made quite an impression with Uncle Steve. I don't know what he was expecting, but you were infinitely better. '"A most pleasantly determined young lady" he called you! And "too intelligent not to be more gainfully employed"'he said.' After a pause Charles added: 'Uncle Steve really liked you, which certainly makes matters easier for me.'

'I'm pleased, because Mummy and I both liked him very much.'

'Interestingly, he said that he thought, if circumstances had been different, you'd have been capable of going a long way in life. Didn't I indicate something similar that time when you told me you were about to start working as just a chambermaid? May be it's not altogether too late to use your latent talents?' he went on without waiting for her reply. 'Uncle Steve said how sensible he thought you were being over our arrangements, and how well spoken he found both you and your mother.'

'How well spoken? What was he expecting then, We're not like Daisy, dropping our "Aiches" if that's what he meant. My mother came from a good family, you know, and my father.'

'I know your parents did,' he broke in quickly, sensing he might have offended her. 'Sorry, Anne. I seem to have said that all the wrong way around. All I was trying to tell you was how pleased I am that Uncle Steve approved of you so highly. That's all.'

'Oh, well. If that's all you meant, I'm pleased too,' she said.

Ten minutes later the car was parked at the back of Mr Steven's office, and they were soon seated in the waiting room.

'Did Uncle Steve keep looking at his watch when you were here last week?' asked Charles.

'Yes. It amused both of us.'

'Uncle Steve is a bachelor. Not a woman-hater, but he never seems to be wholly at ease with ladies. He's the same with my mother and sisters.'

'Is that what it was?' Anne queried. 'He seems quite keen on his sherry. We both noticed that too. Was that also because of us ladies?'

'No, no!' Charles replied with a boyish laugh. 'Uncle Steve and sherry go together. Quite inseparable. Like bread and cheese!'

'I don't know much about sherry, but I would guess it was a very good one he gave us,' she commented.

'But of course. You won't find Uncle Steve having anything but the very best. Not as far as drink is concerned! I'm told his port is even better, but that's only brought out at his home in the evenings.'

As they were shown into Mr Steven's room, Charles immediately went forwards with an out-stretched hand. 'Hullo, Uncle Steve.'

'Hullo, my boy,' replied the short plump man whom Charles seemed to tower over.

Charles turned to Anne and, with a beckoning arm said: 'You two have of course met.'

'Hullo Mr Stevens,' she said with a smile, holding her hand out.

'Hullo Mrs Banks. Nice to see you again,' he replied.

'Can't Anne call you "Uncle Steve" like the rest of the family do?'

'Well, I don't know about that, Charles.' Mr Stevens turned to Anne and smiled. 'We got on very well at our first meeting, but I am not sure whether it would be quite right for me.' He looked up at Charles. 'For me to treat her as one of the family.' He looked back at Anne. 'I do hope you won't feel offended.'

'As you wish, Uncle,' cut in Charles. 'But you must call her "Anne". "Mrs Banks" sounds awfully stuffy, doesn't it?'

'We will compromise, I will call her "Anne" to please you, Charles.'

The document signing took only twenty minutes. 'What are you two doing for lunch?' asked Mr Stevens once the three of them were alone again. 'Would you both like to join me at my club?'

'Uncle, on any other occasion we would love to. I haven't a lot of time today. I've an important office meeting this afternoon, and I've got a pile of brochures on houses in the car to go through with Anne. Would you think it awfully rude of me if we declined your kind offer?'

'Postponed!' interrupted Anne.

'Clever girl!' beamed Charles. 'That's right, Uncle. May we please postpone joining you for lunch to the next occasion we meet?'

'Very well then,' Mr Stevens replied, moving closer to Anne. 'I don't know if I should say this, but I think Charles here is very lucky to have your company alone for lunch!'

Once more in the car, Charles spoke: 'We'll have to be a bit careful where we go. We must avoid the City and West End, I know too many people from those corners of London. I suggest we go in the Hampstead direction. There are lots of little restaurants there, and we can have a short walk on the Heath.'

At the restaurant, between choosing what they would have and eating it, they spent most of the time studying the particulars of country cottages. 'Most of them sound wonderful!' Anne replied glowingly.

'First lesson with estate agents,' Charles responded, 'is not to believe half their blurb.'

They short-listed three properties, and Charles promised to make arrangements with the agents for Anne and her mother to view them. Then, unexpectedly, he produced his wallet, pressed some pound notes into her hand and told her not to feel embarrassed at accepting them. 'It's all part of our arrangement, remember?'

'And you'll come and see me?' She looked pleadingly at him.

'Of course,' he replied, putting out his hand to take hers.

After a few moments, he looked at his watch. 'You're getting like Uncle Steve!' she teased, and leaned forwards so no one could overhear her. 'Are you afraid of women?'

He sat back and laughed. 'Only one!' he teased. 'Let's hurry. I can spare half-an-hour before having to get you back to Waterloo and myself back to my office.'

'I love you, Charles,' she said, half an hour later, turning towards him as she climbed into the carriage. 'And I know you've got to hurry, so please don't wait for my train to go. It's only a few minutes. I'll be all right.'

'I love you too, Anne.' He said smiling into her eyes. He held out his two hands and took hers. She bent forwards and gave him a fairly formal kiss which he returned. 'Take care, and let me know how the house-hunting goes. 'Phone that private number I gave you when you've got some news.'

★ ★ ★ ★ ★

Together with her mother, Anne devoted the following Friday to looking over the cottages which she and Charles had short-listed. 'Well, dear, this is the last of the three and I think it's the best,' her mother remarked. She had been none too enthusiastic about any of the properties. 'It's a pity it's not got a further bedroom, and that the bathroom conversion they've done leaves one with having to go downstairs to have a bath. But anyway, beggars can't be choosers, as they say.'

'It has got a lot in its favour, Mummy, but I do share your dislike about the bathroom,' acknowledged Anne.

At this point the agent, who had accompanied them to the last cottage, spoke. 'In a day or so I shall have a new residence to offer. We've just had instructions to sell a property known as "Wisteria Cottage". From what you have been saying, I feel it could be just what you're looking for.'

'Could we go and see it?' enquired Anne, her eyes opening wide.

'I can show you only the outside today. We're not permitted to take people in until our particulars sheet has been drafted and approved by the vendor.'

'Let's do that then, shall we, Mummy? Go and look at this new property from the outside?'

'All right, dear,' replied her mother, glancing at her watch.

Fifteen minutes later the agent's car drew up on the opposite side of the road to quite the most enchanting cottage Anne believed she had ever seen. 'I love it and I want it!' she proclaimed. The outburst was spontaneous and the agent, his mouth dropping open, looked at her in disbelief. 'But, Madam....'

Anne ignored him. 'Look at the little dormer windows. And the thatched roof. And....'

Her mother became equally enthusiastic. 'The wisteria climber. Look at it. Your father would love that. Think of how it will look in May with all the blue flowers hanging from it?'

'How many bedrooms? Where's the bathroom? Mains or cesspit drainage? Mains water? Gas? Electricity?' Anne turned to the now startled agent and reeled off the list as if she had been engaged in buying properties all her life.

'I don't know.' Replied the bewildered man. 'As I said, we've not got the particulars sheet agreed yet.'

'That doesn't matter!' Anne retorted. 'Let's go and see the owners. May be they'll let us look around as we're here.'

'No,' said the agent firmly. 'I must insist that we do nothing of the sort. I must get back to the office now.' With that he started the engine and drove off.

Anne looked down the side of the building as they moved away. 'Do you know if those out-houses are part of the property for sale?' she enquired.

'I believe so, Madam,' replied the agent in a less agitated tone of voice. 'There's an acre or two of ground, I believe. Exactly what is being included in the sale we should know in a few days time.'

'Your father would have been interested in the out-buildings and the land.'

'So am I.' Anne responded thoughtfully. 'They have potential.'

Shortly after leaving the cottage they drove through a small cluster of old properties. 'This, presumably is the local village.'

'This is Swallowford, Madam.'

'Are we still in Surrey?' enquired Mrs Jones.

'Yes, Madam,.'

'Will you stop for a few minutes, please,' Anne asked. 'I'd like to have a quick look around the village shops.' The agent glanced at his watch, but made no comment. He parked the car beside an attractive duck pond and his two passengers got out. Amongst the village shops which caught Anne's eye was a bookshop. She crossed the road to it and began to study a pile of business books, one catching her attention immediately. It was entitled "Starting Your Own Business". She promptly bought a copy.

'Despite it being winter time, this really is a beautiful little spot, isn't it dear?' said her mother, taking in the small Norman church, a row of well-kept little cottages, an old coaching inn and several very old oak trees around the pond.

'I think this is us, don't you, Mummy,' she replied, beginning to bubble over with enthusiasm. 'I just feel it is ready made for us. The cottage. This sweet little village. It even has a bookshop to satisfy my librarian and browsing loves.'

'I agree, dear. It's certainly far nicer than any thing we've been shown so far,' nodded Mrs Jones, growing equally excited.

'I shall telephone Charles,' said Anne impulsively. 'And tell him we've made our choice.'

'But you can't say that yet, dear. Not until you've seen the inside and found out all the other details. It may not be nearly so nice inside.' Mrs Jones suddenly looked worried. 'And what about the price? It may be above the amount we've…. You've got?'

'If it is, the limit will have to be increased!' Anne replied with a grin. 'I'm sure Charles will agree to dig a little deeper into the Macaulay bank account.'

'Oh! You can't go asking for more. Not after all that's been promised to you already.'

'Why not? Let's ask the man if he knows what the price will be.'

'I don't know, Madam, I don't know even if an asking price has been agreed yet with the vendor.'

On the telephone to the agents, a few days later, she learned that the asking price had indeed been set beyond the thousand pounds limit offered by Charles. She also learned that in the price would be included two acres of land with the various barns and out-houses which had caught her eye.

'I made him an offer of one thousand, seven hundred and fifty pounds,' she informed her mother unashamedly.

'But where is the other money coming from?' Mrs Jones looked aghast. 'Has Mr Charles agreed?'

'No,' she replied. 'But I'm sure he will! The Macaulay's can afford it.'

'But what if he won't?'

'He will! Because with the aid of this,' she replied, tapping the book she had bought in the village. 'I've worked out an arrangement I think will attract him.'

'Well, don't go and get yourself over committed.' Mrs Jones sounded almost fretful. 'We haven't even seen the inside yet.'

'I know, Mummy. We can go over it on Friday,' she continued dismissively. 'I've fixed it up with the agent.'

'Before then, dear, you have a word with Mr Charles.' Mrs Jones shook her head. 'I don't want us getting mixed up in buying something we can't possibly afford.'

'All right, Mummy. I'll go down to our village this afternoon and telephone him from there if that'll put your mind at rest,'

'I've got good and less good news, Charles.' She began, trying to sound not in the least bit concerned.

'Let's have the bad news first,'

'No! The good first, the not so good second. Charles, the good news is that I've found a dream cottage in a dream village. Just what I and my mother want. I know you'll love it as much as we do.'

'That certainly is good news,' he replied cautiously. 'Now what about the not so good news?'

'The not so good news, Charles, is that....'

'It's going to cost an awful lot more!' he broke in.

'How did you guess?' she questioned, slightly alarmed at his somewhat disagreeable sounding response.

'Intuition!'

Was he not in a good mood, she wondered, or had he a client with him in his office? 'Charles? They're asking two thousand pounds, for the cottage and two acres of land. I said I thought we might be able to offer them one thousand, seven hundred and fifty pounds.' She stopped talking to await his response. 'Charles? Are you there?'

'Yes, I'm still here,' he said slowly. 'That's a great deal more than one thousand pounds, isn't it? Perhaps I can get them down another two hundred and fifty?'

Anne then went on to tell him what she knew of the cottage and added finally that she had not yet seen the inside.'

'You're talking of offering money for something you haven't even seen? What's going on?' His tone, she noted, did not sound encouraging.

'I know it's what I want,' she pleaded defiantly, going on to describe the land and out-buildings. 'Why don't you come down with me on Friday and see the property for yourself? Also, I want to talk over with you an idea I have for buying the land and out-buildings.' A grin spread across her face. 'I think, and hope, that you will find my idea irresistible! I can't go into the details over the telephone. I'll explain on Friday'.

'Sounds intriguing? Are you proposing to set up as a one-man merchant banker?' She did not reply, but heard him move some papers around on his desk. 'My diary's clear in the afternoon. All right, I'll meet you in the nearby village,' he reluctantly agreed. 'Did you say it was called Swallowford?'

'That's right,' she replied trying to sound wholly cheerful. 'I'll see you by the duck pond at…. Shall we say two-thirty?'

'By the duck pond at two-thirty. Will you be alone or will your mother be there as well?' he enquired formally.

'I doubt if Mummy will be there. Not if you are coming, Charles. Nothing personal. But I don't think she's quite reconciled herself to meeting you other than as "Mister Charles", Not as the father of her expected grandchild.' She made a pretence at laughing. 'All a bit much for Mummy, but she'll come round to it shortly, I'm sure. Don't worry.' She changed the subject. 'The agent will be there, of course, as he has to drive me over and show us over the cottage. Perhaps we can then get rid of him, if you could drop me back at the bus stop?'

They talked on for a few more minutes and Anne returned to The Grange with a feeling of accomplishment but not of total confidence. At least, she encouraged herself, Charles had not said "No", and he was going to look the cottage and out-buildings over with her. Both were favourable signs she told her mother. She was fairly sure Wisteria Cottage would be coming her way.

★ ★ ★ ★ ★

At two-twenty the agent's car, with Anne in it, drew up at the side of the duck pond. She looked about for any sign of Charles and hoped he would not be late since she was not entirely sure that the agent was not trying to cut a dash with her. It was clear to her that he had on his best country gentleman type clothes, and a cap which she guessed he might have bought that morning. Its design was straight out of a Beatrice Potter Benjamin Bunny children's book, and seemed to be several sizes too big for him. She hoped it would not fall down over his eyes as he drove them along.

'Mrs Banks, I think I should just warn you that the owner, a Miss White, is somewhat eccentric. You will see what I mean when you meet her. Please leave all the negotiations in the hands of my firm.'

'As you wish,' she replied, shrugging her shoulders as she caught sight of Charles's car approaching them. She quickly transferred herself, together with a carrier bag into the other car and, after exchanging a quick embrace, they were soon on their way to the cottage.

'What's in the bag, Anne?'

'You'll never guess!' she laughed. 'Two things. First, the cuddly sailor doll you won for me, what's it now….More than thirteen years ago?'

'Whatever have you brought that along for?'

'He was the first present you gave to me. I've had him ever since. And he wants to come and see our new home, as much as you do!'

'You're a cure! And I love you,' he laughed again, putting a hand across and patting her on the knee. 'And what's the second thing? Is it what you said I would find irresistible?'

'Yes! It's a book I bought last week in the village here. I have been studying it very closely. It contains a lot of sound business advice.'

'Business? So, you are setting up as a Merchant Banker?'

Please be serious Charles. This is important. The book's all about financing and otherwise setting up a new business. We'll soon be reaching the cottage so I haven't time to go into all the details. But very briefly, what I think we should do, based on the book's advice, is to treat the cottage as a separate deal from the land, barn and other out-buildings. We buy the cottage for the one-thousand pounds limit you mentioned to Uncle Steve. And we buy everything else with capital which we raise separately.'

'And from where does this new capital suddenly appear? Buried treasure in the barn, perhaps?' He continued to laugh at her efforts to interest him.

'Do please be serious, Charles. This is for you as much as it is for me.'

'We'll talk about it after we've seen what is for sale with the cottage itself.'

As soon as Miss White opened the door, Anne saw what the agent had meant about eccentricity. She was a tiny old lady with a kindly but wizened face beneath a mass of snow white hair. Her name, Anne thought, suits her well. Around her neck hung numerous necklaces, and around each wrist she had too many bangles to count. She had several rings on her fingers and her clothes were over rich in colour. On her feet, Anne noticed, she wore an old pair of slippers which she guessed might have been nearly as old as she was.

'You must be Mrs Banks? And Mr....?'

'My name's Macaulay,' replied Charles, smiling charmingly.

'Do come in, all of you.' She turned and led the way from the little porch, through a small panel lined hallway and into quite a large living room.

Everything, Anne noticed, was spotlessly clean. 'Look, Charles,' she said, pointing with excitement. 'Even an ingle-nook fireplace. I've always wanted one of those.' She crossed to one of the tiny bay windows and, bending down to look out through the leaded panes, gazed appreciatively on to the neatly kept garden.

The agent hovered in the background, nervously fumbling with his cap. 'May I please now show my clients over the property?' he enquired timidly.

'Of course,' replied Miss White, 'And I shall accompany you!'

'That really won't be necessary, thank you.'

'But I insist!' With that, Miss White walked towards the hall and led them, in turn, into each of the other ground floor rooms.

'This is just perfect,' Anne whispered for the third time, squeezing Charles's hand as they returned to the hall.

'Now,' Miss White said, revelling in her guided tour duties. 'We shall go up stairs. And mind your head. You, Mr Morley. You, Mr Dawley. You're tall. Mind your head.' Miss White's face spread into a broad grin. 'The beams are harder than your head is, and will give you a nasty crack if you don't look out!'

He caught Anne's eye and winked. The agent, now completely despondent, brought up the rear of the procession in silence.

As they returned to the hall, Miss White turned to Anne. 'I can see you like my little home.'

'I do. I think it is just what we're looking for,'

'Would you like to see my garden, the barn and the other out-buildings? I have about two acres, you know. Not going in for agriculture are you?'

Anne was tempted to tell the old lady that she had hit the proverbial nail on the head, but worried as to what Charles might say. 'What are the buildings used for?' she asked instead.

'I let the farmer who has the adjoining land use them. But they'll not be required for much longer as the farmer is retiring and his fields are soon to go up for sale.'

The lady turned to Charles: 'Would you like a nice cup of tea, Mr Rawley? I'll go and put the kettle on. Then when you come back from looking at the other buildings, but don't hurry. I'll have it ready for you.'

'That is very kind of you, Miss White.'

'Thank you very much,' Anne concurred.

Anne and Charles were glad to get away from the others.

Hand in hand they viewed the outbuildings, and walked around the garden. 'What do you think of the cottage?'

'If you feel it really is what you want, Anne, then....' He tried to stop the grin spreading across his face.

'It is exactly what I want!' Her reply was instant and enthusiastic. 'Let's try the old lady over tea on the question of the price, shall we?'

'Interesting....' She commented, changing the subject and taking care to try and not make her remarks too obvious. 'It's interesting that the next door farmer is selling his land.'

Charles was getting used to her circuitous way of bringing into the conversation topics which engaged her. 'And what little scheme is Mrs Banks up to now?' he questioned, 'Or is this where you don your Merchant Banker's hat? And lecture me on the rates of return I might earn from investing in a market gardening business?'

'I'm sure I could earn you a good return on your capital,'

'Better than I earn at Lloyds?' It was his turn to tease.

'I don't know what that earns,' she confessed. 'But market gardening, well....'

'I suppose you get the gardening interest from your father...'

'How do you like your tea?' Miss White had set it out on her dining room table, placed against the wall under one of the windows.

'Not too strong, please, and milk but no sugar,' replied Anne.

'The same for me, but with sugar, please,' said Charles, seating himself in the remaining chair.

'Do tell me, if it's not a secret.' Miss White lent towards them as if wishing no one to overhear. 'When is the wedding day? Do tell me.'

They glanced quickly at one another. It was Anne who collected her thoughts first and responded: 'There're a few family matters to sort out first.' Then, to try and avert further such questions, she changed the subject. 'May we talk about buying your sweet little cottage?'

'But of course, my dear. That's what we're here for,' the old lady replied with a gracious smile, clearly enjoying the occasion and their company.

The three talked about prices and dates for occupation for some time, during which it was learned that Miss White was proposing to move in with her sister at Newhaven. She explained that she could not move out until she had sold most of her furniture as she would be taking only her own bed and one or two special items to her sisters.

'We might like to make you an offer for your furniture,' suggested Anne, looking around the room. 'We would have to buy almost a complete house full of new furniture otherwise. Could we talk of making you an offer for all the items that you do not wish to take with you? That is, if it wouldn't appear to be hurrying you too much.'

Miss White turned to Charles. 'Quite a business lady is your fiancée, Mr Rudley? Certainly knows just what she wants, doesn't she?' He smiled back at the old lady, not attempting to correct the latest miss-pronunciation of his name. 'I leave all this domestic side to her,' he answered, avoiding Anne's eye.

An hour later they bade their farewells, having secured from Miss White acceptable prices for both the property and for almost all her furniture. 'I'm no great expert on antiques, Anne,' Charles said as they drove off. 'But I reckon there're some really good pieces amongst that lot. You've got yourself a very attractive deal. Well done?'

'I couldn't have done it without you, Charles!' She replied modestly.

'You can say that again!' he squeezed her hand.

'I didn't mean it like that!' she laughed back, telling herself that many of the injustices, which had plagued her life to date, were about to be reversed. Mrs Dulcie had better watch out! Anne was catching her up!

'You're suddenly very quiet, Anne.'

'I was thinking what a lot has happened since a certain afternoon just after Christmas.'

'To change the subject, You have yet to fill me in on which of your Merchant Banking activities you said I would find irresistible?'

'Ah, my very useful book on setting up a business! What we are going to pay Miss White for her land and barn and other out-buildings, you very kindly said earlier would come to our child and to me in various legal ways, as would our initial income.'

The adjoining farmer's land coming up for sale shortly adds endless possibilities long term. Please don't dismiss the idea too quickly, Charles, I have a feeling a partnership, you providing the cash and myself providing the labour and management, could provide us not only with an extra interest from working together, but could give our child and me a profitable income and you a worthwhile return on your investment.

Land and buildings. "Bricks and mortar" my book says are generally the strongest of assets to have. And my book is very keen on the wisdom of not putting "all one's eggs in one basket". You shouldn't invest only in Lloyds. Spread your risks!'

'But we Macaulays do spread our risks. We spread them around Lloyds. We diversify.' Claimed Charles.

'That is the word my book uses, -"diversification".'Anne responded.

'Well, I am pleased to hear I am not being encouraged to buy up the whole of Surrey this afternoon!' He looked at her affectionately, and shook his head with a smile. 'Getting back to reality,' he said. 'If you agree, I'll get on to both the agent and to Uncle Steve, explain the terms we've agreed with Miss White, and ask them to hasten all the formalities. I'll also speak to the agent about a survey. One can't be too careful, especially with old buildings.'

Finally,' he paused and looked her straight in the face. 'I'll sound out Uncle Steve about possible future purchases of the farmer's land.'

He smiled agreeably at her before continuing: 'I guess I shall need, apart from the one thousand pounds to buy the cottage, another one thousand pounds. Most will be spent on purchasing Miss White's land, barn and other out-buildings, and many smaller items which you'll need starting from scratch. Also, living right out in the country you'll need a car and, in your case, you'll need to start off with driving lessons.'

'Thank you, Charles. If everything goes according to what we've been told, it should be possible for Mummy and me to move in in about three or four weeks time.' Anne threw her head back. 'Wonderful, wonderful Wisteria Cottage, here we come!'

He reached across and squeezed her hand again. 'I'm so pleased to see you looking so radiantly happy. You deserve it!'

'Miss White thought we were engaged,' she giggled.

'I know. And I thought you handled her remark very well.'

★ ★ ★ ★ ★

It was four weeks to the day when Anne and her mother moved into Wisteria Cottage, and began their new life style together. Anne was disappointed when Charles told her that he considered it most unlikely that he would be able to spend many nights there with her. 'But I've bought an extra large double bed! It nearly killed the two men getting it up the narrow stairs!' she explained, looking at him in dismay.

'I just dare not risk nights, darling. Day visits and evenings, whenever I can, yes. And we'll try out your bed as often as you want! But nights. I'm afraid not!'

He kept his word during the period of her pregnancy, and many half days and evenings he came to see her. He always gave good warning, and always Anne's mother made arrangements to be out. She had made some good friends in the neighbourhood, but on these occasions went to stay with her sister, leaving Anne alone.

The cuddly sailor doll lived in the other half of the large bed beside her. 'He's a constant reminder of who that half is reserved for!' she told Charles, quite seriously, on the first occasion he climbed the steep staircase with her.

Anne always felt dispirited to see her lover drive away after one of their intimate sessions, and tried to console herself that one day she really would win him for herself exclusively. She thought of Dulcie as little as possible, though frequently she was conscious of her shadow in the background and knew the deep resentment she felt for her was in no way abating. Did Dulcie and Charles, she wondered, still make love to one another? If she had not always been frigid, Anne hoped Dulcie had become sexually irresponsive.

Occasionally, Anne permitted herself a self-satisfying grin in knowing that she derived an extra dimension of satisfaction from Charles's not infrequent attentions. Each occasion, she would metaphorically chalk up in her mind another point scored in the vendetta she was waging against her detested rival.

Chapter Nine – September 1929

Anne and her mother were relieved when the hire car, which had come to collect them, drew up in front of the nursing home, and it was not long before they were being shown up to the maternity wing. Anne was not yet fully in labour, but her local doctor had advised moving her into the nursing home early as the journey from Swallowford would be a long one for someone once her labour had begun.

It was the following evening, after tea, when her waters broke. The birth of her baby happened, quite normally and naturally, just before mid-night. 'He's a fine looking boy, Mrs Banks. About eight pounds I'd judge,' the midwife sister said, handing her the bulging shawl.

Anne smiled broadly and, for the first time, gazed down admiringly at the chubby red-faced person cradled in her arm.

'He's not got much hair,' she remarked.

'That's quite normal. He'll soon grow some, don't you worry!' The sister busied herself for a few more minutes in the delivery room, and then came across to the bed. 'I think it's time we wheeled you back to your own room.'

As her trolley was pushed alongside her bed, Anne glanced happily at the little cot which now stood beside it. 'Does he go in there?' She questioned.

'It's almost one o'clock in the morning, Mrs Banks,' replied the sister with a smile. 'That cot's for day-time use, but I'll put him in there just while we transfer you across to your own bed.' The sister then carefully lifted the baby off her out stretched arms.

When, with the help of another nurse, she was back in her own bed, the sister spoke again. 'Your baby will now be taken away and put in a cot in the night nursery marked with his name. We don't go in for wrist labels here, like the big hospitals do. They sometimes put them on too tight, hurting the delicate new born little ones.' The sister looked at her again with a kindly expression. 'How are you? Tired?'

'Fine, thank you,' replied Anne, feeling blissfully weary.

As the nurse left the room with her baby, the sister spoke again. 'We take the babies out of their mother's room at night, Mrs Banks, in order to give the mothers the benefit of a good

night's sleep and, also, so that we can keep them under observation at night time. Your baby will be brought to you each morning, unless you go and collect him for yourself, which you may do when you've got your strength back in a day or two.

By the time her mother arrived the next afternoon, Anne's baby had been fed for the second time and was sleeping peacefully in the cot beside her bed. 'Oh, he's lovely, dear,' said a delighted and relieved sounding Mrs Jones. 'A really bonny looking little chap.'

'Your first grandchild, Mummy!' said Anne proudly.

'I know. I can hardly believe it,' beamed her mother. 'I know you had several names in mind for him. Have you decided on one finally?'

'I'm going to call him Arthur. Do you like that name, Mummy?' she asked, waiting for her mothers' reaction.

'I do, dear. It's a real manly sounding name, isn't it? Like Charles!' Mrs Jones smiled again, looking from her daughter to her grandson alternately.

'When's your Charles coming in to see you? I know he has to be careful, what with Mrs Dulcie about to come in too. Any news about her yet?'

'I haven't heard a thing, not since Charles told me last week she'd had a false alarm,' she replied, before adding without emotion: 'The first I'll know will probably be when I see a cot with the Macaulay name on it in the night nursery.' Her mother returned to her side and smiled again at her daughter. 'You should look in and see the night nursery, Mummy. It's so sweet. A row of tiny cots.'

Later that day, Anne was again talking to her mother. 'They say they encourage mothers to get out of bed and walk about as soon and as much as they feel able to, from twenty-four hours after the birth.'

'Very different from when I had you and Kitty,' Mrs Jones shook her head. 'Then, they made us rest in bed for days afterwards.'

'Customs change,' her daughter commented, looking with admiration at the cot beside her for the umpteenth time. 'Guess which I think is the finest looking baby in the nursing home?'

Mrs Jones beamed at her daughter.

It was just as Anne was being settled down for the following night that she heard a light tap on her half-opened bedroom door. 'Come in,' she called out.

Charles walked in and, before saying anything, glanced around the room. Spotting the young nurse who was just settling Anne's pillows for her, he spoke formally: 'Good evening, Mrs Banks. It is Mrs Banks, isn't it?'

'Good evening,' she replied, finding it quite hard to keep a straight face. 'Mr Macaulay, I believe. What a surprise seeing you here!'

'I'll come back,' said the nurse, diplomatically leaving the room.

Charles immediately put a finger to his lips to indicate that she should say little. 'Where's the…. Our baby?'

'He's gone to the nursery for the night,' she whispered, at the same time blowing him a kiss as her position could not be seen from the passage.

'I must go and have a peep at him in a moment,' he whispered back. 'How does he look?'

Charles had come nearer to the bed and Anne risked another whisper. 'Just like his father, but a bit smaller.'

'Really? Like me?' he questioned, unable to conceal a look of intense satisfaction.

'Truly, Charles, he's got a strong look of you in him,' she replied, looking admiringly at her handsome lover. They smiled happily at each other.

'I do like your hair, Anne. Now you're letting it grow longer.'

After a few minutes of discussion, he said: 'I'll pop down now and see Arthur if I can.' He smiled at her. 'Dulcie's had to be rushed in. Took us all a bit by surprise. She was due last week, but as I told you, nothing happened. The doctor told her yesterday he didn't think she would come for another two days. Then.... Suddenly....' He gesticulated with both hands in the air.

'I was a day or two earlier than expected,' stated Anne, surprised at momentarily feeling no bitterness towards Dulcie.

'It now looks, Charles, as if just what we didn't want to happen, is about to happen. The two of us giving birth here in the same week!'

He shook his head. 'Don't let it worry you. It's not going to affect any of my promises whether her birth happens this week, next week, or months apart from yours. It's just rather odd for me! There can't be many men who succeed in becoming fathers twice over in the same week, apart of course from when twins arrive.'

'Arthur won the race, Charles. Don't forget that, will you? He's the eldest!' She emphasised, wishing to register the point, but not wanting it in any way to cloud their immediate pleasure. He moved towards the door as he heard footsteps, and blew a kiss. 'We'll have to be careful. I must go now.'

The next morning, as early as possible, Anne went along the corridor to the night nursery and, as if to underline the unusual events of nine months before, the cot next to the one bearing a card saying "Banks – Boy" was one which read: "Macaulay – Boy".

Before taking more than a cursory look at Arthur, she drew back slightly the top of the shawl around the newest baby's face, and looked down at the second of Charles's offspring to be born within the space of twenty-four hours.

She was surprised how like Arthur he looked. But, she reasoned, that was to be expected with a father who is common to both and, after all, most babies probably look quite similar for the first few days, if not weeks of their lives.

As if seeking confirmation, she peered closely at each of the other babies in the night nursery in turn. She then looked back at her own Arthur and back again at Dulcie's baby. She was forced to admit that both babies had acquired the strong male genes from Charles, and were abnormally alike. Added to which, both had exactly his coloured eyes.

'Admiring our latest addition, Mrs Banks?' enquired the nurse she had talked to the previous day, and who had walked quietly into the room.

'Oh! Oh, yes,' she responded, momentarily startled out of her thoughts.

'He belongs to someone special, that one does!' stated the nurse in, Anne thought, a rather offhanded tone of voice,

'What do you mean?'

'Oh….It's perhaps not my place to say anything, but….' The nurse moved closer to Anne and dropped her voice. 'A Mrs Macaulay. Obviously from a very posh family. You should see her room. Like a film star's. Looks more like a flower shop. Can't be good for either her or her baby, if you ask me. All that pollen.'

'A Mrs Macaulay?' questioned Anne, trying to sound only mildly interested.

The nurse continued: 'Funny how one likes some, most of the mums. Not her, though! She's all la-di-dah. Way she carried on last evening when she came in. You'd think no one else had ever had a baby before. And what a fuss her family all made of her!'

'What do you mean?' repeated Anne, unsure whether she was annoyed or just amused.

'Got down one of the top Harley Street gyno's, they did. All in a rush. And what,' queried the nurse in obvious disgust. 'What's wrong with our local man? Most of the mums who come into this maternity wing, like you, we deal with ourselves quite all right. No obstetrician needed. Doing it every day. Most nights as well, we are!'

After a pause, the nurse spoke again as Anne began to busy herself with Arthur. 'I'll take you on a bet? Mrs Macaulay will be one of them mums who never comes in here. I can spot them, I can. No interest in other people's babies. Doesn't want to talk to other mums.'

Six days later Anne was pronounced sufficiently strong to be allowed to return home the following day. She had had enough of the nursing home despite finding good company in the nursery nurse and in several of the other mothers. Her own mother came in to see her most days, but, and this peeved and added to her resentment, Charles paid her only two short visits.

Was he overdoing the need to avoid raising doubts in the minds of the staff? On top of this, the nursery nurse had kept her informed daily of the latest luxuries lavished upon Dulcie by both sides of her family.

Am I, questioned a disgruntled Anne, or am I not getting my agreed equal share of the bargain I struck? And what is to happen in the future? Am I, and more particularly my son, to be given the promised equal treatment?

Now featuring strongly in her reasoning was the fact that her baby had been born first. He was therefore the eldest. Of right, she told herself, he should inherit The Grange from Charles, whose statement, nine months earlier, that children born out of wedlock do not inherit automatically, was totally unjust.

Further more, such iniquity would not only be at her own son's cost, but to Dulcie's son's advantage. She vowed that some occasion would be found to have this matter justly resolved for all time.... against Dulcie!

The last morning, as had become her custom, Anne was the first mother into the night nursery. She had not slept well and had found it impossible to relax and overlook, even for a few hours, the deep and now increased resentment of the woman whom she continued to regard as standing between herself and Charles's undivided affections. Anne herself, she reasoned, was no less a person than this snobbish woman and, of even greater importance, Arthur was no less a person than Dulcie's baby.

Charles had promised that her baby would have no less an opportunity in his life. Was that still to be? Or was it going to be necessary for her to act in some way in order to achieve this and, if so, how?

As she stood in the night nursery looking down at Arthur it was as if she were suddenly gripped by a force over which she had no control. The idea which flashed through her mind, and which seemed to manipulate her limbs, was spontaneous. She looked into the next cot at the baby whom Charles had told her would be christened "Ronald".

The nurse was out of the room taking another mother her baby. Anne glanced over her shoulder at the partly open door leading into the corridor. There were no approaching footsteps. The two babies were in their own shawls, the Macaulay one an expensive embroidered one, Arthur's bought by her mother, and clearly not of the same quality. Anne knew that beneath the shawls each baby was clothed in the nursing home's standard night-dress and nappy.

The few minutes of her life which followed were to haunt her every day and every night for years to come.

The large blanket-covered changing table was close at hand and, though the tension made her become out of breath and her fingers tremble, it took her no more than a half minute to effect the change over of shawls and to replace the babies in opposite cots. Neither baby cried and she had not been disturbed. She was just straightening the bedding in Ronald's cot when she heard approaching footsteps.

'Hullo, Mrs Banks. First as usual?'

'Er…. Er…. What…. What did you say?' Anne looked up sharply and tried to smile at the nurse she got on with well, but her face seemed inflexible. She hoped she sounded a lot less nervous than she felt.

'Are you all right, Mrs Banks?' enquired the nurse, staring hard at her in a suspicious way .

'Yes…. Yes, thank you.' Anne wished she could stop her knees banging together. Would she fall over, she wondered as she clutched at one cot end for support?

'I'm going home today,' she added, trying to sound cheerful.

By now the nurse had reached her side and had taken her arm. 'Yes, I know Mrs Banks. But do you feel you're up to it?' She guided her towards a chair. 'Why don't you sit down here for a moment? There's nothing to worry about. A lot of mums feel a bit dizzy at times,' she said soothingly. 'You may have overdone your exercises. Anne sat down, conscious that the room seemed to be spinning before her.

'I'll get you a glass of water?' the nurse said.

'No. No, thank you,' replied Anne, already feeling the worst effects of the shock wearing off. 'Please don't bother.'

'You go back to your room and lie down on your bed for a bit, Mrs Banks. I would. As soon as I've changed Mrs Macaulay's baby, I'll change yours baby and bring him along to you for his feed. You'll feel better in bed. Do you feel you can get yourself there all right?'

'I'll be all right, thank you,' she replied, thankful for an excuse to leave the location of her impulsive and most traumatic ever deed.

Back in her own bedroom, she lay back on the pillows and closed her eyes, her mind in a turmoil. She began trying to reconcile, on the one hand what she had just done with, on the other hand, the natural affinity of a mother towards her own baby. An unique love which Anne knew in her case, she could neither transfer wholly to someone else's child nor surrender absolutely in her own. What had she done?

She tried hard to justify what she had just done, telling herself that, if brought up in The Grange environment, her baby would want for nothing tangible. He would even inherit the place one day. But would he ever have the total love and care which she could bestow upon him? But were these intangible considerations of any real import? Could they ever be more important than a mother's love and care? Had she become totally paranoiac over the thought of injustices which might never even happen?

Dulcie, she knew, would not bring up the child herself. Momentarily, she half smiled as she envisaged her ever deigning to touch a dirty nappy. Anne was adamant, she would never entrust her baby to Dulcie. The point, however, would not arise, she reminded herself, for she had been told by Charles that a dear old nanny, known to the family for many years, had been engaged to look after the Macaulay baby for the first few months, and that another, younger and trusted, person was then to take charge.

Of course, Anne tried to reassure herself, continuing with her soliloquy, there would always be Charles himself to keep a fatherly eye on her child's well-being. And Anne herself would see the child. Or would she? Could she so arrange events that she was able to see the child periodically to check he was all right? That would need further careful thought and planning.

She shut her eyes momentarily. What had she done? The enormity of her deed threatened to overcome her, and she wondered if she were about to start uncontrollable screaming. She regained control of herself and slowly began to relax. Yes, she told herself, she had thoroughly over reacted to a financial situation she should just have accepted. And accepted gratefully on account of Charles's considerable generosity.

The nurse had not brought her Arthur to have his feed. What was going on? Had the swap been discovered? How could it have been? She sat up in the bed. She must not be afraid. She must go back immediately to the night nursery, confess to her befriended nurse in there what she had done, and have the babies swapped back. How could anyone, let alone someone brought up in a good Christian home, she reproached herself, have been so callous? What ever the provocation?

And yet? Suddenly her mind spun off on the other tack once more. How could she ignore such a once-only chance to better her son's whole life? She herself would be the loser, but would she not gladly suffer such loss in order to better her son his chances? And, in any event, would she experience any worse feelings than the mother of a child put up for adoption? And there are hundreds of them every month,' she told herself.

Motherly instincts were paramount, but were not also possessions and status and opportunity? She had no guarantee that her baby, if she kept him to herself, was going to be treated equally to the Macaulay one.

Then she upbraided herself again. How much of her action had been due to sheer jealousy? Could she really be so hard bitten as to give up her own son just to get back at Dulcie? She had truly become paranoid. Surely she did not have hate of that magnitude inside her? Was she really that unpleasant a person? 'No!' she spoke aloud, answering an unasked question. 'I'm doing it for his sake, my baby's sake. For Arthur's sake.'

The mental turmoil continued to lead her one minute to one decision and the next to reverse it and, did she but know it, the enormity of her deed was to continue to tear at her conscience for the next twenty-three years of her life.

'You do seem quiet, dear,' remarked Mrs Jones as, later that day, they were driven back to Wisteria Cottage. 'I expected you to be bubbling over with excitement, at getting your first baby back home.'

Anne looked at the sleeping baby cradled in her arms. 'He's going to be quite a lot of extra work, I was hoping to start the market gardening soon, get it all ploughed over before the winter comes. With him…. Er, Arthur. I don't know if I shall have the time.'

'I thought a local man was coming in with his tractor to give it a quick plough over for you. It's only half an acre you're starting with, isn't it? It won't take him that long, will it?' questioned her mother in a surprised sounding tone of voice.

'I suppose not.'

'There's no hurry, dear. Enjoy your lovely baby while you can. Believe me, they grow up all too quickly. Kitty and you did.' Mrs Jones went on reminiscing. 'I just forgot the rest of life. Not your father, of course. When you two babies arrived. It was hard work, I acknowledge that, but…. You see. Worth every minute of it!'

Mrs Jones leaned over and drew aside the top of the shawl. 'He's certainly more like his father than he's like you, dear.'

That night Anne lay awake and cried until well after midnight. It seemed to her then as if she had only just got off to sleep when the baby's cry awakened her. 'Oh God!' She sat up in bed and reached out to rock the cot beside her, but the baby was not so easily to be comforted. 'I do hope you're not going to be a difficult one,' She said to herself. 'I bet my baby's sleeping peacefully, Nanny and everyone else all in attendance.' She got out of bed, slipped on her dressing gown, picked up the baby and got back into bed with him.

He continued to cry and she offered him a feed, which he gratefully accepted. As she looked down at his tiny sucking lips, she was once more overcome with grief for her own absent baby and for what, unequivocally, she now knew to have been totally irrational behaviour on her part. The baby reacted to her tension and began to cry again.

'Is everything all right, dear?' Mrs Jones had tapped at the door, and half opened it, putting her head round.

'Yes, thanks, Mummy,' she replied, hoping her sore tear filled eyes would not be noticed in the half light cast by the shaded bed-side lamp.

'He'll soon get used to his new surroundings and new home routine. No baby likes changes, even at this tender age,' comforted Mrs Jones.

'No, Mummy,' she sighed, reflecting on the unfortunate choice of the word "changes". Then, looking at the baby again, she silently promised him that he would not want for love and attention. She would do her best for him and he, an innocent party in the whole matter, would not be permitted to suffer on account of her hasty act. The exchange, she reminded herself, would operate both ways, she must not expect others to give their all to her baby without her reciprocating fully.

He didn't know he'd been swapped, only one person in the whole world knew that. How lonely she suddenly felt. How she would like to share her problem with someone else, but who? Her mother, no? Charles, no? Uncle Steve, possibly?

Yes, he was the family's confidant, he would listen to her and advise her, and keep advising her. Or would he immediately tell her to own up, to make a clean breast of her terrible action? Uncle Steven might think he owed more loyalty to the Macaulay family than to her, and he might tell the family. Then where would she be? No, she told herself, the only safe alterative was to tell no one - a burden she should not attempt to share.

A week later Charles came to Wisteria Cottage. Mrs Jones waited until he arrived and then, discreetly, left the two parents together with the baby.

'I think your son is gorgeous, I really do,' Anne's mother said as he held the door open for her, before she walked away from the cottage.

Charles moved towards Anne, but she did not respond with her customary hug. Instead, she walked to the side of the pram which was standing in the hall. Was there something different in Charles's manner, she asked herself, or was it her imagination?

'How is our Arthur progressing?' he asked eagerly. 'Putting on weight and doing all he should?'

'He's developing very well I think. And how is Ronald?' As she spoke, almost anxiously, she turned and looked Charles straight in the face for the first time that day. 'Is he all right?'

'Ronald's fine also. What Nanny calls "a very good baby." What ever that's meant to mean!' He then began to play with the baby's fingers. 'He may be like me,' he said. 'But he's got a look of you, too, Anne?'

'I can't see it,' she replied somewhat abruptly. 'It's you, Charles, both babies take after.'

'Looking at Arthur now, I could take him for Ronald,' he continued.

'Probably if the two were seen beside each other one would notice several differences. As they grow up they'll develop individual physical characteristics. I was about to make some coffee,' she said, changing the subject. 'Would you like a cup?'

'Yes. Yes, I would. Thank you.' As he stood beside her at the stove he tried again to engage her in conversation about the baby. 'How much does Arthur weigh now? He was about eight pounds, wasn't he?'

'Eight pounds one ounce then, eight pounds five ounces now.'

'Ronald was only a pound lighter at birth, and he's also now about eight pounds five ounces,' he continued, finding the conversation hard work.

'I am glad he's doing well,' she replied, more cheerfully. 'This one played up the first few nights, but he's settling down now, thank goodness.'

'Good. And how are you, yourself, Anne? You look tired,' he enquired, putting out a hand and taking gentle hold of one of her arms. 'No worries?'

'I do feel tired. I can't say I've been sleeping that well,' she dismissed.

'You turned down my earlier offer to pay for a nanny,' he volunteered.

'I know I did,' she replied quietly. 'I.... I wanted to bring up my baby myself.'

They took their cups of coffee into the sitting room and, instead of sitting on the settee as she usually did with him, she sat herself down in one of the smaller armchairs. He sat down in his usual corner of the settee.

'I'm going to take up flying,' Charles suddenly announced, hoping a complete change of subject would ease the tension.

'Flying?' She looked at him with a partly opened mouth.

'Yes. I want to become a pilot. Just an amateur. There's a flying club only three miles from here. I could, as it were, kill two birds with one stone.'

'How do you mean?' she asked, having had her interest kindled.

'Well, firstly I do want to learn to fly. I've wanted to for ages. A new sport. Secondly, if I join the club near here I shall have the perfect excuse for coming in this direction at weekends. After I've finished my flying I can call in and see you and Arthur.' He looked up to observe her reaction.

'That's clever! I like it!' she remarked, brightening up. 'But isn't flying supposed to be dangerous?'

'You hear stories. But the planes I'll be flying are small. And you have a fully trained co-pilot to teach you to begin with. That's until you go solo.'

'Solo?' Anne questioned

'Yes. Fly by yourself.'

He looked up at her again. 'It's just occurred to me. I'll be able to fly low over the cottage. Look down to make sure you haven't too many boy friends in tow! Not got your little estate agent friend around!' He grinned as he noticed a smile cross her face.

'So I'm to be spied upon, am I?' she teased back.

'We'll have to use the fields next door to make an airstrip!' he continued, waving a hand towards one of the windows. 'I'll then be able to land, pick you and Arthur up and take you around for a few circuits of the country.'

'Sounds exciting. But then you're joking,' she replied flatly.

'Perhaps, about the landing strip. But I am serious about learning to fly.'

'Well, if you must.'

Again changing the subject completely, he said, dropping his voice: 'My maternal grandmother, that is my mother's mother, seems to be about to end her days.'

'Oh, I am sorry to hear that, Charles,' Anne responded, genuinely saddened. 'You mean Mrs Thompson, don't you?'

'Yes. You remember her coming to stay at The Grange?'

'Very well. She was a sweet old lady,' .

'She's very frail now and,…. Well, when she does leave this life I shall come into a share of her estate.'

Anne looked more cheerful at once, and moved across to sit next to him. 'Do tell me more, Charles, I'm very interested.'

'I thought you would be!' he replied with a slight sarcastic glance. 'Her capital, now comes to me and certain of my male cousins. I shall use part of my share to pay off some of what I borrowed to purchase the farmer's fields. I shall then put title to that land into building up Arthur's trust.'

'Is Ronnie to have his own trust,' Anne quickly interjected. Charles shook his head.

'He'll inherit automatically from me, just as I shall inherit from my father and so on. When he's older, like me, Ronnie will no doubt be given a chunk of his own capital to do what he wants with.'

'Get nice girls into trouble?' She responded jokingly.

'Look after nice girls he gets into trouble!' He promptly corrected her with a wink. 'And look after them very, very, very well. Even if,' He looked at her quizzically, 'They don't always seem to appreciate all that's being done for them!'

'Which reminds me,' Said Anne. 'Your Uncle Steve.'

'Don't tell me he's got someone into trouble!' Charles's laugh was the heartiest she had heard from him for some time.

'No! Of course he hasn't.' She laughed equally heartily in reply, feeling the tension lessening. 'What I was going to tell you was that he sent me a sweet little romper outfit for Arthur. I thought that was so kind of him. Uncle Steve's a real treasure, isn't he?'

'One of Uncle Steve's greatest strengths is his ability to keep in touch with people, particularly our family.' He put his head back and looked up at the ceiling. 'He follows everything that happens to all of the family with the keenest interest. He has no family of his own, which is sad. He won't forget you either. He now seems to regard you as family, which pleases me.'

After starting their walk, she asked: 'What would happen if you were to lose all your Macaulay money? What would you then have to pass on to Ronald?'

'What would happen?' he repeated the question. 'A certain charming young lady would have to keep me and both my sons!' He looked at Anne with a broad grin.

'I do wish you'd be serious when I'm trying to talk business.'

The visit ended on a very much happier note than it had begun. They exchanged long and sincerely meant embraces on the settee. 'How long will it be before we can resume our visits upstairs?' he whispered in her ear.

'Not just yet. I'll let you know. A little longer. Be patient. As you've been these last two months when I haven't felt up to it,' she whispered back.

Later in the day, as his car disappeared out of sight, Anne found herself reflecting on the day's events. She felt reassured by the visit, particularly about the financial aspects. Charles was going to prove true to his word and continue to look after her and both of his sons. With a bit of careful handling, perhaps a touch of guile, she reasoned, might also be necessary, she would be able to build up quite a nest-egg for Ronald, for Charles, for herself... And for Arthur. She must not forget little Arthur. She looked down once more at the little figure still sound asleep in his pram. And once more she felt deeply ashamed. She told herself that Arthur, merely a pawn in all that had happened, must.... No, she impressed upon herself, not just must, "will" be well looked after by her, to the best of her ability.

Chapter Ten – 1930

Life at Wisteria Cottage settled down to a steady routine after the baby's first month. Charles resumed his not infrequent visits, and Anne looked forward to these both for the physical pleasure of his company and because the two of them were enabled to progress their plans for the future market gardening business.

One pleasure she lacked, which continued to weigh heavily on her mind, was her inability to see, to pick up and to cuddle Ronald. She hoped her anxious enquiries as to his progress each time Charles arrived, did not seem overdone to him. 'Could we not get the two babies together?' she asked tentatively one day. 'Wouldn't it be nice if they could grow up together? After all, they do have something rather special in common!'

'I don't know how we'd do it, Anne. Not without giving the whole game away,' he replied, looking at her quizzically.

'Game?' she exclaimed.

'Well, you know what I mean.'

'What about a joint holiday,' she suggested, beginning to build up to her most recently devised scheme. 'You, me, all of us. All together in one hotel?'

'What? You and Dulcie? You wouldn't agree to that would you? Surely not?' He looked at her, an exaggerated grimaced expression on his face.

'If it meant we could all get together, yes!' she replied thoughtfully. 'Besides, I'd like to get to know Ronnie. And the girl you now have looking after him, instead of the old nanny, sounds very nice from what you've told me about her. You call her "Bett" don't you? She and I should get on well together.'

'Are you really suggesting that she and Ronnie, and you and Arthur, should go away together?' He sounded only mildly interested.

'Not quite,' Anne corrected. 'I suggest us four, plus you…. And Dulcie!'

'Now who's the risk taker? Lloyds would never insure such a risk!' he began to laugh lightly.

'Please be serious, Charles. Dulcie is most unlikely to agree to your going away without her and alone with an attractive young nanny!' She paused before adding: 'I might not approve of that either! Therefore, the only way you and I, and the two babies, can get to be together is the way I suggest. You four, plus Arthur and me.' She paused again, then sighed. 'My having Dulcie in the same hotel is my sacrifice for getting you for part of the time. And seeing Ronnie. So, where are we going to go for our holiday?' She asked, disappointed at his initial negative reception of her carefully developed idea.

'You scheming old thing! Never stop do you?' He laughed, putting out a hand to take one of hers and giving it a gentle squeeze.

'I try. I do try, Charles. For the good of us all,' she replied, looking dutifully into his face.

'We were talking the other evening in Kensington, as it happens. About taking a holiday in June, perhaps at Frinton. The beach up there is wonderful for children. A very nice place according to Dulcie, who knows it well.'

'Let's make it Frinton, then,' urged Anne eagerly, agreeable to any venue.

'But I still don't understand how it would all work. How, for instance, would we all go there? Do we just pretend we happened to meet up, quite by chance? Or what?'

'That's what I had in mind,'

'So you have schemed it all out?'

'I suggest you, Dulcie, Bett and Ronnie all go there as one little group. Arthur and I go as another. How observant is your wife? And how much have I changed since the Christmas before last?' Subconsciously, she put her hands up and touched both sides of her head before continuing. 'Would I, with my now much longer hair? And smarter clothes. Will I be recognised by Dulcie as the short-haired uniformed chambermaid she barely condescended to look at in the half darkness of her bedroom?'

'Oh dear, oh dear, oh dear!' he laughed aloud. 'And you were afraid when I first said I wanted to go flying.' He paused, the grin leaving his face. 'Do you know, I think we might just get away with it.'

'Let's try,' she replied, cuddling up closer to him.

Anne's journey to Frinton turned out to be more than she had bargained for. The drive was longer than she had expected, and she had had to stop twice in order to attend to Arthur. She was relieved when, at last, she drove the car in between the impressive gates of the hotel, and parked it in a space immediately beside the steps leading up to the large revolving front doors.

'I'm sorry, Madam,' said the smartly uniformed head porter, running down the steps towards her. 'This space is reserved for chauffeur driven cars coming in just to drop or collect passengers. Would you mind parking over there, please.' He touched the peak of his cap and said: 'I am so sorry.'

He did not sound in the least bit sorry, she thought, restarting the engine. She was annoyed, but decided not to make a fuss.

'If you like to go in and register,' the head porter continued, holding the car door open for her. 'I'll get one of the porters to take your luggage to your room.' She then noticed his expression change as he peered at all the baby equipment wedged tightly in the back of the car which was itself splattered almost all over with mud from her market gardening activities. She had meant to give it a wash, she recalled, as she noticed its grubby appearance in relation to all the other gleaming clean cars there.

The porter's tone became somewhat scathing. 'I'll have the pram placed in the garden room for you, Madam. That's where those sort of things belong.'

As Anne manoeuvred herself with Arthur in her arms through the revolving doors and entered the old fashioned and richly decorated hall, she wondered if she had come to the right place. Had they ever had a baby here before, she wondered? It seemed to Anne as if, the staff apart, everyone was either ancient or crippled and most were both.

'Yes, we have a first floor sea-facing room for you, Mrs Banks,' said the man behind the reception desk, eyeing the baby. 'Room one-o-four. Would you please sign here. Dinner begins at seven-thirty.'

Her arms seemed extra full of Arthur and she wondered how people holding babies and hand bags and other paraphernalia were meant to sign their names. She almost dropped him in the process, but not before she had plonked him down on the man's desk whereupon he had rolled over, to the man's not inconsiderable annoyance, on to his blotter. 'Sorry!' She muttered apologetically.

By now a page boy and an assistant porter were bringing in her luggage. Seeing the steady stream of items being carried to the lift, Anne felt embarrassed at having brought quite so many baby items, and looked the other way as, first the baby's bath, then a set of scales and finally its potty, were ceremoniously carried across the hall. One old gentleman guest, who stood only with the aid of two sticks, watched intently as if mesmerized by the procession which passed him and now monopolized the entire lift he was waiting to use. Wisteria Cottage, Anne thought, must now look positively empty!

The room overlooking the cliff-top greensward with the sea beyond, was everything she had hoped it would be. She had a bath and put on what she regarded as the best of the dresses she had bought with the extra holiday money Charles had given to her. Punctually at seven-thirty, she heard the gong sound in the hall below and tip-toed out of the room, shutting the door quietly behind her.

'Good evening, Madam,' said the head waiter as she entered the virtually silent dining room. 'What room number is it, please? And for how many?'

'Good evening. One-hundred-and-four. And I'm by myself,' she replied, trying to pretend she was used to having staff running around her.

The head waiter consulted a large tome lying open on a lectern near the door. 'This way, please Madam.' She was shown to a table against the wall away from the windows. She was immediately concerned to notice that the adjacent table to hers was laid up for two, and offered a silent prayer that that would not be where the head waiter put the Macaulays.

She had almost finished her soup course when she heard a familiar voice in the background. She turned too suddenly and the contents of her spoon went down on to her lap. An attentive waiter, who had seen what had happened, immediately came forward and presented her with a clean napkin. 'Thank you,' she gasped, feeling that she had become the centre of attention.

When she had collected herself again, she glanced sideways at the adjacent two-person table and was relieved to find it still unoccupied, as was the single-person table the other side of hers. She raised her head and slowly surveyed the room. Her heart seemed to miss a beat when she spotted Charles and his wife sitting together at a table on the opposite side of the room. She was offering a silent prayer of thanks when she sensed someone at her elbow.

'Excuse me, Madam.' The head waiter was leaning over her shoulder. 'The duty chambermaid has reported that a baby in room one-o-four is crying.'

'Oh, thank you,' she said, glad of an excuse to think about something else than Charles and his wife. 'I'll go up right away and see. Thank you.' She rose rather too quickly, having not noticed that since she had taken her seat, an elderly man had been seated close behind her. As she stood up, her chair went back and the man was jolted forwards. She turned to apologise and, as she did so, he turned and looked up at her with a pained expression.

He opened his mouth wide as if he were about to shout something. Instead, and much to Anne's horror, his top set of teeth fell out of his mouth, bounced off the edge of his side plate and landed on the floor at her feet. Unsure what well-mannered ladies were expected to do on such occasions, she picked up the teeth and placed them back on the table beside the man's soup bowl.

'Oh, I am so sorry,' she spluttered, aware that by now she really had drawn the entire room's attention to herself. She hurried for the door, feeling that all eyes were upon her. 'It's just my baby…. He's crying,' she blurted out as she passed one old jewellery-laden lady who glared at her through a pair of lorgnettes, clearly disgusted at the interruption to her usual quiet dinner.

By the time Anne returned to the dining room, she was none too sure she wanted anything further to eat. She was tired after the long journey, and was beginning to have second thoughts as to the wisdom of having ever suggested the holiday.

'Good-evening,' Anne said, with a slight nod of the head, to the lady who now occupied the adjacent single table and whom she guessed was Bett.

'Good evening," replied the lady who Anne judged to be about the same age as herself. 'Is your baby, like my charge, taking time to settle down in his new surroundings?'

'Yes, he is. You have a baby here too, do you?' questioned Anne.

'Yes. I'm a nanny. Is yours your own?'

'Yes,' Anne replied as the waiter approached.

'The beef is very good, Madam. Or, if you'd prefer it, the sole is very popular. Straight out of the North Sea!'

'I'll have the sole, please.'

Ten minutes later, the lady at the next table stood up. 'I'm just going to listen at my bedroom door for any crying sounds. Would you like me to listen at your door as well while I'm upstairs?'

'That's very kind of you. My room number is one-o-four.' Anne smiled appreciatively. When the lady returned to her table. Anne immediately noticed her rather glum expression. 'Is mine crying again?' She enquired anxiously.

'I'm afraid he is,' the lady replied.

'I'll go up to him.'

She did not return to the dining room for the sweet course afterwards, but reflected on the first meal, and felt it could have gone worse for someone not yet used to what, regretfully, she concluded was a very grand hotel. At least, she consoled herself, she had not had to contrive an excuse for a first meeting with the Macaulay nanny.

The next morning she awoke to hear something being pushed under her bedroom door. It was a note from Charles and read:

Glad to see you got here safely. Hope you and I will be able to get away for part of Tuesday. Lots of love. Charles. PS – I think your new boy friend (teeth) is slightly too old for you!"

The note made her laugh, and she immediately felt a lot happier and less isolated. Later on, when she was putting Arthur into his pram in the garden room, Bett appeared carrying Ronald. In her excitement, Anne almost dropped Arthur.

'Hullo,' said Bett. 'How old is your baby?'

'Just nine months,' Anne replied, not taking her eyes off the other baby.

'Ah, about the same as our Ronnie. Are you going for a walk?'

'Yes. It seems to be staying fine, so I thought I'll push Arthur along the greensward.'

'I'm going to take Ronnie that way, too. His mother and father have gone out for the day.' As she put her charge into his pram, she remarked: 'If it stays sunny I'm hoping to get him down on to the beach. His first chance to play with real sand.'

'I'm sure Arthur will love that, too,' replied Anne, still keeping her eyes for the most part on Ronald, as she arranged Arthur's blankets.

'They're too young, of course, to play properly on the beach, build sand castles and all that,' she explained. 'But at this stage I find they just love putting their hands into it.

Running dry sand through their fingers seems to have a strange fascination for the very young.'

'I can see you know all about babies,' continued Anne smiling. 'I've never been to Frinton before. Perhaps you could show me the way down to the beach.'

'Why, of course. I shall be only too pleased to have the company. And so will Ronnie.'

While they were speaking, Anne had managed to edge Arthur's pram into such a position that the two babies were alongside each other. She was relieved to see that, at close quarters, they were no longer nearly so like twins as when they had occupied adjoining cots at the nursing home. Both looked fit and happy as, propped up in their prams, they burbled away at each other. She felt she had nothing to be ashamed of in her bringing up of Arthur. He was a credit to all her time and effort.

The morning was the happiest she could remember. She delighted in everything that the two boys did. Trying not to make it too obvious, she made good of every pretext to touch Ronald, and to help him knock down the miniature sandcastles she and Bett built for them both.

At lunch time the babies were fed in their own bedrooms, and then put down for a sleep. 'Shall we ask if we can share a table for lunch?' Bett suggested tentatively.

'I'm alone, so I shall be very pleased to share.' Anne replied, pleased at the thought of not having to sit through every meal by herself. The two talked, like old school friends who had not met for several years, of their babies. Anne being careful of what she said. She told Bett that her husband was abroad.

'It's a bit embarrassing, I think.' She said as their sweet arrived. 'That there are no other babies, or even children of any age, in this hotel.'

'Isn't it shameful,' agreed Bett, laughing. 'It's more like a home for geriatrics,' She whispered across the table. 'You probably know the joke about Frinton and its aged population.'

'I'm not aware I know of any Frinton jokes, do please tell me yours.'

'It refers to our fellow guests and goes like this – "Harwich for the Continent, Frinton for the incontinent".'

'Oh, I like it! Have you any more?'

'Not that I can immediately recall. One just should not bring small babies away to first-class hotels,' she emphasised. 'Young ones are much better in a hotel which caters specially for children and babies, and where there are all the right facilities for the mothers and nannies. But Mrs Macaulay wouldn't hear of it when I suggested it. Nothing but the very best was good enough for her and her son.' She paused. 'What made you choose this place?'

'Oh, I was given the name by someone who knew someone who had been here,' She dismissed lightly. 'You know how it goes. But I would agree with you, a hotel which caters especially for children would have been much better for all of us.' She paused, wondering whether to ask what had long been on her mind. 'I noticed,' Anne began quietly. 'Your employers didn't appear to be saying much to each other at dinner.' She tried to sound as casual as she could. 'Don't they get on together?'

It was now Bett's turn to pause. 'It's not done to talk behind the backs of one's employers, I know. But....' She lent across the table again. 'To be quite honest.... I don't see what either sees in the other. They don't have rows, but they don't seem to be friends. No companionship.' She paused again and sat back in her chair. 'He's a wonderful, charismatic sort of person, very athletic and.... Jolly good looking, don't you think? A thoroughly nice person.' Anne decided not to interrupt. 'Both seem to have plenty of money. No shortage of that commodity, but little in common I'd say. She lives for her society balls, the garden parties etcetera. You name it, they get invited to it. And she insists on going to them all. Good contacts for his business,

I would guess. But he.... Poor man. He's far happier on the rugby field or doing some other sport. He's got bags of courage. He's even taken up flying.' She laughed lightly. 'You wouldn't get me going up in one of those little planes, not me!'

She paused again, putting her spoon and fork together on her plate before continuing. 'To be fair, I do admire her in many ways also. Hold her own, she would, in any company. Must be a useful asset for him at his City functions.'

'You said "poor man",' Queried Anne. 'You obviously sympathise.'

'Oh, I do.' She dropped her voice before continuing. 'And as I said, he's far happier playing rugby or flying – when he is allowed to get away. She's very selfish, expecting him to dance attendance most of the time. But I mustn't go on.'

Did they, Anne was longing to ask, but knew she could not, share the same bedroom?

The afternoon was spent as the morning had been, with the four of them playing contentedly on the beach.

That evening, as Anne crossed the hall to enter the dining room, Bett approached her. 'I was wondering if you'd mind if I joined you for dinner, as I did for lunch? We seem to have so much to talk about. And you're on your own.'

'That's a very good idea,' Anne replied, wishing it were Charles who wanted to join her, but pleased at the thought of not having to sit out another meal alone.

'We can check on each other's baby then, if one of us has to go up,' added Bett.

After they finished their dinner, during which they had talked incessantly, they went to sit in the lounge. 'Coffee for two?' enquired the waiter as they entered.

'Yes, please'.

'Look! There's a free table over in that corner,' said Bett, pointing to a small table at which four unoccupied large armchairs were drawn up. 'That'll do us, won't it?'

'Yes, let's go and commandeer that corner, shall we, Bett?'

By now Anne was feeling completely relaxed and was, for the moment, beginning to enjoy herself. It was twenty minutes later when she glanced up and caught the eye of Dulcie, who had just come into the room alone and was looking for somewhere to sit. It seemed to Anne that her eyes looked right through her just as if she did not exist. A moment later she was joined by Charles who, it seemed, was bent on finding where she and Bett were sitting.

To Anne's horror, Charles took his wife's arm and guided her towards them. 'May we join you, Bett?' he enquired, keeping his head turned slightly away from Anne. 'The room seems rather full this evening. Probably our fault. I think we were the last into dinner this evening.'

Bett started to get up. 'No, no. Please don't get up.' Charles said, pulling back one of the armchairs. 'You sit here, Dulcie,' he offered, holding out his arm towards his wife who was standing several paces away.

'This is Mrs Banks,' said Bett, pointing her hand in Anne's direction. 'And this is Mr and Mrs Macaulay, my employers.'

Hand shakes were dispensed with. Instead, all three nodded their acknowledgements. Anne felt herself blush, and was relieved when Charles turned and signalled to the waiter that two more coffees were required.

'Mrs Banks,' said Bett, looking first at Anne and then at the other two. 'Is the lady I mentioned to you who has a baby boy almost the same age as Ronnie.'

'How interesting,' replied Dulcie in her, Anne thought, most pretentious sounding voice, at the same time taking an especially long cigarette holder from her bag. She turned to her husband who was seating himself in the adjacent chair. 'Charles, a cigarette, please?'

'Yes, dear,' he replied, drawing out a silver case from his pocket and holding it in her direction. As she took one the waiter arrived with the coffee and produced a light for her. She inhaled deeply as all three of them watched in silence and then, leaning her head back, she slowly and with exaggerated dignity, exhaled the smoke from her lungs.

Anne noticed how Dulcie had seated herself, bolt upright on the edge of her chair with her back leaning against the end of one of the arms. Lady-like and regal that may look, she thought, but it did not appear to be nearly so comfortable as her own way of sitting in all sizes of armchair, which was to sit right back in them, like men did, and like she noticed Charles was now sitting. Was she, Anne wondered, giving her lack of really high-class breeding away by sitting so? Blow it, she thought, at least she was comfortable.

Charles had still not looked Anne straight in the face, and she had not dared to glance at him. 'It must be nice….

For the little boys and for those looking after them, when they find companions of their own age,' he commented in an effort to begin a conversation.

Dulcie did not speak so, after a polite interval, Bett responded. 'You should have seen the two of them in the sand together, Sir. They're a bit too young, but your son was very quick to understand, Arthur also, that a sand castle is made for knocking over.'

'A bit destructive, was he?'

'Where do you come from, Mrs Banks?' Dulcie suddenly asked, staring straight at Anne, making her conscious again of the penetrating eyes.

'Surrey.... Surrey,' she replied, swallowing hard and momentarily afraid her voice might not sound natural.

'Not London?' Dulcie snorted.

'No,' she nervously half laughed.

'Strange,' continued Dulcie, not deflecting her stare. 'I had a feeling I'd seen you somewhere before, in a store? Harrods? Working in Harrods? No?'

'No. I don't think so. Not in a shop.... A store.' She felt herself swallow again. 'I live out in the country.'

'Do you? It must be awfully boring living in the country,' she commented, drawing on her cigarette and aiming her exhalation well above their heads.

'I love it.' Anne sought in vain for more to say. 'Er.... Bett, here, tells me you live in a flat in Kensington?'

'Yes, Very convenient. I don't understand how anyone can live anywhere else. Handy for the theatre, the opera, stores, Barkers, Harrods.... You get everything if you live in London, Mrs Banks.'

'What about your Ronnie?' she asked, not quite sure of why she chose that moment to mention him by name.

'What about Ronnie?' Dulcie almost snapped back.

Whenever, thought Anne, am I going to be able to shake her off? Why does Charles not come to my rescue? 'Oh, I just wondered about…. About where he's going to play when he gets beyond the pram and nursery age. Children, especially little boys, like gardens to run around in. Play games. Be out of doors. Fill their lungs with fresh air.' She shrugged her shoulders and risked a glance at Charles.

'You know a lot about bringing up children, do you, Mrs Banks?' Dulcie's question was blunt.

'Not as much as Bett, here. I wasn't especially trained as she was,' she replied uncertainly.

'How long are you here for?' Charles interrupted, sensing that Anne needed help.

'Just a fortnight. And how long are you here for?'

'We're also here for two weeks,' he stated, then added: 'That is very convenient, isn't it? The two little chaps can play together on the beach every day.' Anne still avoided looking him straight in the face. 'Apart, of course, from your baby, are you here alone?' he enquired in a casual sounding tone.

'Yes,' she replied, again feeling herself swallowing hard. 'My husband's abroad. Singapore.'

'Really? How interesting?' Charles queried, sounding to her completely composed and relaxed. How did he manage it, she wondered? And whenever is he going to stop questioning me? First Dulcie, then him. She felt she could not keep up her pretences indefinitely.

'If you feel the need. To have a day off from looking after your baby. You may perhaps want to go into Colchester or Ipswich. Bett, I'm sure, would be only too happy to look after your baby as well for a few hours. Wouldn't you, Bett?'

'Of course, Sir. I'll be only too pleased to help Mrs Banks,' she readily agreed.

'That is kind of you,' Anne thanked her enthusiastically, quickly appreciating the purpose behind his suggestion. And she was greatly relieved when, a few minutes later, Bett announced that she thought she would go to bed.

'Sea air always makes me feel very sleepy for the first few days,' she stated.

'Is that what it is?' remarked Anne, trying to sound surprised. 'I feel very sleepy myself. I think I'll follow your lead.'

As she went to stand up, Charles jumped to his feet, stretched his arm out across the table and, in his most charming manner said: 'Do let me give you a hand, these chairs are very comfortable, but a bit too deep I think for ladies.'

Anne wondered whether this was intended as a mild rebuke for the way she had chosen to sit. She dismissed the idea and grasped his hand. The extra little squeeze he gave her did not pass unnoticed. She looked him in the face, smiled and said: 'Thank you, Mr Macaulay. Perhaps we shall meet again tomorrow?'

'I hope so,' he replied, moving his own chair out of her way.

Climbing into her bed fifteen minutes later, Anne congratulated herself on managing to keep her head over coffee, on the concept of her shared holiday idea and, above all, on the way in which it had enabled her to get really close to her Ronald for the first time since he was a week old. Additionally, though of less immediate importance to her, it seemed she was going to be able to have Charles to herself, at least for a few hours.

It was two days later when a further note was slipped under her bedroom door, informing her that Charles had told his wife he had to take the opportunity of being in Essex to call on an important client in Ipswich. If Anne would take her car two miles outside on the Manningtree road, and wait at the Plough Inn, he would collect her at about ten o'clock.

When the time came to leave, she was of two minds about missing one of her precious days on the beach with Ronald. On the other hand, she knew she had found it tantalising to have Charles so close and yet be unable to get closer.

She found the inn and was just locking the car door when he drove up in a large Armstrong Siddley car. 'And how do you consider your holiday scheme's working out?' he asked as they drove off.

'I think most things are working fine, Charles. I like Frinton, and the beach is exactly right for the boys. Also, Bett's very sweet.' She glanced at him. 'I have only one real problem.'

'And what is that?' he asked, not taking his eyes off the winding road.

'Either you're in the wrong bedroom, or else I am!' She laughed lightly. 'I want you, Charles, and its very frustrating to be sleeping under the same roof but in different rooms.'

'I can't do anything about that, much though I'd love to,' he replied. 'But let's make the most of today, and I think perhaps we could do something similar next week. The rest we'll have to keep for Wisteria Cottage.'

The day before they were due to go home, Dulcie woke up with a cold and decided to spend the day in bed. Because of this Charles was able to join Anne, Bett and the two babies on the beach, where Anne was amused to see that he appeared to revel in building giant sized sand castles which the boys were far too young to appreciate. 'They might like to try sliding down them?' he suggested tentatively, admiring his handy construction work.

'They're still a little too young, I'm afraid to say, Sir. Your efforts have been rather wasted!' laughed Bett.

Charles joined them in the bar shortly before dinner, and then shared their table for the evening meal. Sitting having coffee in the lounge afterwards, he suddenly commented: 'It's a lovely evening, I think I shall go for a walk along the greensward. Why don't you two ladies join me?'

'I think one of us should stay in the hotel,' responded Bett quickly. 'One of the babies might need us.'

'Oh, dear!' He sounded, Anne thought, genuinely sorry, though she knew what he hoped would next happen, and it did.

'If Mrs Banks would like a walk, I'm quite happy to listen out for Arthur as well as for Ronnie.'

'Are you sure, Bett?' Anne queried, feigning surprise. 'That is kind of you. As you say, Mr Macaulay, it does seem to be a very nice evening.'

'Just leave me your key, Mrs Banks,' requested Bett.

As soon as they were out of sight of the hotel, she slipped her hand into his. 'Who's the scheming one now? You knew what Bett would say, Charles. Do you think she suspects anything?'

'If she does, I think she's discreet enough not to show it,' he replied, giving her hand an extra squeeze.

They stood close together at the far end of the cliff top greensward from the hotel, and looked out to sea. There was an almost full moon, and its reflection provided an illuminated strip across the top of the water from the foot of the cliffs on which they stood right to the horizon, where it disappeared from sight.

'Holland's over there,' he said, pointing. 'Over the horizon. Too far away to see from here.'

She did not look, but instead turned towards him and put her arms up and around his neck.

'Thank you, Charles, so much for a simply wonderful holiday.'

As they walked back, moving apart as they approached the hotel, she felt the time was approaching to bring up another idea she had been working on in her mind. 'I hate to think of Ronnie growing up in a flat in London, while Arthur's going to have all the fresh air and space he could want. Do you think Bett could bring Ronnie down sometimes to stay with us?'

'It's certainly an idea. And it would seem to be a natural step following the success of the two boys enjoying each others company here. You and Bett also.' He paused. 'I don't mind putting the idea to Dulcie, though what she'll say I just don't know.'

'It would be nice if the boys could grow up as close friends,' Anne continued.

'We have yet to discuss schools in detail,' she said, but I recall your saying you hoped both of them could go to your old school. Charterhouse wasn't it?'

'I hope very much they do go there together. I had in mind, also, my old prep-school. That is, when they're old enough to go away to board,' he added.

'Oh, Charles, they don't have to go to boarding school, do they?' She pleaded. 'Not too young? It's so cruel.'

'Cruel? No, it's not!' he scoffed. 'Boys love it after the first few days. You have to make men out of boys, you know Anne. They can't be tied to their mother's proverbial apron strings for ever. And you're the one who wants everything to be done equally.'

'I know, Charles, but don't send either of them away too young,'

'I went when I was just eight years old. And I survived.'

As soon as she had finished her breakfast the next morning, Anne stopped at the reception desk on the way up to her room.

'Would it be possible, please, for the porter to come up in half-an-hour and bring my luggage down to the car?'

The man at the desk looked at her as if he would never forget the arrival of Mrs Banks and her baby, and a cheeky smile spread across his face. 'Yes, Madam. I'll get the removal men up to your room in half-an-hour.'

The ignominy, she thought, and was of two minds whether to give the man a ticking off. 'I said "the porter",' she replied curtly, trying to emulate Dulcie's superior style of speaking to staff.

'Of course, Madam,' replied the man, nodding his head in feigned supplication.

Her return drive home seemed much quicker and altogether less of an effort for her. She reflected on the accomplishments of the fortnight, and was well pleased with the way her scheme had worked out. And there had been no crises, she reminded herself, regarding Dulcie, though her dislike for the woman had grown no less bitter.

She and Arthur had had a most enjoyable holiday paid for by Charles. She had had two, also most enjoyable, days out with her lover, but dwarfing all these pleasures was the fact that she had seen, cuddled and played with her Ronald every day.

She had been able to satisfy herself that he was being well looked after and was growing up a healthy and loveable little boy. Her pleasures in this direction would have been just that much more complete, she reckoned, if she had only been able to bath him herself but, regrettably, she had not even had the opportunity to see him in his bath. She would have liked, she decided, to have seen the whole of her own little baby person in his birthday suit again.

She had been sorry to say her "good-byes" to him, but had come away with the assurance of future visits to Wisteria Cottage by Ronald and Bett, The future, she told herself, was indeed brighter for her visit to Frinton.

Chapter Eleven – *1930/1940*

The remaining years of the thirties, up until the outbreak of the second world war in September 1939, passed for Anne without any exceptional happenings. Although she saw Ronald on many occasions and was, each time, relieved to be able to satisfy herself as to his progress, no day passed without her impetuous exchange of the babies plaguing her thoughts at least once, and often many times.

Charles continued to pay frequent visits to Swallowford which she always looked forward to and enjoyed though, as Arthur grew older, they had to exercise greater restraint, and their intimate meetings generally had to take place other than at the cottage.

Charles continued to reject all suggestions that he should divorce his wife with whom, it pleased Anne to learn, he no longer shared a bedroom. 'I asked her to marry me,' he would tell Anne, 'and I'm not one to avoid my responsibilities. You yourself are a witness to that. Dulcie would never divorce me even if I were to give her the evidence, and you wouldn't want to be drawn into some sordid publicity any more than my family would. I've tried, to the best of my ability, to do my duty to you also, my darling. Just as I said I would.'

Whenever he spoke in such terms, Anne found it difficult to argue convincingly.

'I am intensely loyal by nature,' he would continue. 'And I try to be loyal to you both. And I have tried as far as circumstances have permitted, to provide for both the boys equally. So, while Dulcie is alive, Anne, you and I, much though I love you, can take matrimonial matters no further.

Blame me, I married someone with whom I'm not compatible. We never were, I now realise, from day one.'

His flying escapades were a constant source of worry to Anne, but she felt to try and insist that he stop the sport would deprive him of one of his now greatest pleasures. It appealed, she knew, to his sense of adventure, and high degree of courage. He went in for many flying competitions and races for small planes, and, as he had done when he was younger in football, in cricket, and in other sports at Cambridge, he excelled , and had many trophies to prove his prowess.

'Charles Macaulay, Madam,' said another competitor to Anne at one of the flying displays she attended with him, 'Is quite exceptional. One of the country's finest small plane pilots.'

Charles came into his expected share of his grandmother's estate and bought, in Anne's and Arthur's trust's names, more land at Swallowford. The slump in the early thirties had little effect on his family's syndicate profits at Lloyds and, with his growing income, Charles was content to increase still further his indirect investments in Swallowford each year.

Anne's profits from her market gardening business, continued to expand annually. She had an increasing number of people from the local village working for her, including an experienced foreman, but it was Anne herself who was the undisputed "boss" and from whom everyone was happy to accept her orders.

Uncle Steve, the Macaulay's solicitor, retired and bought himself a flat overlooking the Hamble River from where he could watch the sailing boats, notwithstanding the fact that he had never put a foot on any boat in his life.

One day he paid Anne a long postponed visit at Wisteria Cottage. To her surprise, he warmly embraced her when she went to help him out of his hire car. He did not seem a day older than when she had first met him.

'Had to come and see it all for myself, my dear,' he said, settling himself down in one of her armchairs after inspecting the out-buildings. 'Whether your business was half as good as Charles keeps telling me it is. And I find it's even better! A shrewd young lady you are, Anne. I told Charles so when I first met you.' A broad smile crossed his face. 'You even remembered which was my favourite sherry,' he added, fondly inspecting the contents of the glass she had put into his hand.

He smiled at her affectionately. 'Please, Anne, do keep in touch. Whatever you do, do keep in touch. It's all I've got to live for now. Hearing all about my large family of clients!' He then added with a chuckle: 'Apart, that is, from my sherry!'

Anne's business activities did not preclude her from giving her time, her love and affection to Arthur, who grew into a fine and happy boy, and whom she grew to love deeply and respect as a person.

Following the sudden and unexpected death of her own mother in 1938, it was Arthur in whom, even though he was then only nine years old, Anne found immediate comfort. 'I'll try and help you, Mummy, and do all the things Granny used to help you with,' he blurted out between bursts of tears.

Bett, who stayed on with the Macaulays in Kensington up to when Ronald went away to his first boarding school, brought him down for several visits following their happy meeting in Frinton. Bett gave no clue as to whether she suspected Anne's on-going affair with her employer, but in order to keep her earlier story credible, Anne made out that she and her husband in Singapore had decided to separate.

Anne had a large sand pit and paddling pool built in the corner of her garden for the boys, and these were particularly popular with Ronald with his more restricted playing facilities in London. These assets ensured that every invitation from Anne for him to come down to the cottage for a holiday was immediately accepted. And when the boys outgrew playing in the sand pit, she bought a donkey and a Shetland pony for them to ride around her land on, which proved equally popular.

The boys grew to become each others best friends and, as soon as he was old enough to go away without his mother, Arthur spent several short holidays in London, where he was taken to see the changing of the guard outside Buckingham Palace, and other visitor attractions, all under the watchful eye of either Bett or Charles.

'Mrs Macaulay never comes with us,' Arthur told Anne one day. 'She always seems to be either going or coming. But never with Ronnie and me.' To Anne's utter astonishment, he then pronounced: 'I hate her. And so does Ronnie!'

The prep-school Ronald and Arthur were sent away to was also in Surrey, only ten miles from Swallowford, but the close proximity left Anne with no less heavy a heart when she came away from the school having left the two eight-year olds there for their first term as boarders.

'They're lucky to have each other,' said Charles as he walked beside her back to their cars. 'I never had anyone when I came here as a boy, and I did feel very lonely indeed for the first few days.'

'I shall worry terribly about both of them,' she replied, feeling as if she were about to copy the two boys and begin to cry. 'Couldn't Dulcie find time even to come and see her son, her only child, safely into his first boarding school?'

'No,' Charles replied without emotion. 'She had some Red Cross…. Or other whist drive she had to go to.'

'Had to?' scoffed Anne. 'Had to!'

★ ★ ★ ★ ★

It was just two weeks before the start of the autumn term when war was declared. The boys had been away to the Isle of Wight with Anne for a fortnight, and Ronald was due to be collected from Wisteria Cottage the following day by Charles, and taken back to Kensington.

'Would there be any chance of your keeping him for a few more days, Anne?' he questioned on the telephone. 'Just until we see how things sort themselves out. This horrible business, the war, may then all be over.'

'Don't worry, Charles,' she replied immediately. 'I'll be only too happy to keep Ronnie here. Arthur loves to have his companionship at any time, as you know.'

Ronald did stay at Swallowford until the term began. Charles brought his ready-packed trunk down from Kensington, and collected Anne and the two boys on the way to the school.

'How nice it is not to see any tears these days,' she remarked as he drove her away after leaving the boys. 'They really do seem to love their school.'

'I told you they would!' he replied, half laughing. 'They're both Macaulays, remember?'

'As if I could ever forget!' she laughed in reply.

Later, during their return drive, she suddenly remarked: 'You seem unusually quiet, Charles. Is something on your mind?'

He paused before answering slowly and hesitatingly: 'I don't expect you to be exactly pleased, Anne, but I've joined up!'

'Joined up? What, in the forces? The army? Where? When? What are you going to be doing?' The questions were fired rapidly and with a sense of growing anxiety.

'I'm joining the RAF. Next week. Only as a flying instructor,' he replied coolly, aware that her eyes were on him.

'Does that mean you don't have to go fighting?' Her voice expressed her deep fear, and she kept her eyes glued on his expressionless face.

'It means, as far as I know, that I shall spend my time teaching young trainee pilots how to fly aeroplanes. At thirty-five, I'm considered too old to be a fighter pilot.' He tried to make the statement sound like a joke, but she was not deceived.

'Thank God for that,' she interrupted, letting out an audible sigh.

'Though I do have to admit,' he continued, without removing his eye from the road, and sounding more apologetic than blasé, 'that that is what I volunteered to be!'

'Oh, Charles!' she pleaded. 'How could you? And without even consulting me?' She looked hurt and unnerved. 'I'm jolly glad they thought you were too old. Where are they going to send you? Does this mean I shan't see so much of you from now on?'

'It so happens that it's going to be reasonably convenient,' he replied, trying to make light of the whole matter. 'I'm likely to be stationed in Wiltshire, probably no more than an hour's drive away.'

'What's going to happen to your London flat, Anne enquired?' Is Dulcie going to stay there, or will she move to

The Grange or her own parent's home? Both are safely out in the country.'

'Dulcie's staying in London. She's been getting more and more heavily involved with her Red Cross work. And the war's only going to add to it.' He paused before continuing in a quieter tone: 'As you can imagine, the Red Cross come into their own in situations of war. Dulcie's quite senior now and will be kept busy organising this and that in London.'

He then dropped into silence for the next few minutes. 'In this war there are bound to be air raids. There have already been warnings. It's not going to be like the last war, when almost all the direct unpleasantness happened across the channel in France and Belgium.' He paused again before continuing even more quietly; 'This time, I reckon, English civilians are going to be in the front line. There are bound to be lots of casualties, and the Red Cross will be one of the groups called upon to help. Frankly, I don't envy Dulcie her job.' He shook his head as if the thought pained him.

'Nor do I,' repeated Anne quietly, Her head buzzing with disturbing thoughts. 'How horrible it all is.' They drove on in silence and, as they approached Swallowford and went along by the duck pond, she stared out of the window at the water which that day seemed like the proverbial mill pond. 'It's hard to believe, when you look at this place,' she commented. 'That a war's being fought. That men are fighting and killing one another.'

'I agree,' he said, taking his eyes off the road to glance quickly at her. 'I'm only so thankful you've got your market business based well away from any towns and likely targets.'

'What targets do you mean?'

'Well, factory areas, army camps, RAF stations.' He shrugged his arms.

'What's going to happen to market gardening, do you think, Charles?' she asked, her mind filling with foreboding thoughts.

'It may be that yours will be one of the few trades to which the war will actually be kind. The demand for home grown produce is bound to increase. It may pay you, Anne, to take the initiative and approach some of the military camps over in, say, Aldershot. I can see a heavy demand for fresh food coming, especially from the Officer's Mess in each camp.'

'That's a good idea, Charles. I'll follow that one up.' A moment later she raised another question: 'But what about our staff? Will they be called up? No one's said anything to me yet.'

'I just don't know. The older ones won't be, but they may conscript the younger men even if, as I think yours will be, market gardening is classified as priority work. You'll have to see as the war develops. You may have to employ more women to replace the men.'

'You say "as the war develops", Charles. How long is it going to last, do you feel?' she asked anxiously.

'Anyone's guess,' he shrugged. 'People are talking hopefully of it all being over by Christmas. That's what they said about the beginning of the four-year long first world war. I think it's being very optimistic this time around.' She noticed how drawn his expression had become.

'You'll stay for dinner, won't you?' she enquired as they reached the cottage. 'If I'm not going to see so much of you,' she continued, unsure of his precise mood. 'And with the boys no longer here, why don't we make the most of the evening?'

'And of the double bed?' he teased, as they entered the front door, anxious to relieve the tension which he knew his news had brought. She put her arms up and around his neck as soon as they were in the hall. 'Where else?' she whispered.

★ ★ ★ ★ ★

By September 1940 the war had lasted a year, and life at Wisteria Cottage had settled down to its new routine. Anne's market gardening business was, as Charles had predicted, prospering.

The boys were still at their prep-school which, being in the country and well away from London, had remained operative.

Ronald was not allowed back to Kensington, and divided his holiday time between The Grange and the cottage. He seemed unhappy at suggestions that he should sometimes also visit the Rathbone's stately home and other members of his mother's and father's families.

Charles had completed almost twelve months in the RAF as a flying instructor and Anne was immensely proud of him in his light blue uniform. He managed to visit her about once a month, but was not always the best of company when he did so. 'It's criminal,' he stated on more than one occasion in disgust. 'It really is. And I don't like it. The trainees are little more than boys, and they're only half trained when they are taken away from us. Look at last week's figures of pilots lost. Churchill may call it the "Battle of Britain", but I call it unnecessary slaughter.'

'Well don't you go joining a fighter squadron,' Anne would argue, at times emotionally, 'Don't you dare!'

'I wish I could,' he was always threatening.

'Well think of me. Of Ronnie. Of Arthur. We all depend upon you too much. Promise me you won't go and volunteer for something dangerous?'

'Someone's got to do the dangerous jobs,' he would counter argue. 'And if it shortens the war, then the country, you and everyone else, benefits.'

'Charles,' she would plead with him. 'Charles, please, please leave it to the younger ones. The ones who haven't yet got family commitments.'

'They're all sons of mothers, Anne. Think of it that way.' He used to cut off suddenly into a pensive mood, and she was never sure if her point of view had fully registered.

It was at the end of the first week of September, towards the end of the school summer holidays, when Anne answered the telephone late one morning. Charles's voice sounded to her quite different from normal. 'Anne,' he paused, as if finding difficulty in going on. 'Anne?'

'Yes, I'm here. I can hear you, Charles,' she confirmed, intuitively knowing that something was wrong. 'What is it? You sound troubled. Or have we got a bad line?'

'Anne? It's Dulcie,' he breathed out heavily

'What's happened?'

'Anne. She was.... She was killed last night!'

'Oh. My God!' What, Anne wondered quickly, was she supposed to say? It was a shock to her but, she quickly realised, it must have been a much greater shock to him.

'You've got the boys with you?' he enquired, becoming more composed.

'Yes. We were just about to start lunch,' she replied, hoping the children were not within earshot.

'Don't say anything to Ronnie,' he asked. 'I want to break the news to him myself. I'll come over about four o'clock. Can you and Arthur arrange to leave us alone?'

'Why, of course. Whatever you want,' she agreed, again wondering what one said to a newly widowed man, unusually one who, over the past decade and more, had taken few steps to disguise the lack of affection he had for his wife.

'Charles? I am sorry,' she added, aware of how inadequate the words sounded. 'This must have come as an awful shock for you'.

'It was,' he agreed. Once more she was aware of his finding it difficult to speak. 'I shall know more details in an hour or .so,' he continued. 'The Red Cross have promised to telephone me again. She…. She was killed down in the East End. On duty. Last night was the biggest raid London has so far had. You probably heard about it on the wireless.'

'If it will help, Charles,' she volunteered. 'I shall be happy to talk it over with you after you've spoken to Ronnie?'

'Thanks' he replied, so quietly that she hardly heard him. 'I'm not looking forward to telling Ronnie.'

'Would you like…. Would you like me to tell him…. Very, very gently?'

'I think it's my duty as his father, but thanks all the same,' he replied firmly.

'He wasn't.' She began tentatively, wondering whether to continue. 'I don't think Ronnie was that close to Dulcie.'

'I know he wasn't. You could say I wasn't either. But I can tell you, Anne, it makes it no less easy to accept. Dulcie was his mother, after all!'

She hesitated momentarily at this poignant remark, and then replied softly: 'I understand, Charles. Do let me know, though, if I can help in any way.'

'I will. Thanks. I'll see you later.' His voice died away.

She found lunch with the two boys a considerable strain, knowing what they were yet to be told, and was glad when, as they were finishing their sweet course, they announced their intention of taking their fishing rods down to the nearest stream. 'I want you boys back here by four o'clock.'

'Oh, why, Mummy?' Arthur's voice sounded almost indignant, as did Ronald's.

'Why, Aunty Anne?'

'Because Ronnie's father is calling in to see us. And as you know, his visits are less frequent these days…. What with all his RAF work.'

She then watched the two boys walk away from her, each with his rod over one shoulder and tackle bag hung over the other. They were talking happily to each other, seemingly without a care in their heads.

In Anne's head there was turmoil once more, and she was somewhat surprised to feel that the horror briefly recounted by Charles made her years of deep resentment seem no longer of consequence. But were these quite unexpected happenings, she also wondered, going to give her what she had waited for so long? To have Charles all to herself? Intuition told her that events were not going to tidy themselves up so neatly.

Charles said little to her when he arrived, and she stood aloof, unsure how he wished to greet her. A shallow smile, a peck rather than a kiss, followed by a few strides took him, with Anne following, into the sitting room. She went towards the window. 'They're coming now,' she said, looking out. Then, turning to face him she asked: 'Do you want to go and meet them?' She went up close to him and took his hand.

'Send Arthur in to me. Then why don't you take Ronnie for a walk and tell him as you go along?' She spoke in as encouraging a manner as she could, feeling genuine sorrow on account of the difficult minutes which she knew lay ahead of the man she loved deeply.

'That's a good idea,' he replied, heading for the door.

'You could be a sort of mummy to Ronnie as well?' Arthur's touching words a few minutes later, in reply to her telling him why Ronald had been taken for a walk by his father, were as music to Anne's ear. 'We'll see, darling,' she replied, drawing him close to her. 'You mustn't worry if Ronnie seems quiet and, perhaps a bit bad tempered for the next few days. Try to keep him occupied so that his mind's on other things.'

Later that day she left Charles to go up and say goodnight alone to the boys. 'I think it's much better that Ronnie sleeps on the other bed in Arthur's room tonight, rather than go into one by himself. He needs company.'

'How are they?' she enquired as Charles came down the stairs five minutes later.

'Fine. Fine at the moment at any rate. You may find Ronnie has a good cry tomorrow after it's properly sunk in.' His own expression, she noted, was still grim.

'Try not to worry, Charles. I'll keep a careful eye on Ronnie. And I've asked Arthur to keep him as occupied as he can,' she said, taking Charles by the hand and leading him into the dining room.

They sat down on opposite sides of the table to plates of cold chicken and salad, and it was quite a few minutes before either spoke. 'She was driving ambulances herself,' he recounted quietly, breaking the silence.

'What, Dulcie? Driving herself? I didn't know she could drive?' Anne was quite taken aback at learning this.

'Nor did I!' Charles exclaimed, shaking his head from side to side and staring at the almost untouched food in front of him. 'It's just dawning on me that. I may have misjudged Dulcie, all along. It's as if I hardly knew her. The real Dulcie. The person below the exterior ultra smart façade. The person behind that at times vicious tongue.'

'How do you mean?' Anne enquired gingerly, knowing it would be better to let him talk his feelings out of himself.

'The Red Cross woman on the telephone. She told me quite a lot.' He again paused shaking his head slowly from side to side. 'None of which I knew before.'

'Do tell me, Charles,' she asked, stretching a hand across the table and placing it on top of one of his. 'If it helps to talk it through? But don't reproach yourself.'

'It seems,' he began again, 'Dulcie had only administrative duties until the air raids began. She then insisted on becoming an ambulance driver. In the thick of it she was apparently. She always did make light of what she was doing when I telephoned. That is, when I found her in at home, and that grew less and less frequently. All the time… She was in the thick of it, poor darling.'

Anne noted in silence the unexpected term of affection.

'Last night, as I told you on the 'phone, was the worst air raid yet on London, and she had to drive through the streets, down near the docks…. With bombs dropping, the buildings on fire, others collapsing, debris falling all round.'

He paused again, and she did not interrupt his thoughts. 'One stretcher bearer, the Red Cross woman told me, was badly wounded with shrapnel as Dulcie drew up in her ambulance. Apparently, she just took over and went into this terrace of houses. There were children screaming inside. They tried to stop Dulcie from going in. Burning like an inferno the woman said. It was some sort of temporary orphanage for the kids.' He stopped talking and took his hand away from under Anne's. 'The building collapsed on them. Buried them all. Oh, my God!' His voice grew louder. 'Oh, Why? Why? Why?'

Suddenly he put his hands up over his face as, for the only time Anne was ever to see him, he cried openly. His hands went white with the grip he was exerting on himself, and his body shook as if caught in an uncontrollable fit of convulsions. Without warning, he suddenly lifted up one clenched fist and brought it down so violently on the table that the smaller items of china and cutlery literally jumped into the air.

Anne stood up and stepped to his side. She rested a hand lightly on his shoulder and drew his head against her body. 'Don't worry, Charles, darling. As you said to Ronnie…. It's better to let it come out. I'm proud of you.' She began lightly to stroke his hair. 'Your emotions show what a very sensitive and tender hearted person you are. You feel very deeply for people. You always have. And I love you for being so caring.'

He did not reply, and after a few moments appeared to recover his composure. 'I'm sorry, Anne. Truly I'm sorry to behave like that. I shouldn't have done that…. I…. I…. Well, it's the tension of the war. My own work with novice pilots and….' She looked down and noticed how his lips were quivering and noted his occasional attempts to hold them still with his teeth. 'Nearly had myself killed more than once! And now Dulcie, and all those orphanage kids on top of it all. It's almost too much. More than the human body and mind were made to take.' He reached out to lift his tumbler of water, but his hand shook so much he put the glass down again.

He glanced up at her. 'Don't worry, I'll survive. I'm not cracking up.' He got up and walked across the room, then suddenly turned, and proclaimed vehemently: 'I'll avenge those bastards for taking all those innocent lives. If it's the last thing I do. I'll get my own back. Just you see!'

Anne was momentarily taken aback, then remarked: 'I've got a bottle of scotch hidden away under the stairs. The one you kindly brought for me last Easter. Spirits are still like gold dust, one can't get a bottle now in any of the shops. I've been keeping this one either to celebrate victory or for an occasion, an emergency such as this. I'll get it out.'

'Thanks,' he whispered. 'I could do with a stiff one if I may. Just neat.'

Two minutes later, when she returned with the bottle, she was glad to see he was in control of himself. He was standing by one of the windows, staring out into the darkness.

'Black-out, Charles!' she cried in horror, 'Black-out' putting the bottle down on the table. 'It's more than half-an-hour past black-out. Quickly, pull the curtains.' They had no more than just completed the covering and checking of all downstairs windows when, as if to underline the events of the last twenty-four hours, the distant but unmistakable throbbing drone of enemy bombers made both of them catch their breaths, and glance quickly in each others direction.

'Jerry's coming this way tonight,' she whispered, putting a hand to her mouth. 'The children?'

'Yes, but listen…,' he whispered back. They remained silent, their ears sensitive to the slightest change in note of the planes' engines. 'Jerry's not interested in wasting his bombs on fields of cabbages, so don't be too concerned.' He then added: 'Sounds as if they might be heading Aldershot way. The army barracks. Poor chaps.' He paused again before continuing in the same quiet tone: 'Aldershot's got off surprisingly lightly so far.'

They listened again. 'They're getting further away,' said a relieved sounding Anne. 'I hate Germans,' she stated defiantly, following him with the bottle.

'I don't understand, Charles,' she said some minute later, when her heart was again beating normally, trying to change the subject. 'Why we can't buy spirits any more. One can now get them only on the black-market, and that at exorbitant prices!' He looked up at her but did not reply. 'Where does it all go?' She went on, taking a glass from the cocktail cabinet and filling it half full with whisky for him. 'Just because there's a war on!'

A minute later she joined him on the settee. 'I thought it took good scotch seven years or so to mature.' She continued. 'If I'm correct, what was made seven years ago should be on sale in the shops now? Is it the forces who drink it all? Do you ever have any shortage in the Mess?'

He looked at her, half smiled, and shook his head. 'I've never known a shortage. We run on it in the Mess! Keeps half the boys going.'

'They shouldn't drink before they go flying, should they, Charles?'

'Quite literally, it's all that keeps some of them going.'

He left the cottage at ten o'clock, having assured Anne that he was capable of driving. 'Do be careful, darling,' she said, holding on to his hand after their final embrace.

'And please don't worry about Ronnie. I'll go and have a look at him now and make sure he's sleeping soundly, and

I'll watch him extra carefully for the next few days. You take care, too,' she added.

'Bye Anne. I'll telephone you tomorrow,' he called out as he shut the car door. She watched apprehensively as his car, with only its dim war time black-out driving lights on, disappeared around the corner. Life had the habit, she reflected, of producing many unexpected turns.

She tip-toed into the boys room and was pleased to hear heavy breathing from both of them. A shaft of light from the passage fell across both beds, and she stood for a few moments beside Ronnie. Very gently with her finger tips, she brushed back a forelock of hair which partly hid one of his eyes. Though he looked contented, she longed to pick him up, to put her arms tightly around him, and to tell him that he had not really lost his mother.

It was after mid-night before sleep came to Anne that night. She had been concerned by Charles's behaviour and, despite his assurance to the contrary, prayed that he was not cracking up. It had happened to pilots, she had read. Was it natural for him to have reacted quite as he had? Raw young trainees must frighten the life out of him at times.

She lay restlessly turning the happenings of the day over and over in her mind. Clearly any discussion of her matrimonial prospects was going to be out of the question for the present. She also worried as to how long it would be before he would again be capable of discovering with her their wonderful and so often passionately fulfilled relationship. She must be patient, for Charles's sake, she told herself. At least she could see herself having more or less permanent custody of Ronald, as well as of Arthur, for the duration of the war, and that aspect alone was grounds for no small measure of gratitude.

Chapter Twelve – 1940/45

In September 1940, Charles felt he would like to recognise how well he considered Anne and the boys had coped with the discomforts of the first year of the war. 'I'd like to take you three out for a day on the river. How would you like that boys?'

'Rather, Dad," responded Ronald,

'Just what the doctor ordered, Uncle Charles" Arthur replied.

'Can one still take boats out on the Thames was Anne's cautious response. to the idea.

'I checked up yesterday,' Charles reported. 'The boatyard at Taplow is still hiring out skiffs, but not their motorboats. They can't get the petrol. I've booked a skiff next Saturday for four hours from mid-day.'

All four of them were in a happy frame of mind when they reached the cottage the following Saturday evening.

Later, when they were alone, Anne turned to Charles. 'I think that was one of the happiest days we've had together. The four of us. We make such a perfect family'. He rested his hands on her shoulders and smiled down into her face, but did not speak. 'Charles,' she continued, 'The boys get on so well together, and we all sort of fit in so well - as a family?'

'Yes, we do all fit in very well.' He agreed, turning his head away from her and towards the window.

She so longed to extend the conversation into including their marital relationship, but she held back. It was for him, she reminded herself for the umpteenth time, to make the proposal. She hoped her waiting would not be long delayed.

★ ★ ★ ★ ★

Charles next came for a weekend at the cottage shortly after the boys returned to school. 'Oh, you're hurt!' Anne commented anxiously as soon as she opened the front door, and saw him with one arm in a sling. 'What's wrong with your arm?'

'Oh, nothing. Just got a scratch. That's all,' he replied with a flick of the head as he almost pushed past her in an effort to try and avoid any further inquisition.

'A scratch?' she snapped. Anxiety and disbelief showed in her tone, as she followed him closely into the sitting room. 'And it was thought necessary by someone to put your arm in a sling? Come here, Charles, and let me look at it. I know you. It's something much more serious, isn't it? You look pale, too.'

'Nothing to make a fuss about.' he dismissed, sinking into one of the armchairs. 'Any chance of a cup of tea?'

She ignored his request. 'Nothing to make a fuss about?' She repeated, crossing over to him and gently removing the arm from its sling. He did not try to prevent her as, even more gently, she peeped below the end of the bandage and gazed at the wound in horror. 'That's no scratch! That looks as if something jagged has cut into you.' She looked at his face and snapped: 'A piece of shrapnel? Where did you get that wound from, Charles? From where?'

'Official secret!' he pronounced, putting on a false grin.

Her suspicions grew. Was he in pain and doing his best to hide it from her? It was unusual, she thought, for him to seat himself so promptly on arrival. Where had he been? 'I'll get you some aspirin to have with your tea, but first, tell me…. Tell me truthfully, Charles. Have you….. Have you been up in a fighter, in combat?' He did not immediately reply and she pursued her line of questioning. 'Charles? Charles, you promised me. Remember?'

'I remember exactly what I promised,' he replied, shifting his position in the armchair with an audible sigh of relief.

Anne noticed this. 'You're in pain, aren't you? Tell me. Please, Charles. Tell me the truth?'

He ignored her question and said firmly as if emphasising the truth of the statement: 'I remember my promise and I can truthfully say I have not been up fighting in a fighter!'

'I don't altogether trust you, Charles. At least not as far as planes are concerned.' She paused thoughtfully. 'Not in a fighter? In something else then?' She looked pensively again at the wound. 'We'll have to keep an eye on that, it's not healing too well. It could get really nasty. Oooooo!' She screwed up her face as if in pain herself from looking at it.

Where, she kept asking herself throughout the evening, had he got that wound from?

'Darling?' she said gingerly, as she climbed into bed, taking his unwounded arm and guiding it across the pillow in order that she could lie with it around her shoulder.

'Charles…. I've been thinking,'

He turned his head in her direction. 'That always spells danger!'

'Now, please be sensible. I want to talk seriously. I want to talk about your sons,' she said firmly.

'What about my sons?'

'Isn't it time to put all the deceptions about you and me to rest, Charles?'

'One day we'll have to put it right then, won't we?'

'I think we should. Particularly for Arthur's sake. .'

'And not for Anne Bank's sake also?'

He took his arm away from her shoulder and pulled himself back into his half of the bed. As he moved she noticed the grimace of pain which crossed his face.

'Anne,' he said slowly. 'Please believe me when I say that I want to do just what you want to do. But….'

'Well?'

'But not yet.' He let out an audible sigh. 'Not while this bloody war's still on.' Then, with some difficulty, he rolled over with his back towards her. 'Now, if you'll forgive me, I feel I must get some sleep.'

When she awoke the following morning, Charles appeared still to be deep in his sleep. When he had not woken up an hour later, she became anxious. She lent over him and realised that he was sweating. She put her hand on his forehead and was startled at how hot he felt. She shook him and he still did not wake up. Waiting no longer, she hurried downstairs to the telephone. 'I'd be grateful if you could come as quickly as possible,' she ended by imploring her doctor.

After examining the patient, the doctor turned to Anne. 'Obviously this wound was not attended to right away as it should have been. It's showing signs of septicaemia and I shall now give your…. The gentleman, a large injection of Penicillin, a wonderful new drug which is saving the lives of hundreds of our men on the battlefield. He's slightly delirious with the temperature. You can hear him moaning every now and again. This is normal, and you should not be worried if he calls out…. Talks a bit in his sleep. It may be just gibberish.' He smiled again at her. 'But it can be a bit unnerving if you've not seen someone in this state before. I'll get the district nurse in to attend to that wound, and I'll come in myself and see him again this evening. If you're worried at any time during the day, Mrs Banks, do please give me another call.'

'He's due to return to his RAF station tomorrow.'

'Well, he won't be driving there in his own car I can tell you,' the doctor replied firmly. 'Not under his own steam, he won't. May I suggest you telephone his station and tell them what has happened. Give them my name and telephone number, and…. Be prepared for them to send an ambulance to collect him. The services don't like sick men in their own homes. They prefer to keep them under their own watchful eye.'

'But do you have to transfer him?' Anne enquired of the station duty officer fifteen minutes later. 'I can look after him here, and we have an excellent local doctor.'

About midday she heard Charles call out. She hurried up the stairs and found him in a state of restless sleep. He seemed to be having nightmares. He was panting and shaking every now and then. Suddenly, as she was just tucking in his bedclothes, he became particularly agitated and, to her bewilderment, cried out: *'Oui Monsieur. Vite! Vite! C'est tres dangereux. Heide! Heide! Yous allez a la maison. Vite! Vite! C'est tres dangereux.'* He took a deep breath and almost as suddenly, relapsed back into a deep peaceful sleep.

She stood open mouthed watching him, trying to make out what it was he had said. Her school French had been minimal, but she remembered enough to know that it was French he was talking. But why? Suddenly she recalled that he had got his Cambridge degree in modern languages. But…..And who was "Heide"? The name sounded female

★ ★ ★ ★ ★

It was six weeks before Anne saw Charles again, and she was more than just relieved to find him back to his usual lively self when he arrived at the cottage. She was determined that he should receive a real welcome.

'Darling, it's so wonderful to see you again,'

'To see you, too, my darling,' he replied, holding her away from him and then drawing her close again. 'How are you?'

'Let's go inside, Charles. We've got so much to talk about.' She led the way holding his hand. 'Are you really fully recovered?' she enquired, studying his face closely.

'Fit as fit can be! How are the boys? Everything going well at school?'

'Oh, fine,' she answered, sitting down as close as she could beside him and giving his hand a squeeze. 'I'll get some tea in a minute, but first…. Do tell me why I wasn't allowed to come and see you in the station hospital? I'd have come as often as you wanted me. I was very cross indeed with your RAF people.' She grinned at him. 'I damn nearly gave them a piece of my mind.'

'Naturally, I was sorry, too, Anne,' he replied softly. 'I can only say that I now operate out of a "hush hush" establishment near Guildford, and no unauthorised people are ever allowed into that place.'

'What place, Charles? And what's so secret about teaching people how to fly fighters?' She did not wait for an answer so anxious was she to get to the bottom of her fears. 'The Truth of the matter….' She almost spat out the words as she stared at him, 'is that you aren't teaching any more, are you?'

She paused, out of breath from her emotional challenge.

'I've changed from what I was teaching,' he replied, putting on a grin, and trying to calm her down.

'I know you've changed, Charles. I know it for a fact!' she exclaimed abruptly.

'Do you? And how do you know?'

'Because you've been to occupied France!' she pronounced triumphantly.

Momentarily taken aback, he paused before replying, and then questioned in as matter-of-fact a tone as he could muster: 'I didn't tell you, did I, that I now teach French as well as flying?'

Had she been mistaken? Had she come to quite the wrong conclusion? 'Teaching French?' she queried suspiciously.

'Yes, Anne, Honestly.' His next words were an attempt at sending her off the scent. 'You've heard, if you've listened to the news on the radio in the last few days, that Germany has invaded Russia. They'll conquer the rest of the world unless they're stopped. We in Britain have been spared by the Channel. The British, one day, will have to land back in occupied France.'

'What's that got to do with it?' she interrupted, still far from being convinced he was not avoiding telling her all the truth.

'Why don't we stop this inquisition and have some tea? I could do with a cup.'

'No Charles!' She placed a restraining hand on his lap as he made to stand up. 'I want to get to the bottom of what it is you've been doing. Think of me and the boys! You come in here with a badly wounded arm. You are very, very ill. You become delirious and….' She turned to look him straight in the face and, with her fingers, turned his head towards her. 'You spoke French!'

He laughed. 'I spoke French? Go on!'

'You did,'

He forced his head away from her restraining fingers. 'They say one's past comes out when you become delirious. It seems, if I really did speak French, my Cambridge days were what I was dreaming about. Or perhaps I was giving one of my French language lectures. And did you understand anything I said.?'

'Enough to know it was French, And enough to ask you who Heide is? Where does she fit into your training? I wasn't aware that we are training women to become fighter pilots.'

'I can tell you one thing, my darling,' he replied, pulling her closer to him on the settee. 'She's not a girl friend!'

'I'm prepared to believe that, but I don't think you're being entirely honest with me, Charles. Are you?'

'Don't you really think I've told you all that's good for you to know?'

'No! In the time while you've been in hospital,' she said 'I've been putting two and two together and....'

'And? Making five again?' he teased.

'This is no time to be frivolous, Charles. I think I have worked out precisely what it is you've been up to.'

'Have you now!' he laughed. 'I make no promises, to tell
you you're right, even if you do guess correctly.'

'France,' she began, taking a deep breath, 'is occupied, as you said. I read in the papers that we have been dropping spies. Underground people. Behind the enemy lines. I gather very small planes are used. Just the pilot and the person to be dropped or picked up. The highest piloting skills are required, the newspaper article stated, because the planes are generally landed in very small fields, during the night and with no lights on.'

She paused for breath and turned her head so as to be able to watch the expression on his face. 'Charles, I believe that that's what you're doing. It seems to me to be just the kind of challenge and adventure which would appeal to you.' she continued as her confidence in her beliefs grew. 'And, what's more, I believe you were doing more than just flying a plane there and back. You got that bullet wound, or whatever it was, because you took part with members of the Resistance in one of their raids?'

Not a muscle of his face moved. He stared for a few moments out of the window before turning and speaking: 'I suggested some minutes ago, that we stopped this inquisition and went and had some tea. I see no reason for deferring action any longer.' He stood up and walked from the room. 'Do you?'

★ ★ ★ ★ ★

It was four weeks later, when a Wing Commander Parsons telephoned one morning and asked Anne if he might come and see her that afternoon. 'I'm a friend of Charles's,' he explained. 'I have a message from him, which he has asked me to deliver personally. Would this afternoon be convenient?'

As she put down the telephone receiver, she stood back but did not take her eyes from it. What made her so sure that she already knew what the Wing Commander's message would be, she did not know. The three hours which passed before his car stopped outside the cottage, were, to her, more like months. .

'Mrs Banks?' His face was kindly, but she felt his pretence at being jolly was not convincing. 'May I come in?'

Once inside the sitting room, he held out a bottle wrapped in brown paper, which she took. 'Charles left this with me for you,' he stated stiffly.

'Thank you,' she replied, her words merely whispered. He watched as she tore off the cover. 'Do please sit down,' she said, indicating with her hand one of the armchairs. She sat herself down in the other.

'What a nice little place you have here,' he remarked, seeming to be as nervous as she herself felt.

'Please,' she interrupted. 'I know it may sound rude of me, but....' She paused and swallowed hard. 'I.... I know what you've come to tell me, and I'd be grateful to keep our meeting short.'

'Very well. I have to tell you that Charles is missing.'

'Not killed?'

'We don't know that. We know only that.... That....'

'That his plane did not come back?' she volunteered, willing the man to get on and tell her all he knew.

'Yes,' he replied,

'Was he on a mission last night?' she questioned, not removing her stare from the man's face for a moment. 'Landing someone or picking someone up in France?'

'He told you what he was doing, did he?' The man sounded extremely surprised and looked at her with an expression of reproachful horror. 'He shouldn't have done that!. It was in fact almost a week ago.'

'I knew,' was all Anne said, leaning forwards and covering her forehead with her hands.

'He was one of the finest members of the S.O.E., the Special Operations Executive.' The Wing Commander spoke slowly, choosing his words with care and becoming almost oblivious to Anne's presence and likely reaction. 'One of the most daring and most courageous. Everyone wanted Charles to pilot them. Everyone had the utmost faith in his skills. If anyone could get a Westland Lysander plane down on to a small patch, Charles was the man to do it. He was truly a remarkable pilot, Mrs Banks. And a truly remarkable man!'

'I know,' she agreed, fighting back her emotions. 'I've known him since he was a young boy. He always was…. Always…. Just wonderful!'

He continued in a more relaxed tone of voice, eyeing her with concern. 'He may be perfectly safe, just hiding up somewhere unable to get a message back to us.'

'You've heard nothing?' she pleaded.

'Nothing except that he landed one agent north of Reims. He was then due to fly to Lyon, and collect and bring back another agent to England. We know he never reached that second rendezvous.'

'Thank you very much for coming, Wing Commander,' she said, rising to her feet and feeling she would not be able to hold back her feelings for very much longer. 'Please forgive me for not offering you any refreshment. I would like to be alone now, if you don't mind.'

As he walked out of the front door the man turned to face her and said: 'We must all pray hard, Mrs Banks, that one day, very soon, Charles will be back with you in this pretty little cottage of yours. I shall, of course, let you know immediately if I get any favourable news. In the meantime, please let me know if I can help in any way. Don't hesitate.'

'Thank you,' she said, catching sight of Charles's chart of the River Thames lying on the hall table in readiness for the boys coming holidays. Its message was as clear to her as it was decisive. There would now be no further idyllically happy days for the four of them together, in boats on the river at Taplow. Nor would she now ever become a formally married wife.

She closed and locked all the downstairs doors and windows and, as she climbed the stairs, her feet felt like lead weights. She was grateful, if for nothing else, that the boys were not due back for their holidays for another week. She would have to work out by then, she realised, what to say to them. For the present it was solitude she sought.

She opened her bedroom door and, as they had for all the years she had lived in the cottage, her eyes fell first on the head of the cuddly sailor doll protruding from between the sheets. Retribution for her wickedness, her deviousness, her years of social envying, she felt, had reached its zenith. She fell on to her side of the large double bed, the haven where she and her beloved Charles had shared so many pleasures. She grabbed the doll and, holding it tightly to her chest, gave vent to all her pent up emotions.

Having the boys home for the long summer holidays helped Anne through the seemingly interminable period of silence. The period when no one, including Charles's RAF unit, knew if he were alive or dead.

The Wing Commander telephoned Anne one day to say the Resistance had found Charles's plane. It had landed in the Jura Mountains, near the Swiss border,'

A few days later, on returning from doing some shopping, Anne was met by Elsie who informed her that the Wing Commander had telephoned to say he would be in the vicinity of Swallowford that afternoon, at about four o'clock, and would like to call on her. The message included a caution not to get too excited.

When he duly arrived, Anne was waiting for him on the front porch and hurried up the path to greet him as soon as he had opened his car door. 'Hullo, Wing Commander.'

'Hullo, Mrs Banks. I do hope you got my message about not getting too excited. We have received only the most slender of information and as you will see when I explain it to you, we are unsure whether the information should be regarded as either favourable or unfavourable.'

'Come in, Wing Commander. I have some coffee on the table.'

'Thank you.'

'Well what have you to tell me?'

'A member of the Resistance reported seeing a person dressed in a British RAF uniform crouching at the road side and described by the Resistance man as seeming to be in distress. At that moment a Gestapo squad marched up the road and when it had passed the airman had disappeared.'

'What do you make of that information?'

'I just don't know. That is why I was anxious that your hopes were not falsely raised. Incidentally, I do have some other news, regarding the condition of the plane. There was no body on board.' He paused and then glanced quickly towards Anne, wondering if his unfortunate use of the word "body" had been noted by her. 'We must draw comfort from this piece of information, Mrs Banks. Of course if they had found... Found.... Someone in the plane. Well. Well..., that....'

'That would be the end of our hopes.' Anne remarked in a daze.

'Precisely, precisely. If Charles had hurt himself when he landed, and we are told the plane was only partially smashed by the landing, though it then burned right through, he might have decided to get across the border into Switzerland. He was very athletic. Capable, I would judge, of climbing over any mountain the Swiss chose to put in his way!' The man's attempt at a joke went unnoticed by Anne.

No further news had come through by the time the autumn term was due to start, and the boys were sent back to school in the belief that Ronald's father was now training pilots up in Scotland, and could no longer get home for short leaves. Life seemed to her almost to have become one long deception. Would she ever stop deceiving people, she wondered, albeit most such deceptions were aimed at indirectly helping others?

'It's odd he doesn't write, Mummy?' queried Arthur one day.

'All the other boys at school get letters from their fathers, even when they're fighting out in North Africa,' stated Ronald. 'They get some super stamps on them, too,' he added: 'Could we telephone him? Perhaps he will telephone us one day?'

'He might do just that,' she replied, putting on a brave face and praying to herself earnestly for such a happening that she felt her body begin to shake.

★ ★ ★ ★ ★

At Easter, after the boys had gone back to school, the Wing Commander paid a further visit to Wisteria Cottage and was accompanied this time by Mr Stevens. 'Uncle Steve! How lovely to see you again,' said a clearly delighted Anne.

'My dear, a visit from me is long overdue. But I am not so young as I was, and I didn't want you coming to see me. I'm a bit too near Portsmouth and Southampton Docks, wedged between the two I am at Hamble.' He looked at her affectionately. 'Targets for the German bombers, you know? Too dangerous for someone as dear to me as you are , Anne.'

He walked slowly with the aid of a stick into the sitting room. 'Just the same sweet little place you've got here,' he said, looking admiringly around the room. 'Quiet isn't it, and so peaceful?'

'Do sit down.' Anne had turned to the Wing Commander who had remained aloof near the door. You've no later information I take it, Commander. Nothing more heard from the Resistance?'

'Nothing,' confirmed the Wing Commander, directing his next statement to Anne.'Mr Stevens and I have been discussing Charles's continuing disappearance. It is a custom in the services. After someone has been posted as missing for a certain time to re-designate them as "Missing presumed dead"'

'Anne, dear,' Mr Stevens broke in quickly. 'Please understand, that this does not mean Charles is actually dead. It is simply that. Well, it's how the services work. We must all continue to pray and hope Charles does turn up safely.'

Anne had been expecting a decision along these lines for some months, and had tried to prepare herself for it. 'I do understand. But what effect, if any, does it have on the family?'

'The effect,' Mr Stevens said, leaning across towards her, 'is that Charles is regarded as having lost his life. The RAF no longer pay him as a serving officer. They pay, instead, war widows and dependants or orphans allowances. And, as far as his Civil estate is concerned, we put into effect the terms of his will.'

'This makes it all sound very final,' Anne muttered almost inaudibly, staring across her visitors and through a window on to her garden.

'I believe, Mrs Banks,' interposed the Wing Commander, 'Charles had just the one son. I know his wife was killed earlier in the war, in an air raid I believe.'

She glanced at Mr Stevens, whom she found looking at her intently. He took up the conversation, addressing his remarks to the Wing Commander: 'As I explained to you in the car, two boys were dependants of Charles. Additionally, Mrs Banks, as his common law wife, was also a dependant.'

'Common law?' Anne questioned,

'Don't take exception, my dear. It's only a legal term. It means that you, Er lived together as if you were husband and wife although you were not formally married. On Dulcie's death you became, in the eyes of the law, Charles's so called "common law" wife.' He gave her a reassuring smile.

'Oh,' was all she said, deliberating on the word "wife".

The three spent the next half hour discussing the allowances which Anne would be entitled to draw in the future. The Wing Commander then indicated his intention to leave, and Anne went to see him off.

Returning to the sitting room a few minutes later, she suddenly exclaimed: 'Uncle Steve, you've been here all this time and I've not offered you a drink. I'm so sorry!'

'Don't worry, my dear. We had many more important things to talk about. Anyway,' he added with a chuckle, 'One can no longer get my favourite sherry. I have to thank the Germans for that!'

'But I have a little left in the bottle!' she broke in, crossing to the cocktail cabinet. 'I don't know if it is still drinkable.'

Once they were both seated again, he looked into his brief case. 'I do hope, Anne dear, this is not going to be too painful for you. But we do have to go through certain formalities on these sad occasions. I have here, drawing out a large already opened envelope from his case. 'Charles's will.'

Mr Stevens put on his pince-nez glasses and began to study the first sheet. 'I will try and explain what this document says, my dear, in as simple terms as I can. You stop me if you don't understand something I say.'

'Thank you, Uncle Steve,' she replied, settling herself further back in her chair, unsure of what was to come.

'Charles, as you know,' he began. 'Comes into his father's estate only on Mr Macaulay's death. What Charles therefore has to give away now, by his will, is only what is left out of what he has earned, been given by way of presents and legacies, and some capital his father gave to him when he was twenty-one and some more when he got married. Less, of course, what he has put into trust for Arthur and…. And given to you.'

'Therefore, the total amount there is now for disposal under his will is, perhaps, not as much as one might have guessed.' Dropping his voice, he added: 'One needs to look no further than Dulcie for the cause of that.'

'Dulcie?' Anne questioned, as a frown crossed her face.

'Yes, my dear. Did Charles never talk to you of her extravagances?'

'No.' She lowered her voice and looked away. 'We hardly ever mentioned her name in conversation. Not unless we had to.'

'I understand. She was not my client, so I am not inhibited by what I may not say. Charles was worried, and discussed with me, on more than one occasion, his wife's personal expenditure. She spent money like fish drink water, he used to say.'

'But she had the Rathbone's money behind her, didn't she?' interrupted Anne. 'I thought their family was supposed to be even wealthier than the Macaulays.'

'Yes and no. Yes, she was a Rathbone and they were an extremely wealthy family. No, that Dulcie had four brothers, and the family practised male lineage. Dulcie was made a modest Marriage Settlement by her father, but that was all. It provided her with little more than pin money in relation to her tastes for clothes.'

'So she cost Charles a lot of money?'

'She did, Anne. Indeed, and I don't see why I shouldn't say this, Charles was worried that she seemed to be spending more than he was earning in those pre-war days. She had been spoilt, the only girl, and four brothers… You know how it is.'

'I do hope Charles never felt that way about me, Uncle Steve. He never hinted at any day-to-day over extravagance at the cottage.'

'I'm sure he didn't, my dear,' Mr Stevens replied. 'In fact I believe he held you up as a good example of someone living comfortably within their means. To be fair though, a smile crossed his face. 'I think he felt you went a bit over the top when buying the cottage and land. But in the long term, he couldn't complain as it soon came right, with your business paying its way at a very early stage.'

'As I have already indicated, Charles's estate is perhaps a lot smaller than one would expect.' He began reading from the document: 'The first £50,000, in gratitude for all she has done for Ronald, I leave to be divided equally between Anne Banks and her son, Arthur Banks.'

Mr Stevens rested the will across his knees, and took up a sheet of plain paper on which he had written some figures. 'I have here an approximate total of Charles's assets, and this figure, apart from a few personal items left to Ronald, is all to be divided between you and Arthur because it is less than the £50,000 mentioned. Arthur is not to get his half of the money until he is twenty-one.'

'Nothing for Ronnie then? Nothing at all? Or have I misunderstood you, Uncle Steve?' Anne enquired anxiously, shifting herself forwards to sit on the edge of her chair.

'No you have not misunderstood the position. Apart from a few personal items, there is nothing for Ronald, not at the present time that is. But Ronald, of course, with his father having pre-deceased him, will now inherit directly from Mr Macaulay senior when he dies. It is the same situation as with the Rathbones, the male line takes virtually everything. Ronald should be extremely comfortably well off when that event does occur.'

Anne hoped her sigh of relief was not heard. Her expression changed. 'Do you think, Uncle Steve, it's a fair will?'

'I do think so, Anne. But you must remember that I advised Charles when he drew it up. We did it together, soon after Dulcie was killed. He always said he would look after you and Arthur, and I believe he did this to the best of his ability whilst he was…. Whilst we knew for certain he was alive. He has attempted to continue that intention in the terms of his will.. You, Anne, have used your business brain and have made the most of what he gave to you. The business is a great credit to you. As also, if I may say so, is your Arthur. You've been a fine mother to him. And what Ronald would have done without you to mother him also?'

'It's been nothing but pleasure.' She replied smiling at her elderly guest. 'Charles was always very good about meeting all Ronnie's living costs here. My worry, Uncle Steve, has always been that some of the other members of Ronnie's family might suddenly appear on the scene and want to take him back to live in their main family circle.'

'I don't think that will ever happen. The boys are what, twelve, not yet thirteen? The family know he is happiest here with you and Arthur, at least for the time being. His grandparents see him every now and again, don't they?'

'Oh yes. He goes over to both the Rathbone's house and to The Grange. Just occasionally.'

'Have you been back to The Grange yourself, Anne?' .

'Never,' she acknowdged, shaking her head. 'It was what I agreed with Charles. That, and never to communicate with any of the staff. She looked at Mr Stevens and laughed. 'I wonder if anyone at The Grange would even recognise me now if we did meet?'

'I stayed there last night,' he said to her surprise.

'What's it like these days?'

'As you would expect in war-time, not a shadow of its previous grandeur. Half the house has been shut up for the duration. Some of the garden has been turned over to allotments, people from the village doing what you are doing here, growing their own vegetables. All in accordance with the Minister of Food's wishes!' he laughed. 'But the Macaulays are both taken care of and have all they need.'

He shook his head sadly before continuing: 'But, knowing the family as I do, I have no doubt but that we shall see all the splendour at The Grange again once the war is over.' He then added: 'And, of course, that magnificent house will be Ronald's one day. He's certainly a very fortunate young man!'

Anne smiled with satisfaction at this confirmation of her contrived highest expectations for her Ronnie. Mr Stevens put away his papers in his case. 'Do tell me, Anne, is everything taken care of for the boys' next period of schooling? I believe they're going to Charles's old school, aren't they? Charterhouse?'

'That's right.' She replied. getting to her feet.

'You will let me know if there are any problems, won't you?'

'Of course.' She looked fondly at the gentleman, now in to his seventies, The man in whom all the family trusted. The man who would never divulge a client's confidence and who now was, almost certainly she reminded herself, the only other living person who knew Charles had fathered two sons. Now, she reminded herself later in the day, in a moment of self pity, that she carried the whole responsibility of bringing up both boys.

As soon as they ended their last term at their prep school, Anne decided to tell the boys that Charles was regarded as being "missing presumed dead" following a flight over France. The two months summer holidays the boys would then have before beginning their five years of public school life should, she calculated, enable them to get over their bereavement.

'You should both be immensely proud of such a wonderful and courageous person,' Anne said, as she sat on the settee with one boy on each side of her. And as she looked at each in turn, she realised how immensely proud she also was of both of them.

Neither boy took the news as badly as she had feared, which she put down largely to the fact that Ronald had not seen his father, and Arthur his uncle, for over a year. Life without him might have almost become the norm for the boys, but never, she knew, would it be for her.

★ ★ ★ ★ ★

Until the last day of the war in nineteen forty-five, Anne still hoped and prayed that her Charles would one day just walk in through the front door. But the jubilation of victory, with the parades in London and other places all over the country, seemed to her like a symbolic drawing of the final curtain. He had been killed and, she told herself, she must resign herself now to accepting this as an indisputable fact. Even if she could not put him entirely from her mind, she must devote her whole time and attention to bringing up his two sons, as he would have wanted her to.

'It still seems strange to me,' she had written to 'Uncle Steve' shortly before the war ended, 'that his body has never been found.'

'I am told,' Mr Stevens had written back, 'that there will be literally hundreds of thousands of persons with no known grave as a result of this most terrible of wars. Trust and believe, Anne, that in some quiet corner of France your dear Charles now lies peacefully where some loyal patriot tends his grave, and gives thanks for Charles's part in buying with his own life, the hopefully lasting peace which you and his two sons will shortly begin to enjoy.'

What a wonderful choice of words Uncle Steve had, she realised, as she read and re-read his inspiring letter with tear-filled eyes.

In nineteen forty-seven the boys left school and were conscripted into the Army for two years National Service. Britain was then fighting no wars in any part of the world so that, though she felt a pang at seeing them off together in their uniforms to their first barracks, Anne knew their lives were not in immediate danger.

Their five years at public school had been an unqualified success for the two of them. Both had excelled at games and emulated their father in being chosen to represent, first their house and then their school, in all the main sporting activities. Physically, they had grown further apart, with Arthur emerging as the slightly heavier build of the two, a detail which continued to puzzle Anne since she herself had been of a heavier build than Dulcie. Academically, there was little to chose between the boys,

In nineteen forty-nine they were demobilised from the Army, in which both had attained commissions in the Royal Artillery, and went up to Cambridge for three years before setting out on their chosen careers.

During the latter part of their Army service, it had troubled Anne to note that Ronald chose to come to Wisteria Cottage less often for his weekend and longer leaves. He had, as his father had many years before, developed a keen liking for fast cars and had met other young men with similar interests.

Ronald often spent weekends up in London. He went to watch car racing and crewed for a friend in several motor rallies. He paid more frequent visits to The Grange where, she guessed, he was probably helped financially by his grandfather. When, one weekend, he drove himself over to Anne, her suspicions had been correct.

'Jump in, Auntie. I'll take you for a quick spin,' he had proudly offered as she stood, disapprovingly, by her garden gate looking at the old pre-war open-top vehicle, and politely declined the invitation. 'She'll do sixty easily. I've had her up almost to seventy…. Going down a hill!' Ronald had added with a laugh. 'Jolly good on corners. Just like a racing car.'

Of the two boys, Ronald looked the more like Charles and now, standing by his car, she felt it was as if the clock had been turned back some twenty years. Of one thing she was certain, Ronald had inherited from his father the love of living dangerously. And that, she reminded herself, had cost her lover his life.

If he must have a car of his own, he could be bought a better one, she reflected, storing the idea up in her mind for a future occasion.

Arthur, it became clear to her, was more home-loving, and of a more solid, dependable character. He rarely stayed away from the cottage when he had the opportunity to come for the weekend. There, he would soon don his thigh boots and, with fishing rod over his shoulder, make for the stream at the bottom of his mother's fields. 'Back for tea, Mum,' he would call out to her contentedly.

Anne was delighted to have his company but would, by choice, have felt a lot happier had it been the other boy who had developed the strong home instincts. It was a disappointment, therefore, when she resigned herself to accepting that the two, whilst remaining good friends, were slowly drifting apart on account of their differing interests, and were developing their own individual, and now increasingly different, adult characteristics.

She had hoped that at least one of them would choose to join her in her thriving market gardening business, but Ronald, no doubt influenced by his grandfather, went into Lloyds. 'Sounds very boring to me, but I'll give it a run,' he had told Anne without enthusiasm. 'If I don't like it I can always join my co-driver, Mike, in his garage business. He says I have a standing invitation!'

'I don't think a garage business sounds quite what someone with your education should be doing,' Anne had replied unhappily.

Arthur decided to become a chartered accountant and began his articled service (reduced from five to three years for those who had gained a university degree), with a firm in London.

'I think that's an excellent idea, Arthur,' she had said. 'I've heard people say that that training is the best you can have for business. I certainly wouldn't know where my company was without my financial advisers.'

'I hope it's as good as people make out, Mum. It's a hard grind.'

'You stick to things better than Ronnie does. I have no fears about you giving up half way through.'

Chapter Thirteen – 1950

Several months before the boys reached their twenty-first birthdays, Mr Stevens wrote to Anne and suggested he should meet her to discuss the financial arrangements which would follow Arthur attaining his majority. 'Why don't I drive down, to see you this time, Uncle Steve?'

'That would be very nice, my dear. I do have all the papers here, and there are some nice little spots to go to in Hamble for a bite of lunch. You'll be my guest, of course,'

'That's very sweet of you, Uncle Steve. Shall we say Wednesday of next week?'

'That will suit me very well. Now, promise me, Anne, drive yourself very carefully.'

On the Tuesday, Anne was about to sit down to a cup of tea when the telephone rang. 'Anne, dear. Uncle Steve here. I'm afraid we're going to have to postpone our plans for tomorrow.'

He sounded concerned. 'Oh dear, what's happened? Nothing wrong with you I hope Uncle Steve?'

'No, dear. It's not me.' He paused before continuing. 'It's trouble at The Grange, I'm afraid.'

'What? Who is in trouble?'

'It's a business matter. I don't know all the facts yet, dear, I know only that I have to go there tomorrow. I may stay two more days. Perhaps I could come on to you afterwards?'

'Yes, by all means. But, please Uncle Steve, do be careful not to tire yourself, and could you please let me know what you find? Anything which concerns The Grange and the Macaulays, Uncle Steve, also affects me.... Or rather Ronnie. And me....'

'If I can telephone you, I will,' he tried to reassure her. 'In the meanwhile, try not to worry.'

She returned the telephone receiver to its place slowly. Uncle Steve was usually so composed. She knew she would not sleep peacefully until she learned what was behind his hurried visit to The Grange.

His next call did not come through until the Thursday morning. 'Things are not too good here, Anne,' he said, sounding very despondent. 'Some of my former partners are coming down, and I must stay for at least another two days.

Ronald has kindly offered to run me over to your cottage on Saturday.' He sounded either out of breath or extremely tired. 'Would that be convenient?'

'Ronnie? What's he doing there?' she immediately queried, alarm now showing in her voice.

'All the Macaulays are involved, Anne. I can't explain now, but I will do so when we meet. Would about eleven o'clock be all right?'

He sounded, she felt, as if he were deliberately trying to cut the call short. 'Yes, Uncle Steve,' she agreed. 'Of course it will, but.... But I'm worried.'

'I'll see you on Saturday,' was all he said in reply, and it concerned her the more when she realised that he had not this time told her not to worry. What was going on? And why was Ronald "involved" as she had been told? How involved was he?

Anne's anxiety had in no way abated by the Saturday. Arthur was home for the weekend, and he stood with her on the porch as the time approached eleven o'clock. 'I suppose,' he said. 'Ronnie's got the same old sporting bus?'

'The little two-seater? Oh dear! Poor Uncle Steve. Anyway, if they've been at The Grange he'll surely have the sense to use one of the bigger cars.'

'Yes, you're probably right. I can hear a car now.' Anne joined him. 'No! Oh dear! You weren't right. Poor Uncle Steve, he's had to come over in Ronnie's old two-seater bone-shaker!'

Mr Stevens was gently levered more than helped from the car. How he's aged, thought Anne, as she moved to embrace him lightly on the cheek and then, taking his other arm, began walking him slowly up the path. 'I'm just so sorry, Uncle Steve, you've had to come to us after all. I was hoping to save you the journey,'

As they guided their elderly visitor in to the sitting room, she turned to Arthur: 'I'm sure Uncle Steve would like a glass of something after his rather uncomfortable journey.' She turned to her much, loved confidant, who fell back heavily into one of the armchairs as she spoke. 'Is it to be your usual sherry, Uncle Steve? Or would you like something stronger, you sound rather tired?'

He looked up at her with eyes he seemed to have difficulty focusing and keeping open. 'If you have a scotch, my dear?' he croaked. 'That would be most welcome.'

'May I have one, too?' Ronald asked.

'You on scotches, Ronnie? At your age? And before mid-day?' she half scolded, noticing for the first time how glum he appeared. 'If you feel you need it, you'd better have one. But no more than one, you're the driver!'

'It looks as if we're all going to need fortifying. Is that right, Uncle Steve?'

He at least, thought Anne, sounded composed.

'Yes, my boy. You're right, I'm sorry to have to say,' Mr Stevens replied, fingering his glass slowly.

As the four sat down, Anne promptly broke the silence. 'You know me, Uncle Steve, I'm all for getting to the point without delay. May we know, please, what has been going on? What the trouble is. Let us know, please, right away. What the worst is?'

As neither he nor Ronald spoke, she added more keenly: 'Well, do we have a problem, or don't we?'

'We do,' Mr Stevens said quietly, studying the contents of his glass and seeming reluctant to unburden himself of the news he brought his audience. 'We have a very great problem, Anne.' He paused to look her in the face. 'Did Charles ever explain to you about Lloyds? How it works?'

'You mean the liability side? The unlimited risk Lloyds "names" take?'

'Precisely, my dear,'

'Don't.... Don't tell me,' she broke in, looking first to the elderly white haired old gentleman and then to Ronald for the reassurance she knew instinctively would not be forthcoming. 'Have the Macaulays exceeded their liabilities, or whatever it's called?'

'It would seem so, Anne dear,' nodded Mr Stevens. 'That is, certain of the various syndicates, in which the Macaulay family has by far the largest stakes, have incurred substantial losses.... Very substantial losses.'

'I'm not broke, but I damn nearly am!' It was Ronald who broke the silence and spoke with undisguised bitterness. 'And I'm not even a member, not a "name". But I gather all what would have been my father's share.... What would have come to me. It may all have to go to help meet the present creditors.' He seemed on the point of breaking down as Anne watched him take an enormous gulp of his scotch.

'Oh, my God!' Anne felt her knees tremble, and put a hand to her mouth as if preparing to stifle a scream.

'Tell them how it happened, Ronald,' he croaked. 'Tell them.'

'It was an unfortunate combination of a number of different things,' he began. 'The syndicates had been doing very well, and had been expanding into new fields, particularly aviation and catastrophes.'

'Catastrophes?' exclaimed Arthur.

'Yes. We accept hazard risks on major hurricane, typhoon and similar disasters. In addition, the family recently also joined a new syndicate, one which undertakes re-insurance. And that's been adversely affected also. In fact, the worst of all. It was just bloody.... Excuse me, our bad luck that we'd just got established in these new markets, when the Gods unleashed themselves disaster-wise.... Hurricanes and so forth, on our particular policy holders. Almost all of them Americans!'

Anne's mind wandered and, forgetting momentarily the horror Ronald was recounting, she suddenly felt proud of his grasp of facts and his skill of delivery. He sounded a real business man, and she nodded her head with approval.

'In short,' Ronald added: 'Our syndicates and, therefore the family, face liabilities in excess of normal. Millions of pounds are involved. And this will necessitate realising all the underlying securities, Grand-Dad's wealth.'

He paused and held out his glass towards Arthur. 'Driver or not, I think I've earned a refill!' He turned to Mr Stevens. 'I'm sure you'll join me, Uncle Steve.'

Anne watched the re-filling proceedings in silence, her eyes staring at Ronald, unable to comprehend the full significance of what he had been saying. She felt stunned. Was this to be the out-turn of all her most cherished deeds and plans and hopes for her baby? Of all her careful nurturing over the years?

Ronald had begun speaking again, Anne suddenly realised. 'And in addition to having to sell all the securities,' she heard him say, 'the powers that be won't delay in starting the sales of tangibles, furnishings and the like. The property will be the last to be disposed of. The Grange, the furniture, the whole lot, will be disposed of. Everything Grand-dad owns. All will probably have to be sold for the benefit of the creditors. The managers have let the syndicates become over-exposed.'

'Oh, my God!' were the only words which again came to Anne and passed, just audibly, from her lips. She felt three pairs of eyes focus momentarily on her. No one spoke for a full minute, each absorbed by his or her own thoughts.

'Could anyone do with a top up of scotch?' It was Arthur who felt the need to take some sort of lead. He got to his feet and carried round the decanter again. 'It's getting on for lunch time. May I suggest that I go, perhaps Ronnie you could help me, and see if we have something in the 'fridge we could all have?'

'Ok, I'll come.' Ronald replied indifferently, struggling to his feet and draining his third glass in one gulp.

When the two had left the room, Anne looked at the elderly gentleman, who now seemed to her to have completely crumpled up in his chair like a punctured balloon 'Uncle Steve,' she began softly. 'I just don't know what to say.' She studied his face for some sign of hope. 'Is it really as bad a picture as Ronnie has painted?'

'It's no good my not telling you the truth, Anne,' he replied, his eyes on the glass clutched in his shaking hands. 'It is every bit as bad.'

'But what are we going to do?' Her eyes pleaded.

'Arthur and you, Anne, as I indicated earlier, will be little affected.' He coughed, and she wondered if he were about to choke and needed her assistance. 'Mr & Mrs Macaulay will lose almost everything barring Mrs Macaulay's own personal possessions, her jewellery and whatever cash she has, and any shares she has registered in her own name.'

'They will have to move into some small house or flat and, for the most part, will live off what investments and cash Mrs Macaulay herself owns. She was of course not a "name" so is not jointly liable. Doubtless, other members of the family, relations, may be able to help, but most of the family are also involved. Mr Macaulay will shortly be entitled to a state pension but, as you can guess, that is likely to be negligible compared with their accustomed level of income.' All that beautiful furniture, the pictures and…. And so many other magnificent things they had. Even the wine cellar, such beautiful wines they always served.'

'It will all have to be sold?' .

'Every bottle of it. They've laid-off half the staff already as a precaution. Broken hearted they all were…. They'd been loyal to the family for so many years.' His voice died away as he added: 'It's such a…. A tragedy. A real tragedy.'

'I feel I want to help them. It's not fair that such nice people should be treated so harshly, especially when they are elderly. I suppose it would not be practicable for me to help. I have never forgotten how Mrs Macaulay found my mother work when I lost my Dad in the war. It would be ironical if I were now to reciprocate by paying her back?'

'It's sweet of you to want to help, but I agree, Anne, it just wouldn't be feasible, and might open up the whole business of Charles's relationship with you. What has been kept quiet all these years.'

'I suppose so.' Then, dropping her voice, she spoke thoughtfully: 'For probably the only time I shall ever say it, I'm at this precise moment glad that Charles isn't here. He was such a sensitive and kind person. He'd have been broken hearted like his parents and the staff are.'

'Yes, my dear, I think he would.' Mr Stevens turned towards her. 'And it would worry him immensely that he could no longer pass on to Ronnie all that he had expected to. His grandfather's money.'

'What are we going to do about Ronnie, Uncle Steve?' she asked almost mechanically, the words coming from her subconsciously.

'He's young, my dear, and he told me yesterday that he has the offer to go into some garage business. He won't have much capital. But he'll survive. The Macaulays are survivors.'

'Is he going to get nothing? Nothing at all?' Anne begged. 'I still find it quite impossible to take in all you've been telling us, Uncle Steve.'

'Alas, my dear, it is all absolutely true,' he confirmed nonchalantly.

Anne stood up. 'I'm going to do all I can for Ronnie,' she stated, as much to herself as to her visitor. 'I shall start with his twenty-first birthday in two months. I know Charles would want me to. Giving Arthur and me half each under his will was not right! I've never thought so. I know, Uncle Steve, you helped Charles with his will. but it expressed his wishes. Charles was wrong! He should have given more to Ronnie.'

'Remember, Anne, That that will was drafted, not against the background of what has just happened to the

Macaulays, but with no Lloyds problems and Ronald coming into a fortune on Charles's death.'

'I suppose so,' she admitted.

'A person's estate, his money, is his to do with what he chooses, Anne, but I do share your view that Charles would be very grateful indeed now to.... To know you were going to look after Ronald. But, and here I will offer the words of a very old genarian, and this week a very, very tired old man. 'My advice, strictly between you and me.' He dropped his voice to a whisper as she bent down beside him. 'Is not to give Ronald a lot of capital. He'll only squander it. He gets that from Dulcie's side of the family. If you remember, we discussed this several years ago. Charles found it difficult to keep up with Dulcie herself.'

In any other circumstances, such a bracketing of Dulcie and Ronald would have provoked annoyance in Anne and a prompt correction, but now she hardly noticed the remark, and merely waited for Mr Stevens to continue speaking. 'Instead, I suggest you confine your help for Ronald to the income side. I don't know anything about this garage business he's begun to get tied up in. Tell you the truth, I don't much care for garages, or their proprietors of any age. Our firm had too many legal cases against garages. I don't trust them!'

'I intend to start,' Anne broke in, returning to the window and gaining inspiration from viewing the straight lines of produce stretching away into the distance of her nearest field. 'By giving him a proper car for his twenty-first birthday. So he doesn't have to go around in the dreadful old grids he does now. Besides.... They always look so dangerous to me.'

For the first time that day, a slight smile crossed Mr Steven's face. 'If he's going to drive me around again, I can't say I shall object to that!'

Ronald entered the room closely followed by Arthur who was pushing a trolley on which had been set out their lunch. Anne looked at the spread with surprise and gratitude. 'Well done, boys! How well you've laid it all out. You've even remembered the napkins!' She turned to Mr Stevens, glad of an excuse to change the subject. 'The boys always were very practical about the house. I don't know how I'd ever manage without at least one of them around.'

★ ★ ★ ★ ★

'And these are my special presents for two very fine boys whom I love dearly!' Anne beamed at them in turn as they entered the dining room for breakfast on Arthur's twenty-first birthday. 'Ronnie,' she quickly added, 'gets his present today as well, even though he's not twenty-one until tomorrow!'

Before opening the envelopes she had handed to each, they both embraced her warmly and stood back.

'Gosh, Mum! Thank you very, very much indeed,' said Arthur, after viewing his envelope's contents and moving again to her side and giving her a second hug

'Auntie Anne! Gosh! That really is most awfully generous of you. Thank you so much,' said Ronald after viewing his envelope's contents.

'I want you, Ronnie, to buy yourself a really decent car with your cheque. And by decent, I mean a new one, a brand new one.' She half laughed. 'I never want to see you again in one of those unsafe, dreadful old sports bangers you've been running about in up to now.'

'All I've been able to afford,' he shrugged, then added: 'But Auntie Anne, with this sized cheque….' His eyes were alight. 'I'll be able to buy a really super car. Perhaps even a Sunbeam-Talbot 90. I've always wanted one of those, and Mike's garage are agents for Roots Group cars which would allow us a very attractive trade discount. I could probably get a six cylinder 90 for about the price of the four cylinder 70.

'By decent car, Ronnie,' she quickly cautioned him, 'I don't necessarily mean a fast car. Do I make myself clear?'

'Sort of!' He looked at her with a whimsical expression. 'I will choose the colour "British Racing Green"!

She was about to repeat her speed warning, but decided not to be too hard on him. 'You've had a rough time, darling, over your grandfather's business losses. You buy your Sunbeam-Talbot if that's what you've really set your heart on, But…. Ronnie, do please, please always drive it carefully. Responsibly!' She rested a hand on his arm. He towered above her and reminded her so vividly of her Charles at the same age. 'Don't take any risks,' she pleaded.

'I'll try to be careful, Auntie,' he replied. 'But with the power there under the bonnet…. Well, it's silly not to use it!' He turned and hugged her, and she longed, as she always did when he overtly expressed his affection for her, to tell him that he was hers, and that it had been in her womb he had been carried.

'I think I'll also buy myself a car with some of your wonderfully generous cheque, Mum,' said Arthur pensively. 'Not a Sunbeam-Talbot like Ronnie. I think I'll get something less flashy. A steady car for getting me to and from the station and so forth.'

'Buy it through our garage, Arthur,' interrupted Ronald. 'At a discount.'

'Thanks,' Arthur replied without showing much enthusiasm. 'I'll see what I decide upon. The Motor Show's on at Earls Court next month. I'll go and have a good look around there.'

'Please yourself,' muttered Ronald, taking a further look at his own cheque before putting it away in his wallet.

'A good idea, Arthur darling,' said Anne, once more looking from one to the other, and priding herself on bringing up two such fine looking young men. How proud, she reflected, would Charles also be on this their day of majority.

'And now for my second present. One for each of you!'

'Second present, Mum?' questioned Arthur in a surprised tone. 'I think you've been too generous already.'

'What is it?' quizzed Ronald, his eyes lighting up for the second time that day and glancing around the room.

'You won't find it in here,' she responded with a teasing smile and a wave of her hand. 'It's not wrapped up in brown paper. It's not that kind of a present.'

'Tell us, Auntie,' .

'Yes, please, Mum,' urged Arthur, feigning impatience. 'You know I can't bear suspense.'

She beamed again at them both in turn, relishing her private joke. 'I'm giving you each forty-nine per cent!' she said solemnly.

'Forty-nine per cent?' The boys questioned in unison.

'Forty-nine per cent of what, Mum?' Arthur asked, a puzzled look on his face.

'Forty-nine per cent each of the company which I have asked be formed to take over my market gardening business,' she replied, 'I've asked Uncle Steve to arrange for the firm of solicitors he was with before he retired, to form a company which will then acquire my business from me.

This way, I'm told, it helps the Estate Duty position on my death, and ensures the bulk of the business value I have built up over the years passes to you two and not to the ever-greedy tax man.'

'You're right about Estate Duty, Mum,' agreed Arthur enthusiastically. 'I've learned that side of tax-planning already in my studies. I know of several clients whose businesses have been turned into limited companies. It's often done.'

'That's right,' she replied, a smile of satisfaction crossing her face.

'But what about you, Auntie?' Ronald asked anxiously, as he weighed the proposition up in his mind. 'What are you going to get out of it? What will you have left?'

'I shall have two per cent!' she said, again with a teasing smile.

'That's not much, Auntie. Not after all your years of hard work,' he commented thoughtfully.

'I shall be quite happy with the arrangement Uncle Steve has worked out,' she confirmed happily. 'Let me tell you a bit more about it. First, I keep Wisteria Cottage out of the deal. Our home remains mine. Secondly, as the company's Managing Director.' She paused and laughed. 'You didn't think you'd ever see me carry that grand title, did you?'

The boys both smiled their acknowledgement. 'As I was saying, as the company's Managing Director, I shall have what Uncle Steve has told me is called a Service Agreement.' She paused and wagged one of her fingers at each in turn. 'That's to stop the shareholders deciding to sack the Managing Director!' She let the joke produce a chuckle from the other two. 'So you see, I'm protected as far as my income from the business is concerned.'

'If I've got in correctly, Auntie,' said Ronald, waving an arm in the general direction of the out-buildings behind the cottage. 'Arthur and I each now own forty-nine per cent of the business.'

'Not quite yet,' she corrected. 'It's going to take a few weeks to get everything sorted out. Then, when the shares are issued, all but two per cent will be put into your names.' She looked again from one to the other. 'Oh, and one other thing. I nearly forgot.' She smiled at each again. 'It's a precaution Uncle Steve suggested we put in for the protection of us all.'

'What's that, Mum?' Arthur enquired, displaying his interest and pleasure at being able to understand what was planned.

'No shareholder will be able to sell any of his shares except with the consent of shareholders owning at least ninety-nine per cent of all the shares issued. This way, since my agreement is required, neither of you can sell any of your shares against my wishes while I'm still alive.' She smiled at both and added: 'As I said, your Uncle Steve advised on that condition being inserted.'

'As a matter of interest,' questioned Ronald. 'Why was the figure of forty-nine chosen for Arthur's and my shareholdings? It seems an odd amount to me.'

'I can answer that,' chipped in Arthur. 'I've covered that point in my studies. If two shareholders each have fifty per cent, and they then disagree over something, you get deadlock. There should always be someone who can break an "equal vote" situation.'

'You're absolutely correct, Arthur. Well done! That is just as Uncle Steve explained it to me.' She gave him a congratulatory pat on the hand. 'You see, your accountancy training is proving to be useful already.'

Chapter Fourteen – 1952

On the Thursday following the funeral, the hospital arranged for a hire car to take Anne to Waterloo. 'Thank you all so much,' she said, warmly shaking the hands of the sister and the various nurses who had attended her, and feeling her eyes beginning to moisten. 'You've all been so kind to me.'

As the train pulled out of the station and gathered speed, Anne was relieved to be seeing, for the time being at least, the last of London. As always when she visited the capital, she delighted afterwards in getting back into the country, where the air was fresh and where there was little of the London dust and dirt on everything. Today, as she gazed through the train's soiled windows and saw the dreary suburban scene as if through a grey filter, she looked forward even more than usual to leaving behind her the impersonal London arena with its recent horrific experiences for her.

Opening her bag, she spotted the letter which Uncle Steve had sent to her in hospital several days before. She re-read it and pondered, not for the first time, on why he seemed to be urging her to visit the grave as soon as possible. "Thursday afternoon might be the best time." His suggested timing happened to fit in well with her recovery as far as the hospital doctor was concerned, and her other planned movements. But why had he been so specific?

On reaching Swallowford, she climbed into her car, which was looking the worse for having stood in the station car park for several unusually stormy days. Twigs, leaves and other debris lay on the damp surface of her car.

As she approached Wisteria Cottage, pangs of remorse once more overcame her. Her sweet little cottage, she reminded herself, had been the main home of herself and the two boys for most of their lives and, also, of Charles for the period between his wife's death and his own disappearance over France, the home in which she had hoped so much they would all four settle down in after the war.

She arrived shortly before midday and, after having a few words with members of her market gardening staff, went in to have an early lunch and to prepare herself for what she knew she wanted to do next and, quite apart from Uncle Steve's suggestion, would not defer another day.

'Mr Stevens, Mam,' reported Elsie. 'Says to give you a message. 'E's comin' up to see you 'ere tomorrow. That is, unless you rings 'im back to say it ain't convenient, Mam.'

'Thank you, Elsie,' she replied, wondering what her trusted adviser had to tell her that warranted his making what, at his age, would be an extremely tiring journey. 'I shall be here tomorrow,' Anne called out to the office staff.

Having eaten, she went into the garden with a pair of secateurs and gathered a large bunch of evergreens. She then went into one of the greenhouses and gathered a large bunch of her choice chrysanthemums.

She put the two bunches on the back seat of her car and drove off. A mile from the church she remembered that, with only a minor detour, she could pass The Grange, and decided to see if it were possible to drive up and look at what remained of the old place. The place which had hidden in its walls so many mixed memories of her and Charles's intertwined childhoods.

The road outside was deserted, and she parked the car near the main gates, which she at once noticed were closed. She alighted and walked up to them. A heavy linked chain, with a large and foreboding padlock on it, was woven in and out of the ornate wrought iron, and just inside the gates. On what remained of one part of the East lawn, a large board had been erected carrying the words: "ACQUIRED FOR DEVELOPMENT".

Standing back, she noticed another board on the other side of the drive on which was painted the words: "TRESPASSERS WILL BE PROSECUTED" in equally large letters. Beyond the boards were parked two enormous bulldozers and, alongside these, various tip-up trucks and other heavy demolition equipment.

The fine shingle drive had never known a weed in those halcyon days, but now weeds grew in profusion as far as she could see. The desolate scene seemed only to confirm that an era had ended.

With a heavy heart, Anne climbed back into her car and continued up the road to St Mary's church.

As she began to walk up the main footpath through the churchyard, she looked away to the left. As she expected, in the distant corner, where earlier generations of Macaulays all had their graves, a blaze of brightly coloured flowers covered a mound and stood out in the otherwise bleak and inhospitable graveyard, with its eerie quietness.

As she walked towards the corner, she passed along the side of the church building itself, close to the vestry door she remembered she used to go through to get to the choir room. She had just passed it when it seemed the lock on the door suddenly clicked. Momentarily it made her jump, until she excused the noise on the wind which, though it had now abated from the previous week's gales, was still strong enough to make itself heard.

In the already fading November light, the wind seemed extra chilling, and Anne was glad she had on her thickest winter overcoat. She approached the grave cautiously, subconsciously making the last few steps on tip-toe.

After stooping to place her own bunches of carefully chosen home-grown flowers and evergreens prominently near the head of the mound, she stood at its foot staring down at the many beautiful wreaths and other flowers. Without disturbing any of them she began to read the cards denoting from whom each had come.

One she read with considerable surprise "from your ever loving "Dad"". She wondered who had placed it there on Ronald's father's behalf, and considered, whoever had written it, that it was a very nice thing to have done. Perhaps, she thought, it might have been Uncle Steve. The kind of nice thing she guessed he would do.

As she stared, in front of her, she found her focus on the flowers slowly slipping away from her and, it seemed for just a few seconds, as if she could see Ronald smiling at her through the flowers. It was not a gloating, but an affectionate smile, which flowed towards her.

'I'm so sorry, my darling,' she whispered. 'Truly I am. I did it only for your sake.' As her focus returned, she knew the illusion had been only in her imagination.

She had chosen to come alone because she feared she would break down, but now an unexpected strength came over her. Ronald had been removed from the struggle of life and was at peace, she told herself. No more harm could befall him, physically or financially.

Unexplainably, she felt that she, too, was about to find the peace which for so many years had alluded her. Though she had ceased to be a regular church goer, being back at St Mary's, where she had worshipped with her parents and had been confirmed as a teenager, was beginning to make her aware of her dormant beliefs. Or was it just her conscience momentarily urging her to seek forgiveness?

As she continued to gaze down at the grave, a feeling of being deeply religious overcame her. Perhaps, she thought, this is usual in the presence of those who had died only recently. Her lonely vigil in the graveyard began to remind her of Sunday School and she remembered the account of Mary Magdalene visiting the sepulchre, and of the risen Christ speaking to Mary.

It was as her thoughts were thus enthralled that she heard a crunch behind her on the chippings path.

'Please don't turn round, Anne.' The voice was little more than a whisper and, against the noise of the wind, it sounded very indistinct. But it was sufficient for her to recognise the speaker instantly. Or, Anne suddenly wondered, was she just imagining another incongruous idea, like Ronald smiling at her from amidst the wreathes?

Her heart seemed to miss a beat and, not knowing whether she were fully conscious or back in hospital under heavy sedation, she raised her eyes up slowly to the head of the grave. As requested, she did not turn around. From her lips came only one word: 'Charles!'

She again heard the shuffle of feet as she sensed someone approach close to her A firm hand on one of her shoulders was no more than she was expecting. A moment later a second hand was placed on her other shoulder. 'Keep facing that way, please Anne.'

The voice, she noticed, sounded slurred, like someone with a slight speech impediment. She felt fingers grip her shoulders as if the person were using her for partial support. Her shoulders, she did not doubt, were up to bearing the extra weight. 'Please don't turn around and look at me,' he repeated.

'Why, Charles? Why ever not?' she questioned in a daze, dropping her eyes down once more to the grave. Then, as no
more was said, it was as if she heard herself comment: 'This is our son, Ronnie, in this grave. Yours Charles, and mine. Our baby.'

'Dear, dear Ronnie.' The words were gently spoken back. Then, coming closer to her, Charles added: 'I know, Anne, that all along you have believed Ronnie was yours. But he wasn't. Your son was Arthur.'

Anne felt startled, and longed to turn round if only to reassure herself that there really was someone behind her, that that person really was Charles, and to learn from him, face to face, whether this was not some cruel joke someone was playing on her.

Joke or not, reality or not, she decided that now was the time to unburden herself. The churchyard of St Mary's would be her confessional stall. 'No,' she said in an even quieter whisper, as if afraid the wind might carry off her secret further than she intended.

'Charles,' she began again, unconsciously choosing to express herself with youthful simplicity. 'I did an awful thing. When the babies were only a few days old.' She hesitated, and then clasped and unclasped her hands several times before continuing. 'They were so alike. I wanted my son, not Dulsie's, to have all the best things, The Grange and the position and the prospects which the Macaulay family could give him. I swapped the babies over. So no one would ever know.'

'I know,' Charles replied, equally softly.

'You knew? All the time?' Anne gasped.

'I learned only yesterday,' he corrected her. 'What a burden, what a terrible heart-rending burden you've carried all these years.'

'How did you know, Charles?' she questioned earnestly.

'I learned the truth from Uncle Steve,' he stated calmly.

'Uncle Steve?' she gasped.

He did not immediately reply. 'It's a long story. And for now I will give you only an outline of what Uncle Steve told me yesterday.' He paused again. 'When the boys were almost twenty-one years old Uncle Steve felt it was necessary for his firm to double check as to which boy was the elder. One of his staff went to the nursing home. When the records were unearthed, an unexpected extra report was found. It said that a nurse entered the room just after you had done it, the swap over.

You were just putting back the blankets.'

Anne became aware, as Charles spoke, how fast her heart was beating. 'The nurse,' he continued, 'Thought you seemed extremely agitated. She sent you back to your bedroom to rest before you went home. The baby she later brought to you was, in fact, your own. She had by then discovered what had happened, and had swapped the babies back again. The nurse's report implies you might have become confused and made a genuine mistake.'

'But how, Charles? How could anyone tell,' she questioned. 'The babies were so alike that first week? Even I, the mother of one of them. I couldn't tell them apart.'

'The nurse, as I've said, was suspicious. She unclothed both of the babies. You had changed over only their shawls, none of the standard hospital clothing, nappy etc'. If you had attempted to change that also, you would have found that Ronald had been circumcised the day before. The nurse knew at once that, for whatever the reason, the babies were in the wrong cots.'

Anne's bewilderment continued as she grappled with the many conflicting thoughts which suddenly ran through her mind, trying to envisage the life time of both boys in their reverse roles.

'The nurse persuaded the matron to give you the benefit of the doubt, and she agreed provided a detailed report was put on the file, and that you were kept under constant observation until you left the premises later that day. Left, that is, with your own baby.'

'God alone knows,' Anne stated, 'What I've suffered. Mothers who give their babies away for adoption must go through hell unless they are totally heartless. Can you imagine what it was like for me in our circumstances?'

As she spoke, Charles lifted the pressure of his hands from the top of her shoulders and slid them forwards slightly. He then drew her gently back towards his own shoulder and, as she felt his chin rest on the top of her head, he hugged her tightly. 'Let's forget the nasty side of all that happened to the boys. No one can change what has happened. You punished yourself many times over. All is now forgiven. Let it also now be forgotten.' He paused. 'Therefore, Anne, sad and heart-breaking though it is, it is Rickie, the other baby, your unofficially adopted son, whose body lies in the grave down there.'

Her reply was spoken without thinking, the words coming spontaneously from her heart: 'In the end, Charles, I loved them both. Just as if both had been my sons, as they both were your sons.'

Anne resumed their discussion, keeping her head facing away from Charles as she had been requested to. 'How long have you been here,' she asked?

'In the churchyard? Since just before you arrived. I heard someone coming. I didn't know then it was you. I slipped into the church through that side door,' he said pointing.

'I heard the door lock click as I passed it. I thought it was just the wind,' she whispered back.

'I watched you standing by the grave and knew I had to see you up close, that I had to touch you and to talk to you once again, Anne, my darling. It was a temptation just too strong for me to contain.'

They both remained thoughtful until Anne again broke the silence. 'It's cold out here in the graveyard, Charles. Why don't we go inside the church and continue our discussion in there? Or better still, why don't we go back together to the cottage?'

'I don't think you'd want me at the cottage with my physical problems,' Charles answered in a serious tone. 'But I shall be pleased to sit with you in the church, in the dark, for a short while longer. I ought then to be on my way back to France.'

'To France? You are English, Charles and you belong here. Here with me and Arthur. It is your rightful place as husband and father.'

As they walked towards the church building, Anne was aware that his leg movements were irregular. It took them several minutes to reach the door, and during the whole time she was conscious also of his keeping behind and to one side of her.

'Now Charles, I'm all ears to hear what you've got to tell me about the years since we were last at the cottage together. But first, please tell me why you are not letting me see you. What have you to hide from me? I can only guess you have had a car accident. Are you disfigured?'

'I was involved in an aircraft accident,' he responded, 'As a result of which one side of my face is scarred.'

It was then a full minute before Charles began to recount the life he had been leading. 'Cleverly, but embarrassingly for me, Anne, you guessed exactly what I was doing,...flying allied secret agents into and out of occupied France and sometimes, though this was not an official part of my brief, I stayed on the ground over there with the Maquis, sabotaging and disrupting German communications.'

He paused again. 'I don't know exactly what I said that time I became delirious. It followed the raid on the Peugeot car factory at Mulhouse, which the Huns had turned over to armament production. Our group was caught in an ambush. I got away with one other person, but got a piece of shrapnel from a grenade through my arm. We had to lie low for several days and the wound went septic. The rest of that little episode you already know all about.'

'I'm going to interrupt you, Charles. Why are we sitting in here? In a beautiful but none too comfortable, and certainly rather cold and dark church. I don't know about you, but I'm frozen. Surely we should be going back to the cottage so that, in front of a nice log fire and with a strong drink inside us, you can take your time in telling me your story in comfort?'

Charles appeared not to have heard her suggestion. 'On my next visit to France we were attacked by German MIGs and shot down. I emerged with no worse than a broken ankle and minor facial burns. I managed to locate and join up with the local Resistance, and hoped then to get flown back to England. But that was not to be. The group of saboteurs I temporarily joined up with had a train to blow up. But unknown to them we had a quisling in our midst.'

'A quisling?'

'Yes. A traitor. A Nazi sympathizer,' he continued. 'I believe he recognised me and gave me away. The Huns went for my burns, threatening to disfigure me permanently unless I revealed certain information they wanted. They also twisted my ankle half off, or at least that was what it felt like, the bastards! That was when I told my contacts not to inform London that I had survived the crash. I escaped again but such was my poor physical condition, chiefly on account of my broken ankle, I was soon recaptured. I was then physically messed about, a lot more intensively this time.'

'"Messed about"? You don't mean tortured, do you, Charles? Surely not tortured?'

'Yes, I do mean tortured. And I was to learn to my cost, that my re-capture had been made by a particularly aggressive local group of the Gestapo. An uncivilised bunch at the best of times. They delighted in scalding my already aggravated facial burns with boiling hot water, their aim being to force me to reveal the whereabouts of the Resistance's local ammunition hideaway.'

'Knowing you,' Anne remarked with a smile, 'I assume their hot water methods did not yield the confidential information they sought.'

'Their methods certainly did not succeed. Indeed, the more they scalded me the more determined I became that they should not succeed. After a time they gave up trying and left me as the prisoner of a very young soldier from whom I was soon able to trick my escape.'

'This latest escape left me with an extremely difficult choice to make as regards you and the boys. And to add to my complications, my mind had to be made up against the background of knowing that at that juncture I was barely recognisable as a human being, let alone as an attractive lover, father and uncle. I had strong doubts as to whether the boys would be capable of stomaching the sight of me were I to be flown back to England. To be frank, I wasn't a hundred percent sure that you also, Anne, might not also feel unbearably queasy when confronted with these difficulties. Put succinctly, I felt Anne, that you would not want me other than in pristine condition,'

She felt a lump swelling in her throat. 'I'd always want you, Charles, how ever badly you had been hurt.'

'Rightly or wrongly,' he continued, 'I decided I had no right to risk ruining the life you three had begun to make for yourselves. Call me a coward if you like, it probably fitted my mental state at that particular time. I can tell you in all honesty I feared rejection, your rejection, more than anything. The enemy's actions against me I could take, but you rejecting me…No. You, Anne,' he pointed out .'Were only just into your thirties then. Certainly not too advanced an age to marry. If you had the chance to make someone deserving of a sweet and attractive and wonderful loving wife, I hoped you would feel free to accept the offer.'

'With the objective of causing all of you the least distress, I elected to stay in France as this seemed marginally to present the least unpleasant alternative. I say only marginally because it would leave you initially with having to live with the distressing "missing" uncertainty. If I had been able to avoid you living through that period I would gladly have done so.'

'Please try to understand the mental burden of my looks and of finding myself, if not a complete cripple, at least not ever able to be fully active again, as I had been.'

'And it was not by an accident I'd become inhibited,' he emphasized but by the hand of human beings. Sadists, albeit they were the enemy!' He spoke with a bitterness she had never before heard from him. He became even more vehement: 'But as I said I would, I did avenge what those bastards did to those poor orphanage kids and to Dulcie. Many, many times over! And I'm proud of the fact!'

'That is why you volunteered?' Anne sought confirmation of what she had long been aware, 'Why you were no longer content just to teach flying?'

'Yes, Anne. I just had to!' His voice changed. 'War is a terrible, terrible business but, believe me, the undeclared war, the underground one is the worst of all. It's certainly more exciting, but more cruel if you're caught. There are no rules of mercy. No protection for prisoners. No Geneva Convention to say the captor must not do this or do that with his prisoner.'

'But how awful, Charles?' Her comment sounded to her so inadequate. 'And you were in the middle of all of this?'

He ignored the question. 'If you take part in this type of action you have to be prepared to take everything the enemy throws at you. I was lucky. I escaped the firing squad. Just!'

Anne changed the subject; 'can we talk about this afternoon's meeting Charles? Clearly, Uncle Steve deliberately, and, as it worked out, very successfully, stage managed both of us in the hope that we would bump into each other.'

'You make it sound as if we literally met head-on. like two bucks fighting a rut!' replied Charles as Anne smiled broadly.

'Please come with me to the cottage where we can have a meal and talk over our respective problems in comfort.'

'I fear,' he replied, 'I've talked too much. And you've become chilled?'

'I'm OK, but some heat would certainly be welcome. Meanwhile, Charles, I consider we've played this game of charades long enough. Please let me see your scars in the flesh.'

'All right Anne, my darling one. I have no wish to add to your temperature discomfort, though I would point out that my intentions have all been in your best interests. I wanted only to protect you from your first sight of my scarred face.' He immediately released her and turned her around to face him. Unfortunately, the evening sky was covered by thick clouds preventing her seeing his scars clearly.

'Thank you, my love. Thank you.' Then shaking herself lose, she spoke with a broad smile. 'I was beginning to feel like a trussed up oven-ready chicken!'

'Did you come over from France this morning, Charles?'

'No. Uncle Steve kindly let me stay the last two nights with him in his flat at Hamble, a pretty little spot.'

Anne was immediately interested: 'Staying at Hamble means, Charles, that Uncle Steve must have seen your scars in both artificial light and full daylight, what I myself have yet to do. Do tell me, did he pass any comments? For example, on the scars being more or less conspicuous than he was expecting.'

'No, he made no such comments. It seemed he just accepted the situation of my scars as they were.'

'Rather as I thought,' muttered Anne to herself.

'What was "rather as you thought"Anne?'

'Oh nothing. Unless that is you will permit me to carry out a very simple experiment. May I just touch, very lightly, your facial scars?'

'No you mustn't. Other considerations apart, they are wet and sticky, and there's nowhere around here for you to wash your hands afterwards.'

'I don't believe I shall need to wash my hands afterwards. They will not be wet and sticky,' Anne affirmed. 'Please let me show you. Come outside. It won't hurt, I promise.'

A few minutes later they emerged from the church and Anne noticed, in the semi-darkness, that he held his head proudly high. He had, she acknowledged to herself, lost none of his remarkable courage.

Reluctantly, he let her raise her hand slowly and then lightly touch his face with her finger tips. 'Now, Charles' she asked. 'Unfortunately there is no moon to help light us, so you'll need to feel my fingers. Are they wet and sticky? Please examine the tips of my finger very carefully.'

'That's strange, Anne;' he answered. 'Your fingers are quite dry. How do you explain that?'

'I'm no psychiatrist, but it is a subject which has always fascinated me. Over the years I've probably borrowed from the local library more books on this subject than on any other.

'So you now fancy yourself as a psychiatrist, do you Anne, as well as a merchant banker? Is there no end to your talents? So tell me, please, "doctor Banks", what is your explanation?'

'I would hazard a guess that it has something to do with the shock, Charles, which you sustained when the Gestapo poured boiling water on your scares. That was nearly ten years ago and parts of the clock mechanism of your brain stopped on that day. The effect is that whenever you do something now that reminds your brain of that shock it sustained, your brain immediately tells you the time is ten years ago. I may not have got it correct and I think it is essential you make an early appointment to visit a psychiatrist and let him sort out the remnants of your gruesome sounding war time appearances.'

'Time has moved on, Charles.' she continued. 'And surely so has the drying up and fading processes of your scars moved on. Neither I nor Arthur should be the least bit worried by now seeing your well-weathered dry scars.'

A few minutes later Anne pointed to her car; 'It's over there,' and put an encouraging arm around him. 'Have you had time to visit The Grange? I passed there this afternoon. The main gates are padlocked up with horrible notices about trespassers being prosecuted. They seem to be about to demolish the whole place.'

'Hopefully not the house,' queried Charles.

'Why should they not include the house?'

'Uncle Steve is in touch with a charity, a children's home. He told me about his idea last evening. It will be a wonderful end to a great career if he can bring the deal off. I don't know all the details, but I gather his scheme involves the various developers each paying a little more for their plots of land than they would do otherwise, and the balance is then handed to the charity which spends it on buying the house at a special price.'

'Sounds typical Uncle Steve,' commented Anne.

She was understandably tired, but in high spirits, as she drove the car, with its unexpected passenger, away from St. Mary's. 'Is there anyone at the cottage? Is Arthur there?'

'No Charles. Arthur's away on an audit, up in the Midlands for a few days, We'll have the place to ourselves.'

Both became engrossed in personal thoughts until Anne broke the silence. 'Charles, getting back to Uncle Steve and the part obviously he played today in us meeting. Has he known all along that you were alive?'

'No, not all along. I didn't write to him until well after the war was over. Long after he had dealt with my will and all that. He and I have written to each other regularly ever since. At first, naturally enough, he tried to persuade me to return to England, but accepted that my decision was final. It was through him that I knew just how you and the boys were, what you were all doing. How successful you were with the business. But his masterly activities, today bringing us together, were entirely of his own doing.'

'And now, Charles, that you have been well and truly landed, I trust you are back in Swallowford for good.'

'I want to be. God alone knows how much I would like that. But first I need to check with all the parties who would be affected, especially Arthur, the only one of the family left of his generation. We'll all have a lot to digest, so I suggest we place further deliberation "on the back burner" as they say. In other words, I need time to think.'

'Charles, you've not told me where you've been all this time. Who has looked after you? Where would you have returned to in France had Uncle Steve's churchyard scheming not worked out?'

'Apart from the first few months after the war finished, I lived with a sweet, now alas very elderly, French couple in their small bread shop up in the Juras, the mountains near the Swiss border.'

He paused. 'I saved their son or, rather, refused to give his whereabouts away to the Huns. He was a fine chap, younger than me. He did a grand sabotage job. The Huns caught me again, and it was then that they had a second go at me, this time trying to get me to give away Pierre's hide-out.' He raised one arm dismissively. 'His parents say they can never thank me enough.'

'Where is Pierre now?' she asked.

'Alas, he was killed in a later raid,' he answered without much feeling. Anne felt herself take a sudden breath at the bluntness with which he spoke and, as if reading her thoughts, he added: 'I'm sorry if I seem heartless and lacking in any deep emotional feeling for the war dead. My experiences hardened me against what became everyday happenings.'

He paused again leaving her to wonder if he could ever become the same understanding and sympathetic Charles she had known. As her mind reminisced, he began speaking again: 'But seeing you, Anne, and being with you again, and being accepted by you, may well alter my whole outlook, and give me back my old sense of values.'

'I hope so, Charles,' she whispered. 'I do so hope and pray so.'

'Yes, I agree.' Remarked Charles. 'What an eventful and happy day this has turned out to be.'

'And it's not over yet!' commented Anne.

'You can see therefore,' he said, changing the subject back to his own activities. 'The French couple look upon me almost as a son, a replacement for their Pierre. They were marvellous when I was wounded. They nursed me under the eyes of the Gestapo at great personal risk to their own safety.'

'It won't be easy then for you to leave them now, Charles?'

'They sold their small bakery business several months ago. It was getting too much for them. Otherwise it would not have been easy for me to leave them. I believe I have even more to thank them for than they have to be grateful for to me over Pierre.'

'Perhaps I could go over with you sometime and see them?'

'I don't see why not. I should tell you, though, that they live a very simple life. Like me, they have little money. Together, we three scratched a living from the tiny bread shop. A contrast with The Grange days, eh?'

'You do collect obligations, don't you?' Anne remarked quietly. He did not reply and, after a few minutes she began to wonder if he had fallen asleep.

'Anne, do you know if Ronnie ever made a will?' he unexpectedly asked.

'What a strange question suddenly to drop on me. I'm fairly sure he didn't complete one. In fact, I know he didn't. Arthur and he had wills drafted by Uncle Steve soon after their twenty-first birthdays. Arthur got his signed and witnessed at the office quite quickly. So no, Ronnie's wasn't signed. But why do you ask?'

'It suddenly came to me. Just driving along and thinking. I can't imagine why it hadn't occurred to me earlier. As soon as I heard of Ronnie's accident that is. I always said you did things for me! No doubt Uncle Steve will soon be on to it, if he isn't already.'

'I'm lost, Charles, What do you mean "on to it"?'

'Let me explain. If Ronnie did not execute a will, it is said he died "intestate".'

'Intestate?'

'Yes. It means his possessions are bequeathed to his closest living relatives in a certain prescribed order.'

'Ronnie's hardly got anything, even his car I would guess was a write-off. Though I suppose the insurance on that is worth something.'

'Ronnie's got a lot more than you think!' Charles exclaimed. 'What about his forty-nine per cent shareholding in your company? What you generously gave to him when he was twenty-one.'

At last, Anne gladly acknowledged to herself, that his mind seemed to be off the war and back to practical present day reality.

'As I often used to say, Uncle Steve is marvellous at many things, but none better than keeping in touch. So, you see, Ronnie has that forty-nine per cent.'

'What happens to it now, then?'

'As I said, that and all his personal items pass to his closest living relative.'

'His grandfather?' she enquired.

'His grandfather, yes…. That is, unless I come back officially into the land of the living!'

'You?'

'Yes. Have you forgotten? Ronnie was my son!'

'This is becoming altogether too complicated for me, darling. If I understand what you're saying, it is that if you do come back, officially, you'll inherit from Ronnie?'

'That's right. It's an ironical twist, isn't it?' His tone changed. 'I only wish it had happened in less tragic circumstances.' He paused to collect his thoughts. 'Ironical, yes! In fulfilling my obligations, so that you could become self-supporting financially, I gave you some money to build up a business for yourself and for Arthur. The rest of the Macaulay money is lost, but in your generosity you gave almost half of your business back to a Macaulay, to Ronnie, and that half could now come back to me!'

'I remember saying, Charles, that I would try and build up a little nest-egg for you. For us. You scoffed at my idea, I remember. You always said Lloyds was so much better an investment than anything else! What do you say now?' she teased. 'Other than "Thank you"?'

'It's certainly not an every-day event for a Lloyds member to fail. But I have to admit this time that you, Anne, were well and truly right, and I was wrong!'

'I presume it's possible to reverse such documents as a death certificate and a passport. Uncle Steve I'm sure will know which wheels to get turning.'

'What about the Lloyds insurance business?' Anne queried 'What happens if you do come back, as you call it? The creditors, or other members can't come after you, can they? And strip you of all your possessions, like they did your father?'

'No, thank God. I was never a 'name' at any time. Nor was Ronnie, come to that. So neither his estate nor my possessions can be sued for contributions to any deficits.'

'That's another piece of good news then,' she replied, sighing audibly and turning the car into the yard beside the cottage. She turned off the engine. 'Welcome home, darling. Or should I say "business partner"? Welcome home!' She helped him from the car, and they went inside holding each other by the hand.

In the hallway, she put her arms up and around his shoulders and he put his arms around her waist. 'Darling, darling, darling. I always knew you would come home to me one day,'

Their embrace, the first together for eleven years, lasted some time before they separated.. 'Make yourself at home. You know where everything is. Little has changed inside the cottage, as you can see. For my part, I can't wait to get my hands on a celebration drink. Mine's a really strong one! What's it to be for you? Scotch?'

'I'd love a scotch, please. The first I've had for years. I enjoy the French wines, even *vin ordinaire*, but I must admit, I miss not having occasional spirits.'

'We'll have to start growing vines in the market garden!' she responded, a broad contented grin spreading across her face as she added the soda. 'You must be starving, Charles. I'll get something on the cooker just as soon as I've downed this.'

He took hold of one glass and stepped back behind her as she took a generous mouthful herself without turning round. 'I must light the fire, too,' she said, half turning and taking a box of matches from above the hearth, then bending down to the ready laid pile of logs.

They stood in the middle of the room and, for the first time in fully lit conditions, he slowly turned the left side of his face towards her. She hoped and prayed that he had not heard the quick gasp of breath which passed between her teeth. Hers was more a gasp of horror at what he must have been through than how he now appeared. In the full light, his scars were not nearly as conspicuous as she had feared they might be.

She came up beside him and put her arm around his waist for encouragement. 'I would like you now to try to stop your head turning its better half towards people you are about to talk to.'

Instinctively, she knew that his psychological scars, the greater for his having been such an extremely handsome and athletic young man, ran deep. These, she felt confident, she could work upon and, hopefully in time, erase. The faded physical scars would remain, but with further time, she judged, would come only to remind her of their missing years. The years of Charles's life he had personally sacrificed on account of his love for his childhood sweet heart. The memory would always be especially precious.

She felt his eyes riveted on her, searching for a sign that either he was or was not going to be accepted. She did pause, but only momentarily. Her half full glass went down quickly on to the coffee table as she hurried the three steps it took her to reach him, and to put her arms up and around his neck. Her lips were planted firmly on his. 'Once again, welcome home, my darling, darling Charles. Welcome home!'

He let his stick fall on to the side of the settee as he put his arms around her and, when she looked up into his eyes a moment later, there were tears of joy and relief to cloud both their visions.

As they stood apart, Anne's eyes fell on a massive vase full of chrysanthemums on a table in the far corner of the room. She had not noticed them when she came in. 'Look Charles,' she said with a mild degree of excitement. 'Elsie has kindly picked me some flowers, my favourites, from the greenhouse. I didn't know we had such fine specimens at the moment. We grow a few in one corner, not to sell, but just for our own use and pleasure.' She smiled as she viewed the array. 'No. They can't be ours,' she corrected. 'Not all those colours. The staff must have bought them to cheer me up. How very kind of them.'

Charles pointed. 'There's a card propped up against the vase

'So there is,' Anne replied, hurrying across the room. She picked up the Interflora card and began to read it. 'Oh!' she exclaimed. 'They're from Arthur!' Suddenly she swallowed hard. 'Do look what he's put on the card.' She half choked as she read the words aloud:

"Welcome home to the best mum in all the world.
<u>YOUR EVER LOVING SON</u>,
ARTHUR."

'And just think - He was mine all along,' she repeated to herself twice over in little more than a whisper.

'He was ours all along, my darling.' Charles corrected her equally quietly.

'Yes, ours Charles. And he never had cause to think other-wise. He was ours! Yours and mine!'

As she completed the reading she sat down in the small armchair beside the flowers, and buried her head in her hands. It was several minutes before she felt able to speak again. 'I really ought to go and telephone Arthur, and let him know I got back safely from the hospital, and to tell him....' She turned to gaze again at her favourite chrysanthemums. 'To tell him how much.... How very much indeed his flowers mean to me!'

Ten minutes later, when she returned from the telephone, Anne and Charles curled up close to each other on the settee. 'Just like we used to,' he commented.

'I'll get the meal in a moment. But, Charles.... Do you know something?'

'What?'

'It's 1952!'

'I know it's 1952. What's so special about that?'

'It's a leap year,' she teased. 'And in leap years....' She watched for his reaction carefully. 'It's not considered wrong for ladies to do the proposing!' He did not reply, but grinned at her 'You never asked me to marry you, Mr Macaulay, so I don't see why I should exercise my prerogative now in your favour!'

'Oh dear!'

'I know, Charles darling. Why don't we get a special licence and be married tomorrow?'

'That's pushing it a bit, isn't it?' he replied without losing his grin. 'After all, I've only known you for about....'

'About thirty-six years!' she whispered. 'I've waited a very long time to be called Mrs Macaulay! Mrs Charles Macaulay!'

'What you always wanted, Anne.'

'Yes.' She agreed thoughtfully. 'What I've always wanted. But what a wait.... And,' she added more quietly, 'at what a cost.'

'Anne, darling, to strike a serious note for a moment, I won't have you feeling under any obligation to marry me. As you have said, it's been a very long time. In a few days you may feel quite differently towards me.'

'You, Charles, may feel differently towards me, but never the other way around. Not a day has passed when you have not been in my thoughts and prayers.'

They warmly embraced again. 'You stay in here and rest. And give some thought to marriage,' she directed. 'I must see about our food. I'm starving, and I can't begin to imagine how hungry you must be. And I'll put a couple of hot water bottles in our bed.' She patted him affectionately on top of his head as she got up and walked out to the kitchen. 'It's most appropriate,' she called out, 'that Uncle Steve is coming to see us tomorrow.'

It was past midnight when she helped him up the stairs and into the bedroom. 'Same old bed?' he enquired with a wink.

'Same old bed,' she confirmed.

'And look!' he exclaimed, pointing towards a chair in the far corner. 'If I'm not mistaken, it is the same old cuddly sailor doll!'

'The same old cuddly sailor doll,' she confirmed with a laugh. 'I took him out of the bed earlier on, when I put the bottles in. He's been my constant companion through all the good times and the sad occasions, but now my courageous hero's home for good, my sailor doll can sign off his tour of duty.'

'But what a shame on him,' he teased.

'Not at all,' she said with a giggle. 'I always made it quite clear to him that he had use of your side of the bed on a temporary basis only!'

- THE END -

Printed in the United Kingdom by
Lightning Source UK Ltd., Milton Keynes
139204UK00001B/6/P